## AN EMBARRASSMENT

Lady Sara could survey her list of suitors with satisfaction.

There was Lord Naesmyth, definitely brilliant, if a bit too fond of ancient history. Lord Inglis, truly captivating, though with a troubling taste for gambling. And of course Lord Lambert, most worthy, if a tad stuffy.

But whatever their minor faults, they were paragons compared to the Earl of St. Quinton, with his clear contempt for proper young ladies like Sara and his public display of his mistress, Olivia Smythe-Jones. Why, Sara would not wed St. Quinton if he were the last lord on earth . . .

. . . especially since he did not seem too eager to ask her. . . .

———————————————————

# *Lady Sara's Scheme*

Emily Hendrickson

A SIGNET BOOK

**NEW AMERICAN LIBRARY**

NAL BOOKS ARE AVAILABLE AT QUANTITY DISCOUNTS WHEN USED TO PROMOTE
PRODUCTS OR SERVICES. FOR INFORMATION PLEASE WRITE TO PREMIUM
MARKETING DIVISION, NEW AMERICAN LIBRARY, 1633 BROADWAY,
NEW YORK, NEW YORK 10019.

SIGNET, SIGNET CLASSIC, MENTOR, ONYX, PLUME, MERIDIAN
and NAL BOOKS are published by NAL PENGUIN INC.,
1633 Broadway, New York, New York 10019

First Printing, June, 1989

1 2 3 4 5 6 7 8 9

PRINTED IN THE UNITED STATES OF AMERICA

# 1

Entering the library at a desultory pace, Myles slapped his gloves impatiently against his impeccably clad thigh. Glancing back at the long-case clock in the hall, he noted the time, then, with a shrug of resignation, selected a book from the excellently stocked shelves. The large, rather shadowed room was empty, just as he preferred.

Myles relished his time alone, being by nature quite a private person. His aura of reserve made him a challenge to all the matchmaking mamas and their determined daughters who each year made calculated bows to society with the aim of capturing a husband. Myles tended to look down his nose at those scheming women. No simpering miss just escaped from the schoolroom would ever catch *him*! He had become quite adept at depressing the interest of the cunning young things.

Sauntering down the length of the room, he found a comfortable wing chair. It was drawn near to the window that faced the rear of the house and the wealth of spring blooms to be viewed. He settled down, knowing his cousin, Kit Fenwick, could be depended upon to be at least half an hour late for their appointment. If Kit had not insisted it was of dire import, Myles would have let him stew. But a fondness for his ebullient young relative brought forth unusual tolerance, in Myles. Besides, staying with his relatives while his own town residence was under renovation added a certain obligation to indulge Kit. He crossed his polished Hessians, opened the book, and began to read.

The book did not live up to his hopes. Perhaps the very late night he had spent at White's contributed to his feeling of fatigue. He found his head dropping against the high back of the chair, sliding toward the broad and nicely padded corner. With a soft thud the book fell unnoticed to the Turkish carpet. Myles Fenwick, the Earl of St. Quinton, had dozed off in a light slumber.

With unusual stealth, two young women entered the Fenwick library. Corisande Fenwick shrugged and gestured her companion to be seated. Her gold-on-white spotted-muslin dress was heedlessly crushed as she plumped herself on a dainty chair. "I wonder what Sara wants?" she asked. Her china-blue eyes were puzzled as she gazed thoughtfully about the deserted room. "Why the need for such secrecy?" Her voice dropped to a whisper, as though afraid she might be overheard. "What do you suppose has happened?"

Lady Amanda Tynt seated herself with quiet composure. "You know our Sara. She is ever up to something. Remember the pranks she led us into while at Miss Tilbury's?" Her eyes lit with mirth as she contemplated some of Lady Sara's past ideas. Drawing off her gloves, Amanda settled back on her chair. Soft brown hair peeked from beneath her demure bonnet. Her dress of figured pink jaconet fitted gently about her neat figure. Although as curious as Corisande, she contained it well, waiting patiently for the others to arrive.

There was a stir at the front entry, a flurry of movement, then a dashing redhead in green-striped muslin rushed into the room. "Am I very late?" The breathless inquiry was followed by a heartfelt sigh as Fiona Egerton sank onto a chair. "Oh, I had the veriest devil of a time getting away. Mama was wanting to scold me and I simply couldn't listen to another of her tirades." Fiona pulled at the green ribands of her bonnet, then carelessly tossed that elegant creation on the floor beside her. She settled back on the cushion with another dramatic sigh.

"What is it this time? Another escapade in the park?" Lady Amanda smiled indulgently at her dear friend. "Your mother does not understand how much you love to ride."

"I daresay she would be in alt if I had your feminine grace and charm, dear Amanda." Fiona shot Amanda a rueful smile, one totally lacking in envy. "Indeed, I had intended to ride with utmost care, but the morning was so fine after all that rain we have had, and my horse is such a sweet goer. It was too, too much to expect to plod along like some utter flat!"

"Given time, I am certain she will reconcile herself to your, ah, talents, Fiona." Amanda was renowned for her diplomacy. Indeed, Fiona could only wish she had Amanda at her side when attacked by her mother's angry temper.

"Does either of you know why Sara wishes us to meet?" Fiona looked to the others for a clue to the mystery. "I vow her message brought all manner of questions to mind."

"Since she is not one to keep us waiting, I suspect we shall know soon enough," said Amanda with her usual calm.

As Amanda spoke, a soft murmur was heard in the hall; then a figure in blue entered the library, closing the door firmly behind her. "Oh, good, you are all on time," she said with evident pleasure. Violet eyes sparkling, Lady Sara Harland strolled across to lean dramatically against the imposing walnut desk. She removed her bonnet, setting it carefully aside. Ebony curls modishly framed the piquant face that was lit with impish delight. In a low voice, reminiscent of Sarah Siddons at her most expressive, she announced, "I have the greatest scheme, my dears." She gave them a teasing look from mischievous eyes. "Perhaps we ought to have a cup of tea while we discuss this wonderful idea I have."

Corisande bounced on her chair, pouting adorably. "You know how I simply cannot wait for treats. Do tell us this very minute."

"Well . . . it must remain a secret. Will you agree?"

"Sara," urged Amanda, curious to know what Sara had concocted this time. Never were her plots dull.

"If you insist. You know we must all marry. Our families expect it of us and none of us desires to remain on the shelf." The other three exchanged glances at that most obvious statement. Sara cleared her throat. "Be a love and order tea, Corisande. I'm simply perishing for a cup."

Fiona clasped her hands in her lap as though restraining herself. "Sara, dear, we are waiting with baited breath for this momentous notion you have conceived. No more roundaboutation, if you please."

"I would never wish to tease—you know that." Sara chuckled at Fiona's answering sniff of disbelief. "Very well. If you are agreed, with the expert help and guidance of my aunts, each of us shall be able to marry the man of her choice! Think on it—to marry a man you admire and cherish rather than someone you may dislike, even detest! We shall have all prospects carefully scrutinized and matched to our tastes by my dear aunts. Is this not the most modern, scientific way to find a husband?" Sara paused, tilting her head like a violet-eyed pixie. She gave them an engaging, persuasive grin. "After all, this is 1816, not the Middle Ages. Why should we sit helplessly by and let someone else do the choosing for us?"

Amanda gave a cautious nod. "It sounds like a lovely idea, but I would not wish to be thought forward."

Nodding vigorously, Fiona added, "No scandals, please."

Sara gave them a reassuring look. "No one else shall know a thing about it but us, I promise you. Tell me, is this not precisely what you have secretly longed to accomplish?"

Amanda's eyes sparkled with mirth as she said, "And how do you propose to do this marvelous thing?" She waited, knowing Sara would reveal all in her own good time, after her bit of drama.

Sara turned to her closest friend, red-headed Fiona, to demand, "Tell me what you think."

Fiona hedged. "Mama will not be best pleased if I land

myself in the suds once more. Will your scheme get me in trouble? Your aunts are dear, dear ladies, but even you must admit they are, well, a trifle eccentric."

At the sudden rise of Sara's chin, Amanda inserted, "They are charming and knowledgeable about the *ton*, though. And they would of a certainty know all there is to know."

Corisande, whose family library was being pressed into use this fine April day, bubbled a delighted laugh. She toyed with the artful blond curl draped enticingly over her shoulder with one delicate finger. "I think it is a famous scheme. I ever fear my mother will take a horrid notion to settle me on Sir Cedrick Fenton. Though I suppose he might have to apply to my brother, Kit, it would be Mama who decides the thing." At the bewildered expression on the faces of her friends, she explained, "I *would* like to change my last initial, you see. Shall we have that cup of tea while we hear what Sara has to present? I fear she will not tell us one more word unless we appease her." At the general nod of agreement, Corisande rang for a tea tray and settled back on the little chair her mother had favored when joining her husband in his room.

Sara slipped onto the leather-upholstered chair behind the grand desk, appearing slightly lost in spite of her taller-than-average frame. She drew several slips of paper from her reticule, looking about her with an air of suppressed excitement.

"I do hope you will all go along with my idea. I discussed this proposal with my aunts this week past. As Amanda said, they delight in knowing everything about everyone." She gave a reproving look at her dearest friend as Fiona choked back a laugh. "Here are their lists of the most likely candidates for conquest. The men on each of your lists are based on your interests and expressed past preferences. Since I do not agree perfectly with the first choice for me, I cannot expect you to totally fall in with every name on your list either."

Amanda leaned forward, one dainty hand extended. "Do we get to see these exciting lists before we all perish from curiosity?" Gentle humor lurked in the gray depths of her eyes.

Rising from her place at the desk, Sara walked around with the slips of paper in her hand. She was about to hand them out, then quickly hid them behind her as a footman entered with a large silver tray holding an elegant tea. Amanda sighed with unusual impatience and placed her hand in her lap once more. The tray was placed on the desk—for lack of a more convenient spot—with great ceremony. James bowed from the room, closing the door behind him with a muted snap.

Sara cast a guarded look at the door, then declared in soft but firm tones, "*No one* must get word of what we plan. You do realize that all will be ruined if anyone learns of our scheme. Not only will our chosen partners be lost to us, but we will be the laughingstock of the *ton*!" She was well aware she must impress the importance of secrecy on Corisande or that lovable widgeon might bubble over with their plans and the game would be up.

Glancing at the others, Amanda nodded thoughtfully. "Of course you are right, dear Sara. Certainly *we* shall never say a word!"

"Too true. I would not wish to be thought *coming*." Fiona shifted uneasily in her chair. Memory of that last dust-up with her stern mama still rang in her ears. One more madcap lark and Fiona would be sentenced to marriage with the dullest, most staid eligible male who could be found.

Corisande bounced a little on the dainty chair, resembling a pretty gold-and-white bird on a nest of chintz flowers. "I intend to look on this as far more than a lark. I was quite serious when I said I feared someone like Sir Cedrick Fenton. Mama said she thought him to be a fine upstanding man. He is as dull as ditch-water and twice as hard to understand. I should very much like to find a mate who shared at least a few of my interests. And not too clever, if you please. I am not at all inclined that way, you know." The others heroically refrained from replying to this obvious statement.

"Now, dear, you are the most tenderhearted of women and that is important too," consoled Amanda.

Fiona added, "It is difficult to imagine you as mute as a fish regarding any plan, Corisande, love. But then, I expect even you can accomplish the impossible, given a motive."

Darting a glance of offended pique at her friend, Corisande was prevented from retribution by Sara. If she could keep Fiona from teasing Corisande into a tantrum, it would be a miracle. "Now, you two, we must not make mice feet of this! Fiona has made an excellent point. Unless we are to be thought quite coming, we must keep this strictly to ourselves. And that *especially* means our maids, as well as our families. Not a word to your rattle of a brother, Corisande." Sara's look defied Corisande to any defense of her brother, known to be up to every wild rig and row in town.

Amanda nodded, again reflective. "And I suppose your aunts will be as silent as the grave as well?"

Corisande poured cups of tea, then offered them around while they waited for Sara's answer.

Sara spoke slowly, and with caution. "I believe my aunts look on this as an adventure of sorts. Relegated to the drawing room as elderly widows often are, it offers them a chance to live through us, you see." Sara recalled that the estimable Lady Jersey had been given the name "Silence" in great jest, as the lady in question never appeared to stop talking. "Unlike Lady Jersey, they will remain dependably silent."

A gasp escaped the pouting coral lips of the adorable Corisande. "Oh, dear! We should never see the inside of Almack's again if word of this got out!"

"Serious consequences, indeed!" Fiona had thrown off her former uneasiness and now chuckled. Glancing to where Sara once again leaned against the desk, Fiona inquired, "Are we ever to see the lists? If I loathe the names on mine, I might as well settle for the baron Mama has been urging on me."

Sara looked confused for a moment, then recalled where she had placed the lists before tea was poured. She was more nervous about this scheme than she had anticipated. She'd best take care that no one saw *her* list. "Very well. I trust you will find them quite acceptable."

Amanda extended her hand as though she suspected the list might bite, while Corisande eagerly tugged hers from Sara's hand, quickly perusing the brief collection of names with an excited gaze. Only Fiona held her slip of paper a moment, watching the others. Each read her list before looking up to ascertain what reactions her dear friends had had to their own lists of names. Then Fiona, too, looked to the slim piece of paper in her hand with four names neatly written out in spidery copperplate. "Purple ink? Must have been your Aunt Millicent who wrote this."

"Dear Aunt Milly." Sara laughed softly with great affection in her voice. "She is ever the romantic. I confess I went to her with my idea first, knowing how zealously she follows all the romances of the *ton*." Sara felt it prudent to spare her friends the first skeptical reaction the aunts gave her scheme. It might very well lead to withdrawal before they even gave it a test.

Fiona shot them a mischievous look. "Ah, yes, we could truly say she is awake to every suit?"

Amanda groaned, while Corisande merely looked puzzled. "What does she mean by that? I wish people would not say things I cannot understand."

Shaking her head at the intended pun, Sara explained, "She means 'suits' as in engagements, love interests, and the like."

Corisande gave Fiona a cross look. "Then why didn't she say so?"

"Peagoose," answered Fiona with a fond regard for her dear, if not overly bright, friend. "I shall try to remember not to upset you in the future."

Sara took a deep breath. "Well?"

Fiona spoke first. "Viscount York. It seems to me I saw him once. He has the same rusty color hair I have, as I recall," she mused in a pleased voice. "They note he is excessively devoted to his horses."

A gurgle of gentle laughter escaped from Amanda. "It would seem to me that the aunts chose well for you, Fiona. Any man you married would have to be devoted to horses."

"Just as long as he is devoted to me as well!" Fiona shot back in amused accents.

"That is why I wanted to do this, you know," Sara said in a confiding manner. "So that each of us might stand a chance of a happy marriage, rather than the common sort of tolerated situation where each mate goes a different direction." She gave them an earnest look. "I would so hope to find a man I can admire, and whose good nature would make him an excellent companion."

"Well," Corisande said enthusiastically, "I quite like their first choice for me. They note Sir Percy Wolrige is not only highborn, rich, and exceedingly good-looking, but agreeable as well. If only he is not too clever!"

"Seems he is well-matched, for I believe he is considered quite unliterary," Amanda said, reaching over to place a comforting pat on Corisande's hand. "I must agree to my choice as well. Though I have but seen him once, Lord Rolfe appears to me to be a refined and considerate man." At Fiona's questioning look, Amanda added, "I saw him assisting an elderly lady from the crush at a rout with great solicitude. His grandmother, I understand."

Dismissing the men named so far, Corisande turned. "What about you, Sara? Who could be found elegant enough for your tastes?"

"Now, Corisande," reproved Amanda, "you know Sara is not at all high in the instep."

Quite affronted at this misreading of her words, Corisande huffed back, "That was not what I meant at all. It is simply that Sara requires a very special sort of man, one who has a good notion of how to go on in the world. I doubt Sir Percy Wolrige would do for her in the least, if you take my meaning."

Nodding, Amanda agreed. "Quite right. Come, give over, Sara."

Corisande bounced from her chair and peeked over Sara's shoulder before Sara realized her intention. The dear, irrepressible girl blurted forth, "Oh, how famous! She has Myles . . . I mean, the Earl of St. Quinton!"

Sara drew herself up, snatching the list away from Corisande's view. "I have no intention of trying to capture the attentions of St. Quinton."

"Why ever not?" queried Amanda. "He is very eligible and certainly the most handsome of men. You could scarcely find a man with more polished address."

"He has wealth enough, and his horses are prime bits of blood and bone," added horse-mad Fiona.

"Myles is the dearest of cousins, though I suppose he can be rather awesome," Corisande inserted with an air of helpfulness. "He never teases me, you see. And he is terribly good about Kit. Honestly, if Kit manages to reach five-and-twenty, I daresay my mother will be most amazed."

"Runs in the family, does it?" twitted Fiona in an amused voice.

"Fiona, leave off teasing Corisande. Rather get to the reason Sara prefers the second man on her list." Amanda wrinkled her brow in bewilderment. "For my life, I cannot think who could surpass St. Quinton as a choice for you."

"I was so certain you had developed a *tendre* for him at that house party this Christmas past," added Fiona. "I recall you murmuring something about how a certain black-haired gentleman with wickedly dark eyes and charming manners had quite stolen your heart. Was I wrong in thinking it to be St. Quinton? No other gentleman matched that description half so well."

Sara's eyes flashed with scorn. "I want none of that man, I tell you. I might have been so foolish as to admire him briefly"—she emphasized the word with particular care—"but hardly enough to truly capture my heart! He can use his so-called famous address to snare some other poor soul. He is too top-lofty, too rakish, too . . . utterly boring for words!"

Fiona's brow cleared. "Now, why did I ever think you might be enamored of him? 'Tis clear you are . . . most unsure of yourself, my love. How can you consider a man too rakish and yet too boring?" Her green eyes danced with mischief.

"Fiona, it is clear Sara has for some strange, unexplained reason taken the most perfectly suitable man in the realm into a peculiar dislike," Amanda stated with quiet firmness. "While I cannot understand such a start, I expect we must allow her to go to her second choice. Who is it?" Amanda steadily met Sara's gaze, silently assuring her that she would drop the subject of St. Quinton once and for all.

Drawing in a careful breath, Sara replied in a hesitant voice, "Lord Naesmyth." She rushed on in explanation, "The aunts declare him to be nice-looking and of respectable birth and wealth. He is a quiet man of scholarly interests that I am quite certain I will enjoy sharing. Who knows, with his reputed study of Turkish antiquities, I might travel with him, as did Lady Elgin with her husband to Greece. We could discover some lost city with spectacular remains . . . or something." Her voice trailed off in a vague whisper. Sara didn't know why it was so important that she convince her friends she was set on this second man. Perhaps because it might help to persuade herself.

Fiona had watched this odd performance with skeptical eyes. "Strange, I never knew you had a fancy to travel. Nor was I aware you maintained a partiality for Turkish antiquities. As I recall, Amanda had a difficult time prevailing upon you to visit the Elgin Marbles."

Sensing the distress Sara was experiencing, Amanda intervened. "I am certain the aunts would not have selected his lordship without due consideration, and Sara will make a lovely Baroness Naesmyth."

Corisande gave a sniff of disagreement. "I would far rather see her a countess. She would be, you know, if she were to wed my cousin. I simply do not understand you, Sara. How you could prefer Lord Naesmyth to St. Quinton . . . Well!" She gave an irritated flounce of her skirts.

This time it was Fiona who scolded gently, "Leave be,

Corisande. You admitted your dear cousin is a bit awesome. Perhaps Sara finds him too much so."

Tossing her head with a fine disregard for the elaborate arrangement of her curls, Corisande added, "Yes, well, I should like to point out that she has not captured Lord Naesmyth's heart, nor has she *met* the gentleman in question as yet. Time enough to talk about becoming a baroness when he asks her."

With an attempt to appease, Sara nodded. "Corisande has the right of it, you know. While the aunts have selected gentlemen who closely match our ideals, it does not follow that the same gentlemen will fall into our arms."

"Sara!" Corisande gave a shocked exclamation. "I should hope I know better than to permit such a familiarity."

Fiona's eyes sparkled with humor. "I believe it is quite acceptable to allow an embrace after the engagement."

"I am not so certain of that, dear Fiona. Witness with what speed the mamas and papas rush their daughters into marriage once the engagement is announced. The last two I noted were no more than four and five weeks at the most between the notices in the *Post* and the wedding dates. It seems to me there must be some reason for the haste."

Bursting into quiet laughter, Amanda added, "No one can accuse you of not being observant, Corisande. I believe Sara meant her words figuratively."

"Then why did she not say what she meant?" Corisande gave Sara a cross look, then smiled. "I forgive you. It must be terribly difficult to give up the thought of Myles as a lover. Were he not my cousin and so excessively clever, I would not mind having him at the top of my list, you know. Ah," she sighed wistfully, "he is so handsome and cuts such a fine figure. Have you ever seen him waltz? Utterly divine!"

Sara cleared the strangled sensation from her throat before addressing her friend. "Corisande, love, I think we had better adjourn this meeting of our little conspiracy before I succumb to the urgent desire to throttle you." Turning to the others, she added, "Do you all agree that we shall meet here every Saturday to apprise each other of our progress—with our targets or lack thereof? I know we will see one another at the various balls and routs and such, but with the need for secrecy, we'd best not speak of it unless private. Are we of one mind in this?" She sought Corisande's gaze, wondering not for the first time if they would be able to depend on the darling blond to keep her lovable mouth shut.

"You all stare at me so." Corisande pouted. "I should never do or say anything which might harm my chance at marrying a nice man. The alternative gives me the shudders."

"We shall hold you to that, dearest," Fiona rose from her armchair, placed her cup and saucer on the tray with a sharp clink, then brushed down her skirts. "Amanda, perhaps you will come to Hatchards with me? I have a desire to see the latest offering from Minerva Press." She crammed her bonnet on her head with little regard for how it sat.

Amanda rose to place her china on the tray as well, then nodded. "Very well, though I suspect you have an abundance of wild ideas without the need for further stimulation."

Nearly upsetting her Wedgwood teacup when she gave a delighted bounce, Corisande managed to rescue it in the nick of time, then also surrendered it to the safety of the tray. "I think this is a splendid way to begin the Season. Oh, I hope it goes well."

Sara, thinking of the probable choice of mate her uncle would select for her, agreed. It was well enough to reside with her aunts, sisters of her dear departed mother, and enjoy their company as she went about, but her uncle, her father's brother, was not at all in sympathy with her aunts, and he was the one to decide her future. He would carefully sift through any proposal. No fortune hunter would be allowed to get his hands on the sizable portion left to Sara following her parents' death. Thoughtfully she tied the blue ribands of her bonnet after setting it just so on her short curls.

The young ladies gathered up their reticules, tucking each list with great care to the very bottom. It was a wonderful secret, and they relished the thought of so daring a scheme. Chattering about the promised treats in store, they sauntered from the room.

The new footman, James, hurried forward to assist them from the house to the various carriages that patiently awaited them. He cast a speculative look at the ladies, wondering if one of them might use his services as a butler before the Season was over.

Back in the library, a shadowy figure rose from the wing chair facing the window and gave his body a lazy stretch. Myles Fenwick had the look of a panther about to embark on a hunt. His eyes narrowed in concentration.

So the exquisite Sara Harland thought him a bore, did she? The other epithets hadn't stung. He was aware some mothers considered him a rake, and that wasn't so terrible. As to being top-lofty, he supposed he might be accused of that—he had been told his manner was a bit off-putting at times. It wounded his pride a little that she could not admire him, true. But boring! Now, that was quite the outside of enough!

It didn't concern St. Quinton that he had been deliberately listening in on a conversation quite definitely not intended for his ears. The old saying that the eavesdropper never heard well of himself was totally lost in his rising ire.

When he woke to the chatter from the young women, his first impulse had been to rise and depart as gracefully as possible. Then he heard his name mentioned, and nothing could have pushed him from the chair. In all his nearly thirty years, he had never been so insulted. How dare that young miss presume to speak of him so! Boring, indeed.

Myles had been quite aware of the incomparable Sara's interest in him at that Christmastime house party. Not to mince words, it was a matter of habit with him to put down any young miss who dared flirt with him. Far safer, especially in the dangerous environs of such a setting. House parties were notorious as a convenient means of arranging an engagement.

With all due modesty, the Earl of St. Quinton knew he was quite the most eligible of men. He was accustomed to lures being cast in his direction. He was certainly not familiar with the sensation of being rejected as unworthy!

That she might consider David Naesmyth as a substitute really stung! Myles conceded Naesmyth was a well-enough-looking fellow, certainly well to grass and not given to gaming. But Myles had heard him nattering on and on about this Turkish nonsense. He was a demmed prosy bore!

Though he tried to banish his anger, it remained, simmering just below the surface. Why he simply didn't laugh and sneer at the amusing pretensions of the four young women, especially Lady Sara, he did not pause to consider.

The elegant Lady Sara was about to discover she was not the only one who could scheme. She would find St. Quinton a master at the art. Forgetting his promise to meet Kit Fenwick in the library, he decided to leave, only to discover his cousin in the process of entering the house.

"Thank heaven you waited, St. Quinton," Kit declared. "I have had a devilish time of it this afternoon. Some female thinks I should wed her simply because I held her hand too long. Now, I ask you! Women!"

"You have come to the right man for help, coz. I am well up on women, particularly at the moment." An unholy fire gleamed in St. Quinton's eyes as he gestured toward the door. "Come, let us put our heads together and see what we can devise."

# 2

S ara gave a gentle nudge to the rather fat smoky-grey cat who was perched on a chair by the breakfast table. "Maurice, you know Aunt Eudora does not like to find you at the table. Be a love and disappear."

"Hmpf." The youngest of the three aunts, Millicent Garvagh, reached out to scoop up her precious animal. "If she forgets to put on her spectacles, none need worry about whether he sits here or not."

Sara smiled at the sight of her Aunt Milly, morning cap askew, with wisps of gray and black hair escaping in all directions. Her frilled-muslin chemisette peeked lopsided over an enormous Kashmir shawl and her India muslin dress in her favorite shade of purple. Aunt Milly settled Maurice comfortably on her plump lap, fed him a tidbit of kippers from her half-empty plate, then gave her niece a piercing look.

"Did you reach any decision yesterday when you met with the girls?" Aunt Milly nibbled at her third muffin.

"Outside of agreeing to the scheme, no. They believe the best thing is to leave the planning in your capable hands." Sara glanced sideways at her aunt to catch the elderly lady's complacent smile.

"Well, if I do say so, Tilly, Eudora, and I will do the thing better than anyone else," Milly said in a smug voice. "I daresay there is no one in London with greater knowledge of the *ton*."

A rustle at the door and Aunt Tilly entered, smartly dressed in the latest mode. Her spare frame was crowned by snowy hair, which gave the impression of age. Only her sisters knew that vital information, but it was generally agreed that Matilda Kerr was young at heart and awake to every suit. Her keen mind knew the exact standing of everyone who was connected with a coronet, the value of his property, how deeply the estates were mortgaged, and what claims were placed against them. It was also suspected she knew the amount of credit attached to each name, as well as the balances kept in the bank.

She briskly helped herself to her usual egg and toast, then joined the others at the table. "Miserable day. I have decided we must give a ball for Sara. If the scheme is to succeed, we need waste no time about it. I propose no more than two weeks. Where is Eudora? She will know what date is free."

Aunt Milly languidly stroked Maurice, adding, "I will happily address the invitations. How many should we invite?"

At this point Aunt Eudora drifted into the room, wrapped in a Kashmir shawl of smaller proportions than Milly's, and graced with an elegant mobcap of lace that Sara quite admired. Eudora selected a modest breakfast, then joined her family, casting a frown at Milly and the cat.

Aunt Eudora was a trifle shortsighted. In her advanced years she had yielded to necessity, and now wore delicate gold-rimmed spectacles perched on her aristocratic nose. They gave her the effect of an elegant owl.

"Millicent, dear, must you?" Eudora complained in a very refined tone as Milly gave the cat more kipper.

Gathering herself up in a soft, indignant huff, Aunt Milly replied, "Maurice is no greater trouble than that monstrous parrot you persist in foisting upon us. It continually upsets Maurice. 'Tis most unfair."

Aunt Eudora paused to stare down her nose at her younger sister. Being the eldest of the family brought grave responsibilities, one of which was to set a fine example. Glancing significantly toward Sara, she replied in stately tones, "Xenia is a quite unexceptionable parrot. I have eliminated nearly all the vulgar language she acquired from that awful man who owned her before."

"That name is another thing. Xenia! Whoever heard of a parrot with a name like that?" Aunt Milly sniffed disdainfully as she fed Maurice another piece of kipper.

"It means 'the hospitable one.'" Aunt Eudora cast a disparaging look at the cat, who blinked haughtily back at her from the safety of Milly's lap. "That is far better than a name that merely means 'the dark one.'"

"Sisters! We have more to do than listen to your daily argument about your pets." Aunt Tilly fixed them all with her shrewd gaze, then returned to the inspection of the list before her. "Since Sara, for reasons unknown to us"—she stared at her niece with an uncomprehending glare—"refuses to accept the first candidate on the list, we must go on to the second. I believe I have made myself clear on this point before, but it bears repeating. I take a very dim view of second-best!"

"Now, dear," Aunt Milly inserted, "Sara's heart rebels against St. Quinton as a husband. Poor child cannot bear to think of a lifetime with that scamp."

Aunt Eudora announced in her most cultivated tones, "Only you would call the most eligible of men who is of the highest *ton* and has such a polished address a scamp. St. Quinton is all that is unique in this age, most *recherché*, my dear."

"Sara does not care for him, and that is all I need to know," replied Aunt Milly with her usual tenacity.

Aunt Tilly cleared her throat in a menacing manner and the others fell silent once more. "As I said before being repeatedly interrupted, we must give a ball for Sara and invite all the girls' candidates. Milly will address the invitations once you let us know what date is open, Eudora. Sometime in the next fortnight. Although I expect success with the introduction of our girl, we must be prepared for possible failure. I am not all that settled on Lord Naesmyth. Second choice, you know." She cast a dark look at Sara again, then continued. "Eudora, you draw up the list of those to invite. I will attend to Gunter's and any other catering to be done, the florist, and the orchestra. Sara will see to Cook."

All gazed at Sara with respect. She was the only one in the unusual household of women who could manage the temperamental but outstanding cook. If a party were to be held, Cook would need careful handling.

Aunt Milly's soft, high voice was heard. "Sara will need a new gown for the occasion. May I go with her to select it?" Though Aunt Milly dressed in a somewhat bizarre fashion herself, she knew to a pin what style was the latest mode.

"Of course, dear. I quite forget how fond you are of fabrics and fashions." Aunt Tilly smiled affectionately at her sister. In spite of frequent branglings, they were as close as pages in a book, and twice as loyal.

"Let me see," mused Aunt Eudora, closing her eyes in deep thought. "Today is the fourteenth of April. The ball shall be held on Tuesday, the thirtieth. Sara shall attend Almack's this coming Wednesday so she will have the necessary permission to waltz." She snapped her eyes open and pronounced, "First thing tomorrow you may order the invitations printed, Matilda. I am certain we shall have the list ready by then. While you, Millicent, may go with Sara to order her ball gown. I believe white satin trimmed with violets would be an agreeable choice. Although Sara has had to delay her come-out, she is only nineteen, a most proper age for white satin. I shall attend to her voucher and such trivia." Thus she dismissed that most sacred of things, a voucher for the hallowed halls of Almack's.

"Oh, I do like violet," Aunt Milly sighed wistfully.

"Almost as much as purple." Aunt Tilly's dry words sailed right over her sister's head.

Sara's faintly slanted violet eyes widened in mirth. "I believe Aunt Eudora feels the color will accent my eyes. Your plans seem most satisfactory. Will you make out the list of what else is to be done, Aunt Eudora? May I help you in any way? 'Tis a rather misty Sunday; there is not much to do."

"I shall manage quite well, thank you." Ignoring the

remainder of her breakfast, Aunt Eudora rose from the table to walk regally toward the sitting room, where she kept the daily papers and her large diary. Every social engagement worth noting was entered in this book, making it a veritable chronicle of society. It was a valuable tool to use when discovering who was doing what, when, with whom, where, and why. Of course the latter was largely conjecture, but nonetheless amazingly accurate, if truth be known. Through judicious and skillful questioning, Eudora Bellew garnered every tidbit of information regarding her world, placing it in her diary for reference. No one was permitted access to that leather-bound volume, so dangerously accurate and damning to the unwary and indiscreet. Had Eudora been of a venal nature, she might have done well at blackmail.

Sara also rose from the table, determined to offer her assistance to her aunts. Her slim, poised form with its restrained manner gave her a faintly regal air, much like Eudora's. Those who were close to her knew that beneath that decorous exterior existed a delightful sense of humor, revealed through the tilt of amused eyes and a captivating smile. Her love of the dramatic had gotten her into a number of scrapes while attending Miss Tilbury's School for Young Ladies.

Aunt Tilly's face assumed a foxy look. "I suspect Eudora will want at least three hundred people. No point in fussing for fewer. You will tell Cook, Sara?"

Chuckling at her wily aunt, Sara nodded and headed for the kitchen. In the distance she could hear Xenia scolding Maurice as another normal day began at No. 23 Brook Street.

The following morning Sara set out in the gray landau, its wheels newly picked out in violet, with Aunt Milly at her side in more subdued garb than usual. Her love for the exotic was suppressed when she knew she was to be out and about with Sara. Today she had naught but three shawls over her purple crepe dress. Sara was dressed simply in a blue-spotted jaconet gown with her velvet spencer buttoned up to the treble-mushroom-pleated frill at the neck.

"Dear girl, this is most delightful, our going off like this. I cannot recall when I have looked forward to anything quite so much." Aunt Milly gave a pat to her elegant turban with purple plumes decorating one side. If one plume had an unfortunate manner of falling before her eyes, it was unimportant to the happy lady, who simply brushed it aside—again and again.

"Yes, well, say that anew after we have spent our time with Madame Clotilde and the milliner, not to mention the stops we must make for new slippers and other necessary items. I mean to embroider a reticule to match my dress, if you must know." Sara patted the reticule in her hand, its dainty embroidery a sample of her skill.

"Delightful. You are such a resourceful girl." Milly was merely fond of her married son, whereas Sara was the joy of her heart.

They drew up before Madame Clotilde's establishment. The groom jumped down, hurrying to assist the ladies from the carriage. Aunt Milly went first.

Sara waited until her aunt had arranged her various shawls about her plump form before leaving the carriage to join the elderly lady on the steps of the building. They were about to enter when she felt a tug on the sleeve of her blue spencer. "What is it?"

"I believe that is St. Quinton over there. I see right, do I not? My, the woman with him looks remarkably like you, my love." Aunt Milly studied the incomparable Sara, then fastened her gaze on the elegant high-flier strolling along with St. Quinton. "Extraordinary! I believe she must be his, er . . ."

"Aunt Milly," pleaded Sara in the quietest of voices.

It was impossible not to take a look at the woman. After all, St. Quinton was the man Sara had fancied herself in love with at one time. The woman was elegant, as Sara supposed that kind of woman to be. Not that Sara had observed great numbers of them, mind you. But she had noticed a few. Ladies were not supposed to be aware they existed. Living with the aunts and their absorption with society, Sara would have had

to be deaf not to have heard all about the various high-fliers,
demi-reps, and cyprians with whom gentlemen spent much of
their time.

"I fear they will see us, Aunt Milly. Best to hurry
inside . . . please." Above all, Sara did not wish to have the
Earl of St. Quinton catch her staring at him and the woman
who was obviously under his protection. It was lowering
enough to know he selected a mistress who so resembled
herself. Was that perhaps why he had been uninterested in Sara
at Christmas? He already had one like her tucked away in some
little house?

"Sorry, my dear. It was the interesting resemblance that
caught my eye. Quite forgot myself, you know." Aunt Milly
huffed her way into Madame Clotilde's shop with Sara's
insistent hand at her elbow. Sara breathed a sigh of relief as the
silk-curtained door closed behind them.

Sara wondered just how unfortunate those ladies were. She
had heard stories from Aunt Eudora regarding the enormous
sums of money expended on those women, nearly bankrupting
some of the gentlemen. While they were young, the women
certainly fared quite well. From the apparent quality of that
blue-and-white-striped sateen dress, it would seem St. Quinton
was an excellent protector. A coy twirl of the parasol carried
by the lady had concealed her face from view, but Sara's one
glimpse of it had been enough. The woman could have
been—perish the thought—her sister!

Sara did not think he had seen her. She hazarded a peek from
the window to see the back of St. Quinton as he ushered his
ladylove into a shop down the street. It was not a sight to bring
joy to her heart.

Soon Sara was agreeably occupied in choosing the fabric and
trim for her ball gown. She refused to permit the memory of
St. Quinton and his mistress to dim her pleasure in selecting
her new clothes. She decided to buy a number of dresses, a
large number, much to Aunt Milly's delight. And not one of
them was blue-and-white-striped sateen. It was fortunate that
Sara had an income of her own to spend. She had not one

qualm about disbursing such an extravagant sum today.

After a short conversation before leaving the modiste, Sara had fabric to take to the umbrella maker. She thought it would be lovely to have several parasols to match her new gowns. Sara denounced her envy even as she left the umbrella shop after placing the order. Memory of the coy twirl given that blue-and-white-striped confection rankled.

At the milliner's, she found several charming bonnets and even persuaded Aunt Milly to try an appealing confection with purple riband adorning the brim. The bonnet was most fetching, and best of all, the right color.

"I do believe this is me, dear girl," cooed Aunt Milly while Sara instructed the milliner to deliver the bonnets that afternoon. Milly complacently observed while Sara paid the bill.

Sara was quite aware that few ladies paid their bills so promptly. However, she had found that a number of shop proprietors offered a discount for cash, and although Sara was wealthy, she was also prudent. Consequently she was given preferred treatment wherever she went to shop.

The following Saturday, the four young women again slipped into the Fenwick library. The gloom of the misty rain outside seemed to have entered the room with them. However, they soon cheered each other with the tales of their shopping expeditions.

Amanda began. "I found a delicious ivory sarcenet with dainty clusters of pink roses printed on it. Mama has given me her pearls to wear with it."

Fiona's infectious chuckle followed. "You might know Mama selected green for me to wear. It is well I like the color. Mama insists everything be in some shade of green. When I get married, the first thing I shall do is buy a pink dress!"

"Oh, surely not the first thing!" countered a horrified Corisande. She sniffed at the others' laughter, then added, "My gown shall be a pale daffodil yellow, though Mama wanted white."

Amanda studied the silent Sara. "What about you?"

Sara summoned a smile. "Aunt Milly helped me select a white satin trimmed in silk violets. I'm to have a crown of violets with white satin ribands for my hair as well. Aunt Eudora offered me her pearls, as Mama's were lost." Though Sara missed her parents dreadfully, her loving aunts had done all they could to compensate for her loss when the packet boat went down with her parents on board.

"The ball will not be many days from now," said Corisande with enthusiasm. "Each of us will meet the first man on her list. Rather than worry about making the best choice—and I would have a dreadful time doing that, you know—we shall know our gentlemen will not only meet with our parents' approval but likely ours as well. While we might do passably on our own, this is far better."

"Trust your aunts to get the jump on the rest of the *ton*," said Amanda, hoping to change the direction of Corisande's thoughts. It failed to work.

"Are you going to invite St. Quinton to your ball?" demanded Corisande, like a terrier with a particularly juicy bone to worry.

Sara frowned. St. Quinton had been the subject of a heated debate when she found he was to receive an invitation. "Unfortunately he is on the list Aunt Milly used. Aunt Eudora insists we could hardly ignore the man, and Aunt Tilly keeps muttering something about not trusting second best. With any luck at all, he will ignore the invitation." Recalling his lovely raven-haired charmer, she added with ill-concealed bitterness, "I have no doubt he has better things to do that evening." A young lady's come-out can hardly be of interest to him." She could not dismiss that sense of pique she had felt at the sight of St. Quinton with a mistress so resembling herself.

Amanda touched her arm in concern. "Sara, love, that does not sound one bit like you. Are you certain you do the right thing to choose Lord Naesmyth?"

Sara shrugged and said, "Remember, as Corisande pointed out last week, while I may select him, he may choose to give me the go-by."

"I never did imply any man in his right senses would do such a thing, dear Sara," protested Corisande.

Fiona gave a pleased grin as she sought to change the subject. "I saw Viscount York in the park yesterday. He certainly is handsome. He has quite the best seat I have ever observed in any gentleman. And you ought to have seen his horse. Such a beautiful chestnut!"

"You would be the one to know." Sara gazed out the window at the far end of the room for a moment. "I hope I like Lord Naesmyth as well."

"I know I shall find Lord Rolfe charming," added Amanda. "When we were at Almack's, Mama commented that the Rolfes are a most desirable family. She hoped I would meet him at your ball, since he was not in attendance that evening."

"He has been invited, as have all your gentlemen. Of course, I cannot promise they will attend, but Aunt Eudora seems to think we will have a good rate of acceptance. My aunts are known for a good party—probably because of Cook and her expertise. I have observed that gentlemen do appear to enjoy well-presented food."

"Well, I can hardly wait to meet Sir Percy Wolrige. Your aunt found out he is partial to yellow. *That* is why I wanted that particular hue. I wonder how she knew."

Sara choked slightly. "No doubt some of her discreet questioning." It would never do for the others to find out that Aunt Eudora knew every modiste in town, and somehow always was *au courant* with who was wearing what color, and that her knowledge included any well-set-up cyprians as well. Possibly Percy favored that color on his bit o' muslin.

"It was clever of your aunt to secure permission for all of us to waltz. I do so enjoy it." Corisande tapped her toe in reminiscent beat.

"I suspect Aunt Eudora is one of the few women the patronesses hold in awe." It was possible Lady Jersey knew of the existence of the leather-bound diary, and for that reason smiled so favorably upon Sara and her friends. On the other hand, the three widows were a formidable force with which to

reckon, all with impeccable backgrounds. They were every-
where accepted and well-liked.

"Well," added Corisande, "I hope my cousin does show up.
It would serve you right to have him ask you for a waltz. Did I
mention that St. Quinton dances divinely? Then you would
know what you are missing!"

Fiona took one look at the dark expression on Sara's face
and hastily spoke. "You did, Corisande. It might be best if we
rule St. Quinton out of bounds for further conversation."

"Well, I like that!" Corisande pouted. "None of *you* has
cousins declared out of bounds."

Amanda smiled sweetly with great forebearance. "None of
us has St. Quinton for a cousin."

They left, chattering on about how exciting the ball
promised to be as they strolled to waiting carriages. Only Sara
felt a slight lack of enthusiasm, which she attributed to fatigue.
The aunts had kept her busy from early morning to late afternoon.

After the door had firmly closed behind the talkative quartet,
the house fell into a more somnolent state. From the wing
chair before the library window a figure uncoiled to stand in
amused disdain. So the delicious Lady Sara had decided he
would ignore her invitation.

Myles Fenwick strolled away from the chair where he had
again been concealed while the four young women held their
secret meeting. He really hadn't intended to eavesdrop a
second time. Yet, when Saturday afternoon rolled around, he
found himself in the library, book in hand, this time wide-
awake.

What the devil had Lady Sara alluded to when she implied
he would have better things to do that evening? Of course! She
had seen him with Olivia last Monday. Trust that bird-witted
aunt of hers to inform her niece of the precise relationship
existing between Olivia and himself. While he would defend
the practice of keeping a mistress, he found himself feeling
oddly uncomfortable knowing Sara's censure. But that was
daft!

Lady Sara had intrigued him during that Christmas house party. She possessed an elegant style. He had caught her as she stumbled on the low steps leading to the salon, and been made aware of the enticing body beneath her gown. The fall was contrived, he supposed. He had heard stories about her flair for the dramatic. Yet from the manner in which she now spoke, he began to wonder. What if she truly had been attracted to him? Hadn't he heard she'd inherited quite a sizable fortune? So she needn't chase after money. That would be a novel situation indeed. He was far more experienced with flirts who sought his wealth and title first, his person second.

Yet, were they not all a clutch of schemers? In his observation, all women were skilled in that art. Scheme, scheme, scheme! Lady Sara even referred to her little plan as a scheme. And he had certainly had his fill of endless wiles, beginning with his own mother.

Olivia certainly schemed, luring him inside that milliner's shop to inveigle the purchase of a new, fashionable, and hideously expensive bonnet.

He supposed that inheriting his title, and the wealth that went with it, at an early age had made a difference for him. It had drawn him into situations he normally would not have encountered until a much later date.

But now he had his chance to even the score, thanks to the scheming Sara. This designing woman would be made to understand that she could not trifle with a peer of his stature. He rubbed his hands together in boyish glee. This promised to be his most entertaining Season since he had first arrived in town as a green lad.

With blind determination he deliberately ignored the possibility that his own interest in Sara had led him to the high-flier who so resembled her. He had spirited Olivia away from another man after catching sight of her at the opera. Early January, as he recollected.

Myles moved toward the door with a jaunty step. Not only would he attend Lady Sara's come-out ball, he would waltz with her, not once, but twice. See what the little violet-eyed

schemer made of that! How he relished the thought of holding
her again, this time in the delicious intimacy of a waltz. He had
learned there was a great deal to be achieved during that dance
if one were skillful and daring. Her gown was to be white
trimmed with silk violets. His eyes gleamed with a wicked
light. He loved a good tease with a dash of mystery. Lady Sara
was due for a surprise or two.

As to Naesmyth, Myles had a scheme of his own in that
regard. First, to see a friend who had connections and a little
information. Then on to the ball!

Slipping from the Fenwick residence without a glimpse of
either of his cousins, Myles set out for the British Museum.

At No. 23 Brook Street, Sara urged herself to greater
enthusiasm for her ball. She had attended several parties during
the week. Never would she admit she sought the tall form of
the Earl of St. Quinton in the throng. Fortunately he was not
to be seen.

However, significant glances were shared as Sara observed
Fiona chat with Viscount York after Lady Haywood's
musicale. It had been a somewhat surprising evening, with
rousing music played by a brass band rather than the usual
series of seranades warbled by some Italian soprano. Rumor
had it that Lord Haywood insisted on the program. Aunt Tilly
had been pleased. It was about time the gentlemen were given
consideration, she stated.

The morning of Sara's party dawned with very ordinary
weather. An early-morning mist was followed by an indifferent
sun and temperatures neither hot nor cool.

Sara bustled about the house in last-minute inspections. The
rarely used ballroom at the rear of the house appeared in prime
looks, with a lavish display of white roses and violet plumes.
The decor had been Aunt Milly's inspiration. Cook had out-
done herself in creating a tasty supper for the guests.

Sara might have wished the arrangements a trifle different,
but never would she have said a word to her aunts. The dears

were so proud of their party for her. And truly, no girl in all of England felt more loved than she did this day.

All too soon the time came when she dressed in her white satin gown trimmed with dainty clusters of deep-colored silk violets. The wreath of violets and white ribands was woven in her dark hair by her maid. Her curls were a soft halo about her head, the flowers and ribands a lovely accent. Sara had to admit the touch of violet was inspired, bringing out the strange color of her eyes.

Those eyes grew wide with excitement and anticipation when a footman brought a small bouquet to her bedroom door. She accepted the flowers from her maid, sure her aunts had arranged this final touch—an exquisite bouquet of fresh, delicately fragrant violets. Yet the card tucked into the silver filigree holder indicated that the nosegay came from "Your Secret Gallant." The script was an elegant scrawl in bold black ink. She stared into the mirror above her dressing table. Who could it be that would have been so knowing? A shiver ran down her spine.

Then she rose from her chair to walk toward the stairs. Tonight she would take the first step toward Lord Naesmyth.

# 3

Sara met the combined gaze of her aunts with a charming rise in color. Reaching the foot of the stairs, she crossed to where they were assembled. There was to be a highly select group for dinner, which St. Quinton was not among, much to Aunt Tilly's disgust.

Aunt Eudora had learned from her esteemed late husband that gentlemen detested that dry aeon of space before dinner. So the guests were sure to be on time, if only to sample the interesting wines available for their delectation. Word had filtered through the male portion of the *ton* that the widows treated gentlemen well. Tiny tidbits to whet the appetite were also to be found, a daring innovation Aunt Eudora had had the cunning to adopt.

Aunt Milly held a nosegay of white roses in her hand. A look of disappointment crossed her face as she beheld the violets Sara carried. "Whoever thought to send you violets?" Milly exclaimed. "Clever, to be sure. Far more suitable than these posies." She turned to place the roses on a long cherrywood table in the hall.

Sara looked at the roses with dismay. "But I had hoped you ordered the violets for me. Only a cryptic signature came with them, and I know you love a tease."

Quick to sense a romantic mystery, Aunt Milly beamed. "How delightfully intriguing, dear girl. Perhaps the gentleman will reveal himself during the ball." She sighed with all her optimistic heart, and patted Sara encouragingly on the arm.

Tilly and Eudora exchanged looks, then swept Sara off to the drawing room to await their guests. All were surprisingly prompt in a day when promptness was not prevalent.

Fiona and her mother arrived early. Sara was pleased to observe that Fiona's delicate sea-green gown was beguiling, and set off her flaming tresses to advantage.

When Amanda entered in the wake of her slim, delicate mother and hearty father, Sara repressed an amused smile. Amanda's parents were so terribly proud of her, and quite determined no one should suspect them of such a thing.

"Does it look all right?" Amanda whispered anxiously.

"If you mean your gown, it could not be lovelier. I vow, that is the most becoming print I have seen you wear." Since Amanda was addicted to dainty floral prints, the compliment was indeed a fine one.

The three girls couldn't hide smiles when Corisande, looking like a fresh-picked daffodil, bubbled and bounced into the room. To be sure, it was a refined bounce, but a bounce, nonetheless.

She hurried up to the three, who stood with unconscious grace not far from the door. "Oh, I can scarcely wait for all to arrive. Am I in first looks? Mama said so, but who can believe one's own mama?" Her hands twisted nervously before she gave the others an anxious look. "Suppose he does not care for me. I fear I have my heart set and I have yet even to greet him." She chewed on her lower lip before turning her gaze to the door. Smedley, the starched-up butler, was standing at attention, two young Corinthians at his side.

"Viscount York and Sir Percy Wolrige," he intoned.

Sara fluttered forward with Aunt Eudora to greet the gentlemen. Following their arrival, Lord Rolfe and Lord Naesmyth entered. The widows had also invited three gentlemen whose company they enjoyed, and soon the party was complete.

Seated beside the man of her choice, Sara was pleased with her initial impression of Lord Naesmyth. The baron was elegantly dressed in dark grey jacket and fawn pantaloons with an embroidered waistcoat of white satin. His air of *à la modalité* was not artificial, nor did it grate on the viewer's eye. While they conversed quietly, Sara had a chance to observe that the other girls seemed to be enjoying similar success.

Following the nicely presented dinner, as only her aunts seemed to plan with an eye to the gentlemen's preferences in mind, they moved to the ballroom. Sara was on edge, not able to relax, yet anxious she should appear serene.

"I say, fetching decorations," Lord Naesmyth ventured to state. "Echoes your gown."

With a desire to discover if the baron might be her secret admirer, Sara replied with gracious charm, "And these dear flowers sent to me add to the delight, do you not think?"

"What? Oh, I say, they do indeed. Most fetching."

She thought with resignation that if he did not excel in conversation, he might perhaps be better at dancing. At least she now knew he had had nothing whatever to do with the mysterious violets. His blank expression revealed his lack of knowledge even without one word spoken. Without a pang of regret, she left him to converse with Fiona and Viscount York while she joined her aunts to welcome the remaining guests.

Standing in the reception line after greeting what seemed like a dreadful number of people, Sara wondered if St. Quinton would show. She sincerely doubted such an event. He made it a point, it seemed, never to attend the banal come-out balls, preferring something more enticing. Yet the cream of society was present.

"Dear"—her Aunt Eudora nudged—"Lady Jersey is nearing us. Smile your prettiest and don't forget to thank her for her permission to waltz. Countess Lieven is following her. It seems they came together. How odd." Her aunt sharpened her gaze on two of the patronesses who ruled at Almack's. Sara said all that was correct, enduring the assessing look from Lady Jersey with equanimity.

As new arrivals dwindled, and Sara was feeling rather pleased in her estimation that St. Quinton would hardly deign to make an appearance, he was announced. She couldn't conceal her startled reaction, and she feared he was quite aware of it.

The Earl of St. Quinton was dressed in black coat and pantaloons with an elegant waistcoat of quilted white satin. One tasteful fob was all he permitted, and a single large diamond graced the intricately tied folds of his neckcloth. Sara firmly refused to allow him to see how impressed she was with his refined appearance.

"Lady Sara, you are as lovely as all the flowers of spring this evening. I count myself the most fortunate of men to have garnered an invitation to your ball." He bent low over her hand, and she forced herself not to tremble as his lips brushed against the thin, delicate kid glove that sheathed her hand. While his touch was light, it sent tremors down to her toes. That rascally man! To linger a moment too long, to press his lips a trifle too much, was infamous. Her instinct was to snatch her hand from his light clasp and hide it behind her back. Since that reaction would reveal far, far too clearly how he acted upon her nerves, she remained stone-still.

Not pausing to consider that Lord Naesmyth had not affected her in a remotely like manner, Sara told herself that St. Quinton must expect her to be a ninny. She glanced up at him, her slanted violet eyes alive with mirth. "Doing it a bit brown, Lord St. Quinton. Surely you must know that any young woman making her bow to society would be delighted to see you attend her ball." She added to herself: I can only wonder what brought you to mine. She narrowed her eyes, giving him a shrewd assessment such as Aunt Tilly might.

He moved in the first circles; he knew very well every matron would send him a card to any event being held. His mail must overflow with invitations to every conceivable manner of entertainment. If he accepted a quarter of them, he wouldn't have a moment at home. And he was here.

"But they cannot compare with you, fair lady."

Aunt Tilly, seeing an opportunity to put an obstacle in

Naesmyth's chances with her wealthy niece, floated over to their side. Conscious that Lady Castlereagh and Lady Cowper watched with eagle-eyed acuity, Tilly offered a benign smile to St. Quinton.

"Would you do our little gathering the honor of beginning the evening's festivities?" At his nod, she sent a look to Sara that warned that young lady not to object in any manner. "Delightful," Tilly pronounced. Her signal to Colnet, the orchestra leader usually seen at Almack's, brought forth the rich strains of a waltz.

St. Quinton bowed and led Sara out on the floor. A hush far greater than the moment warranted fell over the expectant dancers. Sara dipped a curtsy worthy of a royal presentation, and then allowed herself to be gently drawn into his arms.

She glanced to see where Lord Naesmyth had been, and found him escorting forward a dab of a girl Fiona must have thrust upon him. Gradually the floor began to fill with other dancers.

"Did I manage to cut off the hopes of another gentleman?" When Sara refused to answer that leading question, St. Quinton gave her a reply of his own. "But of course I must have done so. Let me see, whom have I so harshly disappointed? I noticed a glare from several gentlemen, Naesmyth for one."

Sara raised her gaze from where she had been studying the intricate folds of his neckcloth to stare into his eyes. She ought not admit to partiality for any one man, yet she wondered.

"You know the gentleman?" There was nothing peculiar in their acquaintance; they belonged to the same clubs and must have mutual friends.

"Fine chap—if you enjoy antiquities. For myself, I prefer the living. So much more rewarding, you know."

There was nothing actually wicked in his words, but the inflection of his voice, his caress of the word "rewarding," shot a bolt of apprehension through her. That those uncomfortable words were followed by a deft maneuver which brought her much closer to him shook her to her core.

His hand, however discreetly gloved, tightened at her slim waist. She could feel the pressure of each finger through the fragile satin of her gown, to her sensitive skin beneath. She found his clasp of her own gloved hand intensely tender, his gaze fraught with a meaning she couldn't hope to uncover. Would the dance never end? Her heart could stand only so much stimulation.

Yet her eyes could not break with his. It was as though some magic he possessed kept them riveted to his devilishly handsome face. She tried. "I must confess I am surprised to see you here."

"You did not intend the invitation? I am desolate."

As an answer it bordered on the absurd. "Oh, come now, milord. You know better than that." Her chuckle was bewitching, and found its way to the heart of the man who had vowed to remain untouched.

"You look entrancing tonight. Your posy is most appropriate. A gift from someone special?" His eyes held a certain intriguing sparkle that captivated her against her will.

"It was a surprise from someone who discovered my intentions for the evening. Whoever it was must have remarkable perception." Her voice revealed her curiosity. She still had no clue as to who might have sent the violets. She had ruled out St. Quinton, as it was well known he never dangled after any emerging bud of society.

They waltzed past the aunts, who all nodded graciously, Tilly with a sly gleam in her eyes. Myles commented, "Your aunts care deeply for you, it seems. They lavish attention on you as though you were their own."

A spark lit her spirit. "I am their own, milord. From the day the news reached us of my parents' death, no girl could have had more loving guardians."

He failed to respond to this remark, simply spinning her around in a series of intricately executed steps that brought her closer to that broad chest of his. She inhaled the heady scent of costmary from his linens and whatever spicy lotion it was he used on his person. Then the dance ended.

Sara hoped her relief was not too patent. He bowed low over her hand, then raised his gaze to meet hers, those wicked eyes sending most improper messages. It was as if he knew how glad she was to be free of him and found her discomfort highly amusing. "I must have another waltz with you, dear Lady Sara." Before she could think of an evasion, he took her dance card and scrawled his initials on the space next to a waltz.

By some odd coincidence, he stopped close to where Lord Naesmyth stood with Aunt Milly while she chatted away in charming confusion. She beckoned and Sara found herself partnering Lord Naesmyth in a country dance.

"I say, I'm surprised to see St. Quinton here. He usually avoids these dos," Naesmyth said as they met in the first pattern of the dance. Sara had no time to think of a sufficiently vague and depressing response.

She was spared a reply, as the dance was a lively one, requiring concentration on the many patterns.

From then on it was a whirl from one partner to another. However discomfiting for her to admit, Sara suspected that the first waltz with St. Quinton had established her far beyond her initial hopes. She was besieged from every side. She made certain Lord Naesmyth obtained his second dance before consenting to any other gentleman's request. It was barely possible to observe what was happening with Fiona, Amanda, and Corisande, but she thought she saw St. Quinton with each of them at least once. His presence had her so bewildered that she scarcely knew what to think.

Sara was still puzzling over the matter when he appeared at her side to claim his second waltz. She had hoped he might forget it, or disappear, or some such thing. Unfortunately, he did not.

"Lady Sara? I believe it is my pleasure to partner you once more this evening."

Head high, her resolve not to be affected by this . . . this rake firmly in place, Sara gracefully extended her hand to him. "I believe you are correct." She didn't make the foolish mistake of checking her card. He would know that a man of his consequence would not easily be forgotten.

If she thought the first waltz had been an indecorous affair, she was certain this must be just short of scandalous. His attentions were marked. Those eyes laughing down at her firm-lipped expression were the final straw. Wicked, they were.

After one of those whirls at which he seemed so adept, he whispered, "Relax, Lady Sara. I promise not to eat you."

Since she had the feeling he might do just that, she found herself giving a reluctant laugh. "I must confess you are a trifle disconcerting, milord. Though I am far from the schoolroom, I am not accustomed to such gallantries as you press on me this evening." Her expression was as wry as her words. She prayed the dance would end and she could find a haven with someone else.

"But you are an exquisite woman, Lady Sara. Surely there is some man who holds you in deepest regard? The sender of the violets, perhaps?"

His voice was too amused to please her. She didn't trust the trace of huskiness in that deep drawl. Sara looked at the charming silver holder where the violets still nestled in simple richness. "He remains a mystery. Mayhap he will step forward before the evening is over."

At the dance's conclusion, once again he managed to bring her to where Naesmyth stood. As St. Quinton relinquished Sara's hand with evident reluctance, he turned to Lord Naesmyth with a polite smile. "Have you heard of those startling discoveries in Turkey, Naesmyth?"

Lord Naesmyth was not accustomed to having St. Quinton address him with such a degree of congeniality. He preened slightly before eagerness overcame his desire to look blasé. "No, I confess I have heard nothing of any new developments. Who mentioned them?"

"Harford."

Since Naesmyth knew very well that Lord Harford was in charge of the Turkish section at the British Museum, he sharpened his gaze, his obvious absorption in antiquities taking precedence over his interest in Sara. "Did he, by Jove? Tell me what you heard."

As the next set formed, Sara was drawn away by Sir Percy, so she failed to hear the remainder of their conversation. A feeling of unease settled over her for one moment before she shook off the ridiculous notion that St. Quinton sought to deflect Naesmyth's interest in her. There was absolutely no reason on earth St. Quinton should do such a thing. She entered the country dance with a fixed smile, determined to ignore her forebodings. Sir Percy was a darling lamb, just the right man for Corisande. It seemed he was quite taken with the lady, for he brought up her name often.

Several dances later, Lord Naesmyth appeared to claim his second dance with her, a distracted look on his face. Sara finally decided that although his body might be there, his spirit was more likely in Turkey.

Thinking perhaps she might further her cause if she could converse with Lord Naesmyth on a subject so dear to his heart, Sar touched his arm lightly to gain his attention. "I believe it is time for supper, Lord Naesmyth. Perhaps while we enjoy the treats our cook has in store for us, you could tell me a bit more about your interest in artifacts and archaeological sites."

He was extremely polite in his attentiveness. First finding her a chair, he set off to fill two plates with the delicacies from the lavish spread set out. Once seated at his side, she attempted to quiz him regarding his abstraction. Then St. Quinton joined their table. He had a quiet miss in tow, a charitable gesture on his part, Sara had no doubt.

Sara gave him a vexed look, and he responded with that lazy, wicked grin of his. "Excellent repast, Lady Sara. I had been told the ladies of your family are well up to snuff on the proper care of a gentleman."

"We are all that is proper, milord." Her answering smile bordered on saucy, with eyes that held a dangerous sparkle in them. Bait her, would he? "Of course, there are some who find propriety quite boring."

"What do you find boring, Lady Sara?"

She caught a fleeting expression on his face that she couldn't begin to identify. Before she could explore it or answer, Lord Naesmyth entered the conversation.

"I must say I am intrigued with the news you gave me this evening. I intend to check it out, you may be sure."

Sara looked from one man to the other, trying to assess the probable results of this conversation. The poor dab of a girl St. Quinton had in tow was seated too far away from Sara for her to rescue. She abandoned all thought of aid, and turned to a subject closer to home, her future.

An enthusiasm such as Sara had not observed in him before lit Lord Naesmyth. "This discovery in Turkey. Some fellow has trekked into the interior and found a city of enormous antiquity. Pre-Roman, likely early Greek. I should dearly like to explore the area myself. I vow, St. Quinton has quite stirred my curiosity."

"We need men like you who have the vision and daring to uncover the past for future generations." St. Quinton's drawl was gone, his voice now reflecting an earnestness most flattering to the younger Lord Naesmyth. To have a man of St. Quinton's caliber show such condescension was enough to put him in alt.

Sara's mouth fell open slightly. Was this St. Quinton speaking? "I was unaware you possessed such an interest in history, Lord St. Quinton."

"Ah, dear Lady Sara, but then, what do you know of me? I find Turkey an intriguing subject." Myles sent her another of those disconcerting looks at which he excelled.

Lord Naesmyth leaned forward, his plate of food forgotten in his desire to converse with a gentleman of like interests. He plunged into a complicated and, to Sara, rather tedious account of other explorations in the area.

Listening with growing unease to this enthusiastic narration, Sara allowed her gaze to flicker from Lord Naesmyth to St. Quinton. There was something terribly odd in all this attention from one who held so lofty a position in the *ton*.

It was time to return to the ballroom. Sara found she had eaten without knowing what she consumed. St. Quinton had quite spoiled her ball for her, she decided.

Naesmyth absentmindedly attended to Sara, chatting about his interest in Turkey and antiquities in general while they sauntered along the edge of the ballroom. It seemed Grecian ruins had the power to attract him, as well as Turkish. Her attempts to steer the conversation around to other channels were futile. Once Naesmyth took up antiquities, there was no diverting him. She glanced across the ballroom to where St. Quinton was taking leave of her aunts. As he sauntered toward the stairs, Sara resolutely repressed the notion that the ball-room somehow seemed a duller place.

In another part of the room the notice paid Sara by St. Quinton was not unremarked by the ladies in attendance. Indeed, Lady Castlereagh had tapped Lady Jersey on the arm, nodding to the two as they waltzed.

"What is that rascal up to, do you suppose?"

Lady Jersey had stared thoughtfully down her elegant nose and commented, "Quite the most interesting sight I've seen in weeks."

Still later, after all the guests had departed, Sara thanked her aunts for her lovely ball, then slowly made her way to her room. To her mild annoyance, the aunts trailed after her.

"Well," queried Aunt Milly, "how did it go with Naesmyth?" Her expression was quite hopeful.

"Noticed St. Quinton paid you quite the honor, my girl," added Aunt Tilly.

Sara smiled wanly and nodded. "Lord Naesmyth is a . . . a fascinating gentleman. He certainly is conversant with the latest techniques in searching for and uncovering antiquities." As an afterthought she added, "St. Quinton seems amazingly well-informed too."

Aunt Milly fluttered along beside her. "You are a very artistic girl. Think how you will enjoy painting watercolors of the ruins in Turkey!" she exclaimed softly.

"Millicent, that is enough for tonight. I suspect Sara is longing for her pillow at this point." Aunt Eudora gestured toward the windows, where the faint pink in the sky gave evidence of a dawning day.

The aunts drifted from the room after each had bestowed a light kiss on Sara's tired cheek. Sara allowed her maid to undress her, then crawled beneath her covers to sleep. Her last thought was one of puzzlement. Why should St. Quinton do Lord Naesmyth the favor of bringing to his attention the news about the Turkish discovery?

Lord Naesmyth was in attendance at Almack's the next evening. Sara was able to enjoy two dances with him. She also had a chance for brief conversations with her friends. Amanda blushed a rosy pink as she revealed Lord Rolfe's most zealous attentions. Anyone could see the marked interest displayed by Viscount York in Fiona. They were deep in discussion about some horse when Sara passed by them.

Corisande twitted Sara about the two dances with St. Quinton the night before. "You must admit what a marvelous dancer he is. Did I not tell you he could waltz better than anyone else? You looked quite well together. I cannot understand how you can prefer Naesmyth to my cousin." She pouted. "To my mind, there is no comparison."

"But then, you must confess to a prejudice, my dear." Sara could not take issue with her friend. "However, one does not choose a mate for life simply because he performs the waltz well."

"If you prefer to dwindle away in some moldering old ruin, it is no matter to me, my love. What pleases you must come first. I vow I am charmed with Sir Percy. Your aunts were exceedingly wise when they matched me to him." She beamed a smile at Sara, then drifted off toward her mother. Sara agreed to a ride with Lord Naesmyth the following afternoon, displaying polite interest in seeing his matched bays.

On the way home, she scolded herself. Surely a time spent in search of antiquities would not be so bad. She could think of it as an adventure. Eventually Lord Naesmyth would settle down on his estate to have a family and attend to his duties as a peer of the realm.

Another dainty bouquet of violets from her "secret gallant" was delivered the next morning. Sara discovered them when she came downstairs for breakfast. Violets were not uncommon this time of year, but these had a just-picked freshness about them, and they were deliciously fragrant.

Aunt Milly beamed from her end of the breakfast table. Maurice was perched on her lip, consuming his second kipper of the morning. "Violets again, my dearest girl? Oh, how I do love a mystery! Who can it be, do you suppose? Lord Naesmyth?"

Sara shook her head. "He gave no indication he knew anything at all about the violets. He merely spoke politely when I pointed them out to him the evening of my ball."

None of the other aunts had any help to contribute. All were intrigued, full of speculation. By the time Lord Naesmyth arrived to take Sara for her ride in the park, Sara was heartily sick of the subject.

The matched bays were worthy of regard, Sara found. She complimented Naesmyth on his excellent equipage, then settled down for the afternoon jaunt through that prestigious spot, Hyde Park, at four of the clock.

She caught sight of each of her dear friends with the gentleman of her choice. There was little time for other than a greeting, but she noticed there seemed a good deal of intimacy between each couple. She tried to engender more enthusiasm for the aspect of traipsing off to Turkey. Beside her Lord Naesmyth continued his monologue (interspersed with soft noises from Sara) on Turkey.

"This fellow I spoke with told me of how important it is to get in with the pashas and the agas. He said the mode of transportation is crude, but the trip well worth the effort. The Turks are not as given to cheating as the Greeks. Still, a fellow has to step fast to keep alive."

"Surely there is no danger of death, is there?" Sara hadn't figured on that aspect of the trip.

"But there is, you know. Aside from fevers, there are other perils. The chap I spoke with told me of the murder of a Greek bishop who refused to pay a janissary monies which he demanded of him. I venture to say there is precious little justice, as we perceive it, in that part of the world. Such an expedition would not be without dangers, my dear Lady Sara." There seemed a trace of pomposity in his words that she could not like.

Friday afternoon Lord Naesmyth presented himself in the drawing room of No. 23 Brook Street. Sara found herself dismayed but not surprised when he informed her with glowing enthusiasm that he was getting together an expedition to Turkey.

"Time is of the essence," he stated with utmost gravity. "Lord Harford assured me there is much to be done at the discovery site. I am to hire a group of diggers to excavate what we are certain will prove to be an amphitheater of the earliest style. After that, he envisions there will be an agora, which will yield much about the life in that city. Who knows, it may be of far greater significance than either of us dreams."

He continued to chat on the subject, warming to it as he went on. Nothing was said about taking a wife along.

"I should think you will find it lonely," she said at last in sheer desperation. "Lord Elgin had his wife."

"Lonely? Well, I expect it may be, you know. But think of the adventure!" He gave her a sapient look. "I hope I am not such a nodcock to expect a delicately nurtured female to attempt such a trip!" His eyes assumed a faraway look, then he continued crushing all of Sara's hopes. "No. I daresay I will devote all my energies to discovery, much as other scientists have in the past."

Sara could see he entertained visions of great importance in the archaeological community. Discovering she had no desire to persuade him to change his mind, she gave up and wished him Godspeed.

Later, meeting Aunt Tilly's censure was the worst of it all.

"I told you to beware of second best, my girl. I hate to think of what the third one will be like!"

# 4

"There was something quite, quite odd about it all." Lady Sara paced before the imposing desk in the Fenwick library as she spoke to her friends. "Consider this: when can any of you recall St. Quinton attending a come-out ball? Or for that matter, paying such marked attention to a mere miss at her introduction to society? My aunts say never! And," she demanded as she paused near the far end of the room, "what about his chats with Lord Naesmyth? Decidedly odd, I say."

Sara had found a great deal of time to ponder the matter after Lord Naesmyth departed from her aunts' home, his face wreathed in an anticipatory smile. That he was eagerly looking forward to his trek to the Turkish interior was most evident. Sara's pretty straw bonnet that now dangled from her hands by its ribands swung crazily as she spun about to return to the desk. "There are so many things that puzzle me." She gave an appealing look to the others, seeking some sort of answer to the enigma that had plagued her these past days. Something simply did not feel right about the entire situation. "There is something decidedly smoky about St. Quinton's part in this."

Amanda sought Fiona's eyes before turning a troubled gaze toward Sara. "I confess it does seem peculiar that St. Quinton was so closely connected with these worrisome events."

Fiona slowly shook her head. "But why? What difference could it possibly make to him if you formed an alliance with

Naesmyth or not? I feel you are making substance out of air castles, Sara, dear."

Corisande firmed her lips before voicing her complaint. " 'Tis most unfair to my cousin. Myles is the kindest of persons. Look how interested he was in Turkish antiquities. He mentioned talking with Lord Harwood, and you must know Myles is not fond of the British Museum. I believe he showed a rare compassion to pass along the news of that dig, or find, or whatever it is called. I do not see anything so remarkable in that!"

Sara rubbed her forehead before lifting her gaze to meet Fiona's in a shared look of dawning comprehension. "I believe I understand . . . now. Only I had so hoped Lord Naesmyth would prove to be the answer. Now my aunts will give me no peace."

Fiona gave Sara a speculative look. She was unconvinced that Lord Naesmyth's defection to Turkey was a bad thing. He might be acceptable, but he wasn't half fine enough for Sara. "Who is the next man on your list?"

Sara had no need to pull the slip of paper covered with elegant purple copperplate writing from her reticule. The names on that list had long since been committed to memory. "His name is Baron Oliver Inglis. I saw him recently at a rout. He is reputed to be a rather dashing man-about-town, attentive to the ladies from what I hear. No need for a fortune, so I needn't fear on that score. You all know how I fear a gamester."

Amanda shrugged. "Seeing him does not tell you a great deal, except that he is not repulsive to look upon."

Toying with the grosgrain ribands dangling from the bonnet in her hand, Sara gave an impatient shake of her head, her shining black curls dancing about her delicately shaped face. "Aunt Milly pointed him out. I own I am vastly pleased with what I saw, though I must know him better before I can decide if we will suit. I will not have the advantage of inviting him to my ball, but you can see to it he is on your guest list, Amanda. Will you?"

"Of course," replied her friend. Her affirmation seemed to release something inside Sara, for she sank onto a chair with barely disguised relief. Amanda was perplexed. "Surely you never thought I might refuse?"

"No," came the thoughtful answer. " 'Tis Aunt Tilly. She was utterly scathing when I divulged the news that Lord Naesmyth was forming a party to traipse off to the inner wilds of Turkey. I have already heard far too much about the folly of second best. Heaven knows what I shall hear regarding the third choice—especially if he proves to be unsuitable."

Corisande gave Sara a puzzled look. "But I thought you said your aunts vetted each gentlemen carefully. So why worry about Lord Inglis? I can picture you with such a dashing man at your side. I do not know if he dances well, but of a certainty he does have a polished address. Though why you persist in ignoring my cousin is more than I can see. I think Myles would suit you to a cow's thumb."

Rising, Sara mangled the bonnet ribands in her hands as she softly stalked to where Corisande sat in innocent bewilderment. "If my suspicions are correct, your dear cousin lured my baron off down the Turkish path. I must guard that he does not come near Lord Inglis when I am with him. Heaven knows where St. Quinton would contrive to send him! I can see it now. Every time I see St. Quinton, I shall divert Lord Inglis and myself in another direction. It ought to be truly amusing." The grim look on Sara's lovely face belied her words. "I can only hope my behavior does not seem odd to Lord Inglis." She gave a rueful laugh, then looked at Fiona. "Forgive my heedless tongue. I am so lost in my woes I forget to ask how you all go on."

Fiona blushed an interesting shade of pink. "Viscount York has been all I could wish. I hesitated to say anything about him for I would never desire to distress you, Sara. But I believe he is quite smitten with me. Aunt Milly confided she heard he had come to town to seek a wife. He reportedly had few hopes of finding a woman who shared his interests in horse raising. And now he has found me. Or at least he thinks he found me," she amended with pretty confusion.

Amanda chuckled, then offered in her practical manner, "What difference does it matter who found whom, as long as you are so right for each other? If ever two people were suited to be as one, it is you and Viscount York."

"Amanda has the right of it, Fiona. But she does not confide as to how her interest in Lord Rolfe prospers," said Sara, with a glance at the quiet one of the four.

"Jason . . . that is, Lord Rolfe, invited me to meet his grandmother at tea. What a charming old tartar she is." Amanda smiled. "Thought I would be intimidated by her lofty address. I have an old aunt who is just like her. We got along amazingly well, which seemed to please Lord Rolfe no end. Mama feels he is becoming most marked in his attentions." Amanda spoke in her usual gentle, soft voice, but her eyes danced with happiness. Sara thought she had never seen a woman more feminine than Amanda in her dainty printed silks and laces.

Corisande had been sitting on her mother's chair in puzzled silence while the others conversed. She turned to face them. "Do you get any more of those violets, Sara?"

Now it was Sara who colored a delicate pink. "Yes, I do. I have tried everything I know to discover who sends them to me. I had my groom hide outside to watch the door, then follow the man who delivered the last flowers this very morning. No success. The clever fellow got clean away. Aunt Milly loves the mystery of it all."

Corisande cocked her dainty blond head and studied Sara. "And how do you feel?"

"I confess I adore them. Violets have always been a favorite of mine. Aunt Milly says violets mean faithfulness." Sara sighed wistfully. "The mystery person is certainly faithful about sending them. The card is always the same, 'Your Secret Gallant.' 'Tis silly of me, but I find myself weaving dreams about this unknown person."

"Well," inserted Fiona with unaccustomed briskness, "you

must tell us how you get along with Sir Percy, Corisande."

"Quite well indeed. I do believe we shall make a match of it. He has hinted of an attachment, nothing more." Corisande gave them a vague smile, her eyes a tender mist of blue as she gazed into the distance.

"You told me," countered Amanda, "that he said you gave him a reason for existence. Surely that is nigh onto a declaration. Did he not say you shared many of the same interests? That he has explained how he feels about every subject on the earth? I say that is of a certainty more than just a hint."

Corisande blushed a demure rose and lowered her eyelids to conceal an exultant look. "He does seem to display an unusual regard, does he not?"

"Well," said Sara in a determined tone, "it is to be hoped that Lord Inglis will not prove to be another disappointment. I vow he is handsome enough to make the thought of wedding him rather appealing. I found his smile most attractive." Turning to Amanda, she grinned. "Just you wait until you see him, and you will know what I mean. He has utterly delicious blond curls which I find as fascinating as his dark brown eyes."

Amanda rose from her chair to walk toward the door. "I am sorry to leave you all. Mama desires I purchase some silks for her this afternoon. You may safely assume we shall all do our best to assist you in any way we are able, dear Sara."

Sara followed after her. "I fear I shall need all the assistance you offer. It is quite lowering to find a man can so easily resist me."

The four drifted toward the front door, chatting quietly as they walked. Fiona offered to accompany Sara to the lending library, and Corisande asked if she might join Amanda in her search for silks. "I am working on a set of chair covers, just the central designs for now, and need more wools. If Sir Percy does ask for my hand, I may choose the background color then. Needlework is one thing in which I excel, thank heaven."

"We shall all see each other at Amanda's ball next week, if not before. I trust I will not need your help in keeping St. Quinton at bay. It's not likely he will attend another come-out ball this season! At any rate, I shall be keeping a wary eye out for your cousin, Corisande."

The petite blond gave a good-natured shrug and nodded her head. "He is one to be cautious of, I suppose. I still say—" Her remaining words were lost as the door closed behind the four with a firm thump.

Within minutes the hall returned to quiet. The butler was called to the first floor, and James, the footman, disappeared on his duties, leaving the lower regions silent. Almost.

The figure in the wing chair sat deep in thought as he shifted uneasily. The tulips that nodded colorful heads in the spring breeze were unseen as he stared out the window.

He had not intended to be so obvious. Instead of being clever, he had been downright ham-fisted in his handling of the Naesmyth affair. Myles drummed his fingers on the arm of the chair as he considered his stupidity. He would need to be far more circumspect in his behavior regarding Lord Inglis. Fortunately Oliver was a friend of his. That made it simple in one way, yet difficult in another. If Oliver suspected what motive lurked behind the ruse to separate him from the charming Sara, he would be perverse enough to marry the girl. It would take some serious planning.

Myles rose from the wing chair and strolled to the library door, deep in thought. He checked to see if the hall remained free of relatives, then walked up the stairs to his temporary room, observed only by the recently hired young footman, James.

James had come to check the library fire and see that all was in order in that room. He had hoped to attend the Lady Corisande as she went on her errands, but had been thwarted by her maid. He found the young lady of the house enchanting, hovering in the hall to catch a glimpse of her whenever he could. Instead, all he got was a glimpse of the house guest, that dashing fellow St. Quinton.

* * *

Later that evening St. Quinton ran Lord Inglis to ground at White's. After a congenial dinner, he persuaded his friend to join him in a game of cards. It was then he passed along the information he had decided to drop in Lord Inglis' ear.

"Looked over this year's crop of beauties as yet?" St. Quinton's voice was lazy, amused.

"I expect there are a few choice misses." Lord Inglis nodded, then studied his cards. "You have the devil's own luck when it comes to cards. Everything, for that matter."

"Perhaps. Saw a little charmer the other night at the Jersey rout. Not in your line, though."

Lord Inglis glanced up, his ears catching a nuance in St. Quinton's voice that quite intrigued him. "How so?"

"The Harland girl. Money, looks, and a dainty figure. Must be a problem somewhere, or someone would have snapped her up before this. I think I may investigate." His drawl was languid, voice faintly bored. Myles dropped the subject of Sara Harland, knowing his few words were sufficient to rouse the curiosity of his friend.

The game continued until its conclusion, Lord Inglis pleased that he for once had defeated—by a slight margin—the usually unbeatable St. Quinton. His step was jaunty as he left his club. If he succeeded in winning at cards, he might also claim victory with the delectable Lady Sara Harland. He was not in the least deceived by the casual ennui displayed by his friend. When St. Quinton was on the prowl, he appeared his most indifferent.

St. Quinton watched his friend leave the club, headed no doubt to the Sefton ball. He had heard Corisande say she planned to attend; most likely Lady Sara would as well. The four seemed to go to the same parties, but carefully reserved their words regarding progress, or lack thereof, for the Fenwick library on Saturday afternoons.

His conscience twinged a bit when he considered his utterly reprehensible behavior. Listening in on the conversations of young women was something he would normally never consider. This was an exception to his rule. Lady Sara had thrown down the gauntlet, unknowingly of course, in her cutting assessment of him. Boring! Of all the words she might have used, "boring" was the worst, in Myles's estimation.

Aunt Milly happily accompanied Sara to the Seftons' ball. It was a glittering affair. Hundreds of candles were reflected in the mirrors, along with the silver, gold, and myriad colors of jewels worn, not to mention the dazzling smiles from the hopeful young girls seeking to find their future husbands.

Lady Sefton beamed a gracious smile on Aunt Milly, exchanging a few words before turning her gaze to Sara. Sally Jersey had chattered about the unusual attention given Lady Sara Harland by St. Quinton. The girl was exquisite, her ebony hair curled charmingly about her face, those strange slanted eyes such a delicious shade of violet. She dressed well too. But then, Millicent Garvagh always had had an eye for design and color, even if she wore rather bizarre creations now that her husband was gone. Sally, in a moment of rare perception, said she believed Millicent to find it a comfort. Her predilection for purple certainly set her apart from the crowd. Her gown this evening was subdued—for her—with only three tiers of ruffles, a sequined panel down the front, plus fan and headdress of moderate-sized plumes—all in purple, of course.

Sara walked close to her aunt as they made their way to the far side of the elegant ballroom. Her dress of pink figured sarcenet swished about her, now clinging, now floating away. She carried today's posy of violets in her left hand again, as ever hoping to discover who might be her mysterious admirer. Whoever it was knew how to capture a woman's curiosity. Sara had never in her life been so intrigued.

The musicians were playing a gay country dance, and couples cavorted through the patterns in happy order. Milly found a vacant chair next to where her dearest friend sat while watching her daughter. Milly plumped herself comfortably down and prepared to elicit every tidbit she could to share with Eudora later.

In moments of collection of fashionable men had gathered about Sara, soliciting her hand for a dance or two. Aunt Milly knew the background of each and every one of them. Tilly had prompted her sister well as to who possessed ne'er a face but his own and was likely to be hunting up a fortune. Sara always deferred to her aunt when seeking permission to dance, and generally it was given. It seemed any young gentleman who felt he might not pass Aunt Millicent's shrewd study did not make the attempt.

About an hour after their arrival, Sara found herself facing the elegant figure of Lord Inglis. He first addressed her aunt, then bowed over Sara's hand as they were introduced. She tensed, her mouth as dry as a piece of day-old toast. He cut out the young sprig of fashion who had come to claim this dance with Sara, much to that gentleman's dismay.

Lord Inglis said, "I believe I must have this dance, my lady. You would not wish me to perish from grief at being denied your fair hand, now, would you?" Those brown eyes were sparkling with gentle humor. His blond curls were carefully arranged to achieve a careless effect. His clothes were all that was correct, tasteful. A very fine gentleman indeed.

This light raillery amused Sara. Since this particular meeting was, above all, what she sought, she gracefully inclined her head in agreement. Tension fled, her body relaxing as he skillfully led her into a waltz. He was charming, handsome, and seemed intent on finding out all he could about her in the shortest order possible. At last she protested.

"Fie, sir, I feel as though you are compiling a biography of me. Such questions are surely not necessary for a simple waltz?"

"Dear Lady Sara, my life has been a barren desert until I met you this evening. It is extremely necessary I find out all I can about your past, for I intend to know everything about your future." Inglis' voice was pitched low, pleasingly husky, as he spoke into that shell-shaped ear so enticingly close to him.

Sara drew in a gratified breath. This was far better than she had hoped for when she first entered the ballroom tonight. Suddenly she caught sight of St. Quinton across the room. When Lord Inglis would have waltzed in that direction, she glanced coyly up at him, indicating a preference for the other, more shadowy part of the ballroom. Bless the man, he was quick off the mark. In seconds they were widely separated from her nemesis. When the dance ended, she nodded to Aunt Milly, then turned to her partner.

"I find the heat of the room has grown oppressive. Would you be so kind as to walk with me for a breath of air?" Sara sniffed her violets, and Lord Inglis envied their place so close to her lips.

"Nothing would give me greater pleasure, fairest lady." He espied St. Quinton making his way across the room, seeming to come their direction. The last thing Lord Inglis wanted was to have St. Quinton join them. The man had too high a score when it came to snatching females from other men. Lord Inglis spirited Sara from the room with dispatch.

"Next time I want to escape, I shall call upon your expertise, milord. That was a fancy piece of footwork if ever I saw one." Sara giggled softly as she found herself whisked around the last corner and into the dim light of the garden. Fairy lights nodded gently above the flowers, and several couples sauntered along a well-brushed path.

Oliver preened a bit before commencing to stroll along the romantically lit way. He felt Sara's hand tremble as it lay on his arm, and he swelled with pride that he had the power to evoke such a strong emotion in an exquisite woman.

"I see we were not the only ones to notice the warmth of the ballroom," Sara commented. She was relieved to see so many other couples taking a breath of air. It would not do to be discovered alone with a man in the Seftons' garden.

"All those candles and people combined, you know." Lord Inglis spoke in a low voice, imparting the conversation with an intimacy Sara found delightful. His talk was mostly nonsense, but she thought him prodigiously agreeable. At the end of the neat garden they turned toward the house, intent upon retracing their steps. Then Lord Inglis saw St. Quinton standing by the door. Dash it all, that deuced man seemed to follow him wherever he went. "Shall we return to the house? I believe it is time for supper, and I would claim the honor of your company if I may."

Sara had also noticed the shadowy form she knew to be St. Quinton. She was becoming far too acquainted with the sight of him. Not desiring his interference in what promised to be a success, she agreed with Lord Inglis.

Sara whispered, "I believe I know another way into the house. If we slip through there, we may avoid . . . the crush of the crowd, perhaps." She was proud her voice was so calm, utterly devoid of panic.

"Guide me, dear lady, and we shall claim the first of the lobster patties." Lord Inglis cast a victorious smile toward his good friend, then disappeared from the garden with the delectable Sara on his arm.

Contrary to what either of the escapees supposed, the Earl of St. Quinton smiled with great pleasure at their joint departure. Inglis' had fallen in with his plan beautifully. Myles figured he could proceed to the next step in his scheme. That twinge over what he intended to do attacked him again. But then he reassured himself. Lady Sara, of a certainty, deserved this little set-down. It wasn't as though the fair damsel could not find another man to wed. Why, from his observation as he entered the ballroom, she had been deluged with simpering fools falling over their own feet to reach her side. He had watched her in Inglis' arms during the waltz. With her ebony curls and those poetic blond locks Inglis permitted to fall over his brow, they made an attractive pair.

He gave a sigh of disgust, then tugged his ear while he thought about the next step to take. All in all, this was becoming a very intriguing Season. He ought to thank Lady Sara Harland for enlivening his days. The nights . . . well, he still had Olivia. Satisfied his friend was in full pursuit of his quarry, Myles sauntered toward the door, bidding his disappointed hostess good evening before taking his leave. The thought of the warm and eager Olivia drove all concerns for his scheme from his mind.

The next morning found a bouquet of delicate pink roses, the precise shade of her gown of the evening before, joining the violets in her bedroom. Sara buried her nose in the roses, then sniffed the delicate violets. Never would she admit the violets won her heart. The roses bore the card of Baron Inglis; the violets revealed nothing of the identity of the sender, as usual. Sara stared wistfully at the dainty petals, touching the soft surface of one with a gentle finger. Who was this man of great mystery? It had to be a man, of course. A woman might have sent one or two posies in fun, but never for weeks on end.

Sara had no illusions about her beauty. She accepted that she looked well enough, given the lovely gowns she could afford and the acceptable background provided by her aunts. But her money posed no little problem. She greatly feared a gambler would seek to marry her, then toss her fortune to the winds. As far as she knew, Inglis was not addicted to play.

That afternoon she found the baron in her aunts' salon, looking quite at ease, as though he confronted the scrutiny of three protective dowagers every day. When he requested Sara's company on a drive through the park, she caught the barely perceptible nod of three lace-crowned heads from the corner of her eye, and graciously accepted the invitation.

It took only a few minutes to run up to her room to slip on her pelisse and bonnet. She was especially pleased with the bonnet. The violet ribbons exactly matched those dainty flowers delivered each morning, the dew still lingering on their petals.

Baron Inglis had quite acceptable chestnuts and a very nice curricle. Sara admired the shiny black surface of the body with its inset of cane edged with bright red. The wheels were picked out in the same gay color. She flashed him a delightful smile.

Smart and most fetching. It was a relief to note he didn't favor the high-perch phaeton she had observed being driven by St. Quinton on more than one occasion. Such a vehicle looked dangerously unstable. It was not unusual to see one on its side, having turned over going round a corner when driven by a careless whip.

Lord Inglis handed her into the vehicle, then after entering gave his groom a nod. The lad let go of the horse, then ran to jump up behind them as they moved toward the park.

Hyde Park was crowded, as was usual. Sara smiled at the sight of Corisande, dressed in a lemon-yellow pelisse that nearly matched her curls, at the side of Sir Percy in his neat gray curricle, its wheels newly picked out in bright yellow. It seemed Sir Percy was showing a partiality to yellow as well as Corisande. Discreet nods were exchanged.

A sudden tensing of Sara's escort drew her attention to a rider astride a superb cream-colored Arab. St. Quinton was stopped by the carriage road in conversation with a lady.

Sara felt a constriction in her chest as she realized the woman seated so graciously in the blue-upholstered whiskey with plain blue sides behind a single gray horse was none other than the cyprian she had seen him with before, his mistress. She was wearing a velvet pelisse the same shade of blue as her smart little carriage. Sara ignored the woman, focusing her attention on the man on horseback. He was laughing, his teeth flashing in attractive amusement.

It seemed Lord Inglis hoped to pass the pair with no notice from St. Quinton, a feeling heartily endorsed by Sara. They had nearly succeeded, when Sara heard Lord Inglis hailed in a too-familiar voice. The figure at her side remained tense. St. Quinton rode up as the blue carriage continued on its way.

"Inglis, old fellow. Heard you made a packet on that race the other day. Clever man! I understand you have done very well at the tables lately. I'll have to look to my laurels, it seems." He turned his attention from his friend to Sara. "Ah, the fair Lady Sara. I need not ask you how you are this afternoon. It is plain from those sparkling violet eyes that you are in first form. Inglis, I hadn't thought you to be so astute with the fair ones. Fancy giving the delightful Lady Sara violets to match her eyes."

Sara flushed guiltily. She had found the notion of pairing her new bonnet with the violets irresistible. "Too kind, milord." Her voice was polite and rather distant—the sort of manner one might use with a relative she would rather not acknowledge but found she must.

"Not at all, I assure you. Enjoy your day." With that jolly comment, he tipped his beaver, then rode off through the park, looking remarkably satisfied with himself.

The atmosphere in the curricle was as dark as the carriage itself. Oliver was cursing himself for not thinking of ordering violets for Lady Sara, and wondering who had. Sara sat fuming at St. Quinton. First he had had the audacity to utterly fawn on that . . . that woman. Then he had twitted that nice Lord Inglis about his gaming.

The latter thought gave Sara pause. Surely this nice gentleman was not a gamester, was he? She resolved to learn the truth without her aunts finding out about it. Perhaps Kit Fenwick might know. The idea of "third choice" hung over her, always remaining in the back of her mind.

St. Quinton *would* bring up the violets.

"I truly do not know who sent these violets, Lord Inglis. They matched the ribands on my new bonnet, so I took them along. The lovely roses you sent are in my bedroom, where I can view them when I first open my eyes in the morning." The appealing smile she gave him was sufficient to wipe away any suspicions he entertained.

Oliver found he rather liked the notion of having the fair Sara see his offering the very first thing upon opening her eyes, and he beamed a smile of forgiveness at her. She really was a fetching little thing.

The drive continued on through the park, each nodding to friends as they slowly made their way back to the gate and the streets leading to No. 23 Brook Street.

At the front door Sara bade him farewell, then thoughtfully entered the house. She wouldn't say anything to the aunts about the teasing given Lord Inglis regarding his gaming. Any words from St. Quinton were suspect. Yet Inglis had previously mentioned beating St. Quinton at cards. She decided she would seek out Kit as soon as possible to discover what he might know. Her brow furrowed slightly as she walked up the stairs, mindless of Aunt Milly's injunction never to do such a thing for fear it might be permanent. Might there be a flaw in the so-suitable Lord Inglis that her aunts had failed to note?

# 5

Flecks of moisture clung to the velvety petals of the richly fragrant violets. Sara buried her nose in the center of that morning's posy of flowers, savoring their delightful scent, wondering, as she did, who persisted with this mystery. Who was the unknown "gallant" who ordered delivery of the flowers so early every morning? Why was it important for those flowers to greet her upon each arising?

Impatiently she thrust aside the notion of a handsome stranger who admired her from afar. It mattered little if he was poor-but-proper or rich-but-rakish. If her aunts had not set forth his name as acceptable, he might as well not exist. Yet, alluring ideas lingered in her mind, and with them the growing fantasies she wove in secret moments.

Sara's love of the dramatic was often a source of teasing by her dearest friends. This mystery of the flowers was straight from the plot of one of the Minerva Press novels she had smuggled into her room—from Aunt Milly, usually. Aunt Tilly deplored such nonsense and Aunt Eudora ignored the matter, claiming the novels beneath consideration. Sara didn't go to extremes, but she yearned to be swept up in the arms of a handsome man and truly cherished. It wasn't unheard-of, this marvelous love between husband and wife. Naturally that was the only sort of loving arrangement she would contemplate. She wasn't so lost to what was proper that she would go out of bounds.

However, if the plot were real, the handsome poor-but-proper suitor (the rich-but-rakish would never do, she decided) would find all obstacles to true love swept aside. Her aunts would deem him worthy, and a fortune would suddenly appear from an Unexpected Source. Rich uncles were the usual means of sudden wealth. She hoped her mysterious suitor had an elderly, very rich uncle who was about to go aloft. Not that she would wish anyone dead. Not actually.

The violets had brought mystery into her life, and she longed to know who shared her flair for the dramatic. Sara was convinced they were most compatible.

Following a late breakfast, Sara, her maid trailing closely behind her, with a footman along as well, set out for the Fenwicks'. The footman was always along just to be safe, urged by Aunt Eudora. After all, Sara was an heiress. She garnered a curious look or two, but the presence of the two servants at her side prevented unpleasantness during the brief walk.

Her simple blue-and-white-spotted muslin was quite proper and her chip bonnet tied with cornflower-blue silk ribands unexceptionable. Her fingers might have worriedly smoothed the silk of her gloves, but outwardly she looked composed enough. Though it was too early to be making a social call, this was nothing of the kind. Sara was determined to find out what she could of Lord Inglis' propensity for gaming. Kit Fenwick was bound to know, considering his fondness for the pastime. Was there any young man who escaped the love for games of chance? How many fortunes were whistled down the wind in an evening of so-called pleasure?

The new footman opened the door, admitting Sara into the entry. When she requested that Kit be called, James first showed her to the library, then hurried up the stairs, his face impassive. Worried she might be caught by St. Quinton as he strolled down to breakfast, Sara eased the library door nearly closed, figuring she could safely hide if necessary.

Quite some time later Kit opened the door with an impatient push. "Dash it all, Lady Sara, a fellow can't be rushed in his

dress, y'know." He entered the library, a yawn barely concealed behind his hand. He was attired in the height of fashion.
High points on his collar threatened to impale his cheeks at any
turn, and fobs dangled at his waistcoat in considerable number.
Sara recalled the restrained elegance of St. Quinton and
shuddered at the sight Kit presented.

She had small patience with the fashionable pleasure of
gaming until the wee hours, and felt little pity for Kit.
However, she decided to approach him with a touch of
flattery. "I know what a popular man-about-town you are, and
I simply had to see you before you took yourself off to the
clubs or somewhere beyond my reach."

At this totally unexpected praise, Kit preened a bit; then
suspicion reared its head. "What is it you want? If it's money,
my pockets are to let. 'Twas a devilishly rum night at the
tables."

Clearing her throat, surprised by a sudden bout of nervous-
ness, Sara shook her head, then plunged. "Have you ever seen
Lord Inglis at play?"

Kit shrugged his shoulders. This feat was accomplished with
some difficulty, owing to the large amount of padding in his
coat, deemed necessary to look all the crack. His mode of dress
failed to amuse Sara as it usually did. She watched him
intently.

"He is found at the tables now and again. Saw him with
Myles over a hand of cards not long ago. Devilishly good
player, a regular knowing one. Never see him sneaking off to
Howard and Gibbs to borrow money. Doubt if you'd have to
worry about him putting a period to his existence over debts, if
that's what you want to know."

Sara twisted the strings of her reticule about in her hand, not
convinced with this faint praise. "I read in the *Morning Herald*
of a gentleman who lost four thousand guineas the other night.
That is a fearsome amount."

"Not Inglis. He's usually in high feather, seldom loses very
much. Not quite in the same league as my cousin Myles, how-

ever." Kit picked a piece of lint from the cuff of his correct blue coat. He wavered between the excesses of the dandy and the elegance of his cousin. Today the war waged between the cut and the color of his coat versus the remainder of his ensemble.

Sara stilled her unsettled pacing about the library to face Kit. "I was not aware St. Quinton was addicted to green baize or pasteboards."

Kit rubbed thoughtfully at his chin. "He plays, but not extravagantly. Never drinks if he intends to really gamble, y'know. Has a remarkable memory and a dashed cool head on those shoulders. Sound judgment too."

Sara flared back, "You seem quite impressed, as if you envy him."

"I do."

Kit's simple reply surprised Sara. Not wanting to discuss the man she distrusted, Sara returned to her former subject. "But Inglis?" she persisted.

"He's no worse than a dozen other peers I know. He's no niffy-naffy fellow, y'know." Kit grew suspicious. "Why do you want to know? What are you planning? You and m'sister up to something?"

Sara feigned innocence. "What could we possibly be up to, Kit? I vow you are the silliest man. Inglis has paid me a few attentions recently, and I was . . . well, curious. Who better to seek information from than you?"

Her artless smile won him over for a moment. Accustomed to being called corkbrained by his sister, he was pleased to have Lady Sara recognize his true worth. Then he recalled her aunts. "Seems to me your aunts would know all this and more."

"Yes, well, I am certain they do, but . . . you see, I would rather not ask them, at the moment anyway." Sara edged toward the door, wanting nothing more than to get home before her aunts could question her whereabouts. "You needn't mention I was here. I shall see Corisande later." With that she slipped around the corner and out the front door, leaving Kit in a puzzle.

When he entered the breakfast room moments later, he greeted his cousin with an abstracted air. " 'Morning."

Myles set aside the morning paper, studying Kit with a knowledgeable eye. "What goes on, coz? Bad night?"

"No more than usual," replied Kit. "Had the oddest conversation just now. Dashed if I can figure out the female mind."

Intrigued, Myles began carving up the slice of roast on his plate while presenting a sympathetic mien. "Do tell?"

"Lady Sara was just here asking all manner of questions about Inglis," Kit said, only too happy to get the listening ear of his esteemed cousin. "Odd thing was, she wanted to know about his gaming losses. He ain't been up to some deep doings, has he?" Kit heaped a plate with food at the sideboard, then joined Myles at the expanse of mahogany.

The butler entered with a fresh pot of coffee, poured two cups for the men, then left them to their conversation.

"Not really. Inglis enjoys a good bet, as don't we all? His luck at cards is not as fine as it could be, but I daresay he'll settle down, given time. He's not up the River Tick . . . yet." Myles thought a moment, then queried Kit. "Lady Sara seemed quite concerned about the possibility that Inglis often gambles heavily?"

Kit nodded sagely. "Come to think of it, seems m'sister said something about Lady Sara having a horror of gaming. That was after old Lord What's-his-name hanged himself in his conservatory. Remember? Lost everything he owned. Ruined. His daughter found him. She was a school chum of Lady Sara's and Corisande's."

Myles changed the subject, but continued to think about Lady Sara Harland. Should he use this knowledge against her scheme? It was undoubtedly not the act of a gentleman, but on the other hand, a true lady did not behave thus. His chance remark about gaming had borne unexpected fruit, and it would be a shame to waste it.

\* \* \*

When Myles bumped into Lord Oliver Inglis at White's, he had pretty well decided on a plan of action. Thus he purposefully invited Inglis to dine with him, then proceeded to tell him a number of innocuous tales before passing along a final tidbit of gossip.

"Saw you escorting the delectable Lady Sara Harland the other night. Surprised to see you two together. It isn't often I get pipped at the post with a fair charmer, old boy."

Inglis, who had decided by this point that Lady Sara possessed all the qualifications his parents would approve in a bride, frowned. "Surprised?"

St. Quinton leaned back in his chair, rolling the stem of his glass of claret between his fingers, staring at its ruby glow rather than at his friend. "Well, you know how talk is. I heard she is fascinated by gamblers. Finds them devilishly exciting, or so they say. Something about the thrill of chance and all that. But I understand how you might feel about overextending yourself, old chap. I daresay it is far safer to be a bit on the dull side than take a risk at the tables. Wouldn't blame you one whit, myself." Myles took lazy note of the sudden glint in his friend's eyes, then changed the subject. No point in belaboring the matter. It was up to Inglis to follow through. Myles would lay odds that Inglis would do just that.

When Sara met Lord Inglis at Almack's that Wednesday evening, the gentleman was prepared. During their first dance of the evening, he casually passed along the information that he had won a terribly amusing bet from his good friend Loftestone. He added a few details and awaited her breathless delight.

Sara smiled politely up at Lord Inglis—and began to worry. However, her attempts to be gay and unconcerned must have succeeded, as Inglis continued to wear that self-satisfied smile on his face the remainder of the quadrille.

A glance across the room revealed Fiona with her mother. At the conclusion of the disturbing dance with Lord Inglis, he returned Sara to her aunt's side. Sara murmured a vague excuse to Aunt Milly, then edged her way around the room until she reached Fiona.

"I must speak with you." Sara's voice was low and urgent.

"Here? I thought we decided to talk on Saturday?" Fiona was puzzled at the agitation Sara could not conceal. She strolled along with Sara to the ladies' withdrawing room.

Sara gave a quick check around, then sighed. "Good, there is no one else here." She twisted the draw cord of the dainty reticule in her hand, while deciding how best to phrase her worries.

"I saw you dancing the quadrille with Lord Inglis. I must say, you perform the patterns of the dance very well. Is that it? Does what you have to say regard Lord Inglis in some manner?" Concerned, Fiona studied Sara closely, aware that Sara was not given to fretting without cause.

Relieved that Fiona had made explanations simple for her, Sara nodded. "A feeling of unease eats at me. Silly of me, I am sure, but he mentioned gaming again tonight." She darted a worried glance at Fiona before looking down at her hands. "I asked Kit Fenwick if he knew about any gaming Lord Inglis did. He said that Inglis played no more than others. What does that mean, pray tell? Does it mean he loses only a *small* fortune at a sitting?"

"Perhaps you are unduly cautious." Fiona tried to soothe Sara. "Men have these little weaknesses, you know. I am certain he will devote himself to you and a family, once you are married."

"Married? That does not seem to stop most men. You must know I have a sizable portion. What money I have will be settled on my husband. I doubt my uncle will reserve any part of it for my own use. While Lord Inglis might be a generous husband and pay all the bills and give me a small allowance for my personal expenses, he would still have the bulk of my fortune to use as he pleases. I cannot bear to think it might be lost at the gaming tables. Kit described Lord Inglis as a regular 'knowing one.' That hints of a close acquaintanceship with green baize, does it not?"

Comfortable with her growing relationship with the estimable Viscount York, Fiona could only give a helpless shrug. She shared Sara's concerns but didn't know what could be done about them. She was inclined to return to the glittering company of the Assembly Rooms and a second dance with her dear Brian rather than dwell on a possible tendency to gaming on the part of Lord Inglis. What with Sara's inclination to the dramatic, it might all be her imagination. Fiona placed a comforting arm about Sara's shoulders and guided her toward the door.

"I believe you are again making much out of little. Let us join the others. I vow I am so thirsty that even a glass of lukewarm lemonade entices me. Remember, Lord Inglis could not have passed your aunts' scrutiny if he were addicted to cards and lost heavily at the tables. Lord York says Inglis is not infatuated with the turf, either. Come, cease your fidgeting over the matter and enjoy the evening."

Sara, suddenly ashamed that she was keeping Fiona from the gaiety of the evening, agreed. The two returned to the tier of chairs, where Aunt Milly noted her niece's preoccupation but didn't interrogate her.

It was nearing the hour of eleven, after which no one would be admitted to Almack's, when a flurry at the entrance caught Sara's attention. St. Quinton! She sent a questioning glance to Fiona that was met by a shrug. Both young women knew his lordship never graced the Assembly Rooms with his presence.

St. Quinton raised his gold quizzing glass to survey the room. Sara detested his air of superiority. Never mind that he put all other men in the room in the shade with his elegance and address. Her spirits sank as he approached the tiers of seats at one end of the room where the dowagers and chaperones reposed in carefully concealed anxiety—or joy—depending on whether their charges were "taking" or not.

He made a bow to Aunt Milly, then, at her admiring nod,

took Sara off for the next dance. Sara's heart sank as she recalled it was to be a waltz.

His mocking smile infuriated Sara as nothing else possibly could. "I am surprised to see you here, Lord St. Quinton. I was under the impression you never attended the subscription balls at Almack's. What could have changed your mind?"

His eyes gleamed with a devilish fire for a brief moment. "I suppose I could say I was drawn to your loveliness, knowing that as a bud of society you would be present. However"—he swept her into his arms, bringing her a discreet bit closer than the usual separation—"I heard that Inglis had made a bet that I wouldn't show here tonight. So naturally I had to come."

"Naturally." Sara felt as though she might suffocate from his proximity. His manner of dancing was impossible to criticize from afar. It was when one was in his arms that one discovered the little nuances he used to make a woman feel deliciously wicked and quite wanton in her desires. It was no wonder that Byron had condemned the dance as a potent aphrodisiac. Of course, it stood to reason the poor man felt keenly his own inability to waltz. Sara pitied Lord Byron as she spun around the room in the arms of the most dangerous man in London. It was a divine sensation, and as afraid as she was regarding her feelings for St. Quinton, she would be a liar to deny her pleasure at being his partner.

Though the waltz had been performed in London for several years, it had not the popularity of the quadrille. While she enjoyed the intricacies of the latter, Sara felt the waltz by far the most romantic—and perilous as well—of the dances. Especially while in the arms of a man like St. Quinton.

"You have enjoyed the company of Lord Inglis this evening? I understand he has singled you out for his attentions." His lazy, hooded look was deceptive in its acuity.

Sara flushed a becoming pink. "Lord Inglis has paid me the honor of requesting my hand in two dances. You must know that is all that is permitted."

"I am certain I shall hear if he asks for a third. Tell me, his flutter at the tables does not bother you? I am aware that not everyone shares the daring attached to a wager."

Sara stiffened perceptibly, nearly stumbling as St. Quinton swept her around in a skillful whirl. Only his expertise saved them from disaster. "I would rather not discuss such things, milord. It cannot possibly concern me."

"Odd," he murmured. "I would have thought you very inquisitive regarding the subject of gaming."

There were moments of strained silence before he spoke once more. "I suppose you have read the latest scandal, that novel *Glenarvon?*" St. Quinton studied the lovely face so close to his own, suddenly wishing he might explore it with greater intimacy than was permissible while on the dance floor at Almack's.

Sara was relieved to have the subject changed. "Aunt Milly bought it as soon as it came out. There is little doubt who the authoress is, is there? Poor Caroline."

"You feel sympathy for her?" Lord St. Quinton raised his brows in surprise.

"I am aware of the spiteful things she has written about many in society, and the cruel portrait of her husband. Still, she is a creature to be pitied. It must be terrible to love, then be rejected." Sara recalled her own fleeting *tendre* for St. Quinton and knew that while Caroline Lamb was to be censured for her bitter novel, a *roman-à-clef* quite thinly disguised, Sara had little heart for it.

"And what would an incomparable like yourself know about such a thing?" Lord St. Quinton found himself wishing that manners permitted the truth to be known. Did Sara Harland nurse a secret affection for him in that beautifully covered heart?

"It is possible to imagine such a thing." Sara dared not look up at him lest he detect the truth. Though she was quite certain that not a vestige of her interest in him remained, she couldn't be equally certain he might not see the past disappointment written on her face. The music drew to a conclusion and she took refuge in silence as Lord St. Quinton returned her to where her aunt was seated in her usual purple splendor.

Aunt Milly fluttered a small fan of purple paper ornamented with silver spangles as St. Quinton smiled down at her. Her romantic heart skipped at the sight of his handsome face and form.

"Your servant, Lady Garvagh." There was no mockery in his eyes as he made his bow to the elderly lady. He quite admired the old girl.

"Surprised to see you here, Lord St. Quinton. What got you inside the doors?" While her heart might be susceptible to a good-looking man, her mind told her to cut the nonsense and fish for the truth.

He gave a modest laugh and then confessed, "It was a simple bet, madam. I heard that Inglis had wagered a generous sum that I wouldn't show up, and here I am."

Aunt Milly frowned, then glanced at Sara. She was well-acquainted with her niece's aversion to gaming. "Is that so?" She studied St. Quinton with care, to see if he might be joking about the matter, then sat straighter as Lord Inglis crossed the room to join them.

He strolled up to where Lord St. Quinton stood by the ladies and gave Myles a rueful grin. "I see you heard about the wager of this afternoon. How like you to show up and ruin my chance of winning."

Myles shrugged. "Nice to know you don't hold it against me. You are a clever one, usually. It certainly is better than gambling to see which raindrop beats another to the bottom of the pane."

"Nor have I lost several thousand pounds betting on a race of turkeys to win against geese, as our dear Prince Regent has done. No, I try to wager on a sure thing." He gave St. Quinton another grin, this one a bit less amiable. "That was why I bet against you, my friend. I was certain you had other, ah, more interesting things to occupy you this evening."

Sara caught the inflection in his voice as he gave St. Quinton that arch look, and knew at once what was meant. Lord Inglis believed that Lord St. Quinton would be with his mistress this evening rather than waltzing around at an insipid ball at the Assembly Rooms. She flashed a look of scorn at St. Quinton before turning to her aunt.

"Dear Aunt Milly, I vow I am overcome with thirst. Shall we make our way to the refreshment table?"

Because she looked at her aunt, she missed the frigid stare St. Quinton gave his friend. His private nature permitted no one to intrude on his personal life. Certainly to imply, while he was in the presence of ladies of quality, that he would rather spend time with Olivia was the outside of enough.

Lord Inglis bowed to the ladies, glancing with resignation at his seeming rival. "Allow me, please. Lemonade or orgeat?" He received their requests for lemonade and walked toward the refreshment room with obvious reluctance.

Aunt Milly narrowed her eyes in shrewd assessment of the two gentlemen, then turned her gaze on her niece. There was something going on, if she didn't miss her guess, and she rarely did. She watched St. Quinton cut out his friend by escorting Sara onto the dance floor as Lord Inglis elbowed his way through the crowd. He handed a glass of lemonade to Aunt Milly, then stood with the other in hand while he observed Myles and Lady Sara in a quadrille.

"Interesting evening, I'd say," Aunt Milly ventured.

"Quite so, Lady Garvagh. Your niece seems most in demand this evening."

"Yes," agreed Millicent complacently, "she is, isn't she? Dear girl. I shall miss her when she leaves to marry."

This statement startled Lord Inglis, and the lemonade sloshed dangerously in the glass. "Has someone spoken for her? I had not heard."

"Oh, no," Millicent said most happily, the plumes dancing around her head as she shook it vigorously. "It is plain, however, that there will be someone before long. I have a feeling for these things, you see."

Lord Inglis glowered at Lord St. Quinton and waited with great determination for the couple to return. He was not going to permit St. Quinton to take Lady Sara away from him. He must think of an amusing way of gambling with which to snare the lady's approbation. Although it wasn't on the betting books, he was willing to stake a goodly sum that Lady Sara would be his before long.

# 6

The ride home from Almack's was exceedingly quiet, as Aunt Milly and Sara were each lost in thought. When they arrived, the sisters were waiting up for them, intent on gleaning every facet of the evening for study. Tilly was anxious to learn of any evidence of change in fortune. Eudora naturally wanted to know who was present and dancing with whom. It was she the two troubled ladies in all their finery turned to when they entered the salon.

"What happened?" Eudora quizzed. She could sense an *on-dit* at twenty paces. "Never tell me Caroline Lamb tried to enter Almack's!"

"No, no, nothing of the sort," said Sara. "No one behaved other than they ought. Fiona was there with her mother." Sara pulled off her gloves and tossed them on a table along with her dainty reticule. "Fiona is being paid court by Viscount York, with nice attention on his part. The evening was much as you might expect."

"Well," said Aunt Milly, "there actually was more going on than that. We had a very interesting evening." She then related what had occurred between Inglis and St. Quinton, omitting not one word. Sara volunteered her chat with Fiona, as much as she felt necessary. She wasn't sure how much she wished to reveal of her conversation with Lord St. Quinton. The aunts had a most disconcerting way of discerning in her speech far more than she liked.

"And what was said while on the dance floor?" asked Aunt Eudora, her eyes fixed on Sara's face with narrow intensity.

"Lord Inglis told me of an amusing tale of gaming and Lord St. Quinton commented on the same, then discussed the new novel *Glenarvon*."

"Scandalous!" breathed Tilly.

"The book, surely, not his comments," Sara teased, forgetting she wasn't supposed to know it was in the house. "He seemed surprised I had read it."

"Well! I never," huffed Eudora.

"Bother the novel," said Aunt Milly, "the problem is that Lord Inglis seems to have developed a propensity for gaming that we knew nothing about!"

"Oh, dear," exclaimed Aunt Tilly, casting an accusing look at Eudora. "I had not heard a whisper about it. You ought to have known, Eudora."

"Well, I did not." Eudora was indignant yet perturbed. How could she possibly have missed this curious bit of information? She took a look at Sara's pale face and began to move the group toward the hall. "I suggest we allow Sara to get to bed, and we can mull this over in the morning. It will take a bit of contrivance to uncover the truth of the matter." So saying, she handed Sara her gloves and reticule, then guided her from the salon and up to her room, turning her over to a sleepy abigail.

The following morning there was relative harmony between the sisters as they conferred around the breakfast table. For once Eudora made no slighting remark about Maurice, seated in Millicent's lap as usual, munching on a piece of kipper. Millicent refrained from complaining about the nip Xenia had given Maurice when he got too close to the stand from which Xenia ruled the salon.

Tilly got to the heart of the matter with no roundabout-ation. "Do you suppose it is a hoax? I, for one, find it difficult to accept that our information was wrong about the gentleman, though I believe I have made myself clear upon more than one occasion about how I feel regarding other than first choice."

Languidly stroking the loudly purring Maurice, Milly nodded, adding, "I am most confused, dear sisters. Sara seemed to get along well with St. Quinton last evening. They were beautifully partnered for the waltz and a quadrille. Though Lady Jersey twitted me about his attentions, I sense he is not seriously interested in Sara. Nor does she seem to have a *tendre* for him. I had thought—from things she said after that Christmas house party—that there might have been an interest in that direction, but apparently not. It is of a certainty confusing."

Studying her nearly empty plate (she did not believe in wasting time over her meal), Tilly mused, "The violets arrived as usual this morning. I wish we could uncover that mystery."

Beaming with delight, Milly said, "I think having a touch of intrigue about the house is rather romantic. Leave well enough alone, sister."

Eudora cleared her throat, then continued as though the violets hadn't been mentioned. "I believe that until other information comes our way, we shall have to go on what we know to this point. There is nothing we can do if Lord Inglis behaves in a manner inconsistent with what we accept to be the facts."

"I suggest we say nothing to Sara. Poor lamb has difficulty making up her mind as it is." Tilly looked at the others for confirmation of her opinion.

"Agreed." Eudora ate the last bite of her substantial breakfast—anxiety always made her ravenous—and took the morning papers with her to her desk, where she combed every page to check for some snippet that might confirm or deny their worst fears.

By the time Sara arose and came down for her breakfast, the house was peaceful, only Aunt Milly remaining in the cheerful breakfast room with Maurice. Knowing her aunts quite well,

Sara assumed that all had been discussed before she made her sleepy way downstairs.

Taking her plate of food, she chose the chair closest to Aunt Milly, then slipped onto it, her unease evident. "Well, what has happened?"

"We discussed the evening and Lord Inglis, as you suspect. Men have these little humors, dear. It is our considered opinion that there is nothing to worry about . . . yet. A small wager now and again does not make one a knight of the elbow, you know. With all the talk centered about the forthcoming marriages between Princess Charlotte and Prince Leopold, I doubt that Lord Inglis will cause much gossip."

Milly reflected a moment on the coming marriage of the Prince Regent's daughter and all that it promised, before bringing herself back to the subject at hand. "That may be well and good, yet it does not give us much chance to get to the heart of the matter. Perhaps it is best to ignore the entire event. I suggest you try a little harder to fix the gentleman's attention." Aunt Milly fastened a penetrating gaze on Sara, trying to ascertain precisely how this advice was received.

Sara sighed, then nodded. "I expect I dwelt upon it far too much. Lord Inglis said we are to receive invitations to a *fête champêtre* at the Countess of Langholm's country house at Richmond. She is his sister, as you probably know."

Aunt Milly beamed. "A fine family, as I mentioned before. I expect it will be my lot to attend with you. I do so enjoy these romantic gatherings in the countryside. Think on it—dancing in one of those clever striped tents, and archery, or other amusing activities. You know you would enjoy using a bow and arrow again, my love." She frowned, adding, "Such a strange diversion for a woman. Though I am certain it is quite proper." She patted Maurice on the head, then dropped the cat unceremoniously to the floor as she rose. "I had best see to my gown. I wonder what I ought to wear for the occasion?" Milly drifted off to her room, leaving Sara behind, wearing an abstracted expression on her face.

"Well," Sara confided to Maurice, who had resumed a comfortable position on the chair vacated by Milly, and was consuming the last of this morning's kippers, courtesy of Sara, "I doubt that Lord Inglis will have an opportunity to gamble while at an innocent breakfast. Though why it is called a breakfast when we do not get fed until five in the afternoon, I am sure I never understand. At least there ought to be plenty of activity to keep him occupied."

The day of the outing dawned uncommonly bright and clear. It seemed the weather had decided to favor the countess by being on its best behavior.

Sara dressed in a very pretty gown of striped pink-and-white silk muslin and tied on a chip bonnet with matching pink ribands. Her pink parasol was of the latest mode, with fringe around the scalloped edge.

One look at her niece and Eudora said, "Best take a shawl with you. That dress doesn't look as though it would keep a body warm in the middle of a sunny day. Millicent, do you not think she ought to wear a chemisette with that low neck?"

Affronted that her taste was called into question, Aunt Milly replied somewhat huffily, "And destroy the line? Nonsense. A shawl, perhaps. I have a lavender one you may use if you like, dear."

Tilly bustled in at that moment with a white *cachemire de laine* shawl over her arm. "I believe this will solve the matter quite nicely. Have a lovely time. Eudora and I are invited to the Graftons' for a card party this afternoon. We can compare notes later."

With that, Sara and Aunt Milly joined the gratifyingly on-time Lord Inglis in his carriage for the ride to his sister's house in the country. The shawl proved unnecessary for the moment and Sara placed it aside as the three sped along the cobbled streets and out of the city.

Once beyond the noisy confines of the city, Sara appreciated the beauty of the rural scene. They crossed over the Thames at

Fulham, passed the Hare and Hounds, continuing on the main road, turning off just before Richmond. The Earl of Langholm's country house was a charming place. Wisteria draped over a brick fence at the gate, and lilacs bloomed in wild profusion, earning the ecstatic approval of Aunt Milly.

"What a sweet little home. Your sister must enjoy herself out here." Millicent Garvagh was not one to cavil at simplicity.

"Not above fifteen bedrooms, but it does, she says. We are to go around to the rear, I believe." Lord Inglis smiled at the older lady's enthusiasm.

They swept around the rambling brick structure to the courtyard behind the house. There, stablehands ran forward to take control of the horses as Lord Inglis drew to a stop with a nice flourish. He assisted both ladies from the equipage with an elegant touch, tucking Sara's gloved hand into the crook of his arm before setting off in search of his sister and the other guests.

A broad, pansy-bordered lawn was the scene of a lively, if unfashionable game of pall-mall. A snappy game was in progress, judging by the way the ladies squealed so prettily as a gentleman sent a wooden ball skimming across the green with a tap of his wooden mallet. Sara glanced at the group, stiffening as she saw St. Quinton send a ball through a wicket. He glanced their way and grinned at Sara.

Oliver noted the presence of his rival as well, murmuring, "Dash it all, the fellow could have declined."

Confused at this odd remark, Sara concentrated on studying Lady Langholm as she approached them. She was a lovely woman some years Oliver's junior, with the same golden hair and large brown eyes. Her dress of blue calico was of the latest stare of fashion, and most becoming. The tall gentleman drawing his bow at the archery target was pointed out as her husband.

"Oliver, how pleased I am that you have finally arrived. But then, I can see what might make you wish to dawdle. Hello, my dears. I am Oliver's sister, Catherine. My husband, Langholm, you can see over there, proving his skill with the arrows and bow. I hope you have not had a tiring journey out here to our little retreat." She beamed a smile, then fluttered her hands in the air to indicate where the various tents and amusements were located. "There are all manner of things to do. Please do wander about and try whatever takes your fancy." With that she smiled again, and drifted off to visit with another arrival.

"My sister is a bit of a rattle, but a dear soul nonetheless. We could take a stroll through her gardens. I believe you will find them quite unexceptionable this time of the year." He cast a hopeful look at Aunt Milly, who took the hint to decide she simply must have a glass of ratafia at the charming refreshment tent, and walked in the opposite direction.

Sara was undecided as to whether she was pleased at this turn of events or no. She assayed a smile at Lord Inglis, then accepted his escort to the gardens.

She saw a colorful array of lavender and white stock contrasted with cheerful deep yellow wallflowers and primula of various hues. Wisteria cascaded from an arbor beside a bed of roses now sending out shoots. Langholm must have a staff of very fine gardeners.

Sara was content to stroll with Oliver in the spring-scented air. Hope stirred within her.

"You fit into these surroundings well. My manor is not unlike this, aged brick, many-paned windows, and rather nice gardens, if I do say so. The house is perhaps larger, but my sister shows a hand with decorating that my bachelor establishment lacks. What I need is a feminine touch to the place." Lord Inglis looked down at Sara with a gleam in his eyes that she found rather appealing. Hope rose.

They had reached a wooded dell where a stream wandered through the property. Before them was a wooden bridge spanning the meandering waters just over the spot where a waterfall had been created for all to admire. Masses of primula bloomed along the creek bank. A warbler darted across the glade to where trees screened it from view.

Oliver drew her to the center of the bridge, where they stood quietly taking in the beauty around them. It was peaceful and serene, a most romantic place.

"Lady Sara, I believe you know what is in my heart. I hold you in the highest esteem." He took her hand in his and earnestly searched her face for some sign of acceptance or rejection. He saw her faint smile and took courage. He was about to continue when a sound was heard. Someone was walking along the path directly toward them.

"Hallo, there. Don't tell me you two are not going to try your hand at one of the events of the day. Inglis, you would never be so cruel."

The hearty voice stopped Oliver's speech abruptly. Sara and Oliver shared a look of dismay. How had St. Quinton found them out, and, what was more important, why?

Oliver took a calming breath and turned to face Myles, who was lounging casually against a post at the foot of the bridge. "We felt it adequate to admire my brother-in-law's garden. It is quite unnecessary to concern yourself with our welfare." His tone sharpened slightly as he concluded.

Myles gave them a devilish grin and extended his hand. "Come, join us, do. The archery range awaits. A little bird told me that Lady Sara is a dab hand at the bow and arrow. I wish to see her prowess for myself."

Sara gave Oliver a resigned look, then nodded, still clinging to his arm and ignoring St. Quinton as they retraced their footsteps. Near the house she met Aunt Milly's raised eyebrows with a faint shake of her head.

"I see Lady Corisande has been babbling again." Sara glanced at St. Quinton, wishing she might send an arrow, not to his heart, but perhaps at a less vital part of his anatomy.

Myles gave her a conspiratorial smile and said nothing. He gestured as they reached the now-deserted archery range. "Perhaps you can show us your skill, Lady Sara?"

Not understanding in the least why St. Quinton had sought

them out—much less insisted she use the bow and arrows—
Sara selected a yew bow with strong linen string. She guessed it
to be the weight she used when in the country. There Aunt
Tilly had ordered an indoor range to be set up for her so she
could practice in the long gallery. Archery, though not
unladylike, was not common either.

She took the accepted stance of right angle to the target,
notched the arrow, drew back, and aimed. The arrow hit just
at the edge of the center circle. Sara gave it a vexed look. She
was off center a little, what with having been in town and out
of practice.

"Not a bad shot, my lady. Your point-of-aim was a little
low, I think." Myles bowed to Lady Sara.

Sara seethed as she caught the glint of mockery in St.
Quinton's eyes. She bowed slightly in his direction and
prepared to leave the range with Lord Inglis. They had some
unfinished business back at the bridge, if they could recapture
the mood.

Myles continued, "What say you, Inglis? Care to make a
small wager on the lady's skill?" That shaft of fire Sara had
seen before gleamed in his eyes before he turned away to face
her escort.

Sara stiffened as Lord Inglis turned to confront St. Quinton.
He couldn't possibly know how she detested gaming of any
kind. It was not a thing of which she spoke to others. She
didn't want to participate in anything that might contribute to
the downfall of anyone, either. What an odious fix to be in. If
only Lord Inglis would ignore that wager.

Lady Langholm floated across the lawn in time to hear the
challenge. "What fun! Oliver, never say you will ignore this
scoundrel. Take him on. I know Lady Sara will uphold our fair
sex in the contest."

Sara could never afterward figure out how so many people
suddenly converged upon them.

Lord Langholm called out, "I'll wager ten guineas Lady Sara
can hit five out of six."

A man Sara didn't know said, "Four out of six."

"I say three out of six," called another.

Before Sara could stop the silliness, someone had arranged to take the bets, and all were watching Oliver, who stood glowering at St. Quinton.

Lord Langholm strolled to where the three stood in tense silence. "Surely you will place a bet on your charming lady, brother? I have heard of your good luck of late. Test it now on Lady Sara."

Sara found her heart chilled at the look that crossed Lord Inglis' face at those words. He glanced at St. Quinton, then at his brother-in-law, and nodded.

"Why not?" He walked at their side to where the man stood who was accepting the wagers. He named his sum and the odds, then stood to one side to see what Myles would do.

St. Quinton grinned slightly, then added his own more modest bet to the others. "After all," he confided softly to Oliver, "I have nothing to gain from this bet. You do."

Oliver frowned, wondering why Myles would assist him in winning Sara's hand. The fellow was a good loser, he'd have to allow that. It was a famous notion, one he'd not seen before, betting on his lady's prowess with a bow. If she liked a gambler, he was only too happy to comply. While he was not a dedicated knight of the elbow, he enjoyed an evening at cards or the tables. How nice to know she'd not complain once they were wed.

Sara had quailed further when she heard the sum of money placed on her skill by Lord Inglis. Even St. Quinton was not so extravagant in his betting. To wager that she would score six out of six hits was asking a great deal of her skill.

Again she notched the arrow, drew, and aimed, this time a touch higher. The arrow went home sweet and true to the center of the target. The group ceased their raillery, and attention became more marked. Sara shot again. Once more the arrow shot true. The third as well hit the center, and Sara drew a breath of relief. If she must participate in this awful contest, at least she might win and thus save Lord Inglis from losing such a vast sum of money.

St. Quinton moved slightly to where she could see him. He sent her a taunting smile, one that shook her. This time the arrow was slightly off, nearly missing the center, and she glared at St. Quinton. If only she could order him away. Yet that might reveal more than she wished, at least to Lord St. Quinton.

The crowd had swelled to everyone in attendance. Sara feared she was well on her way to becoming the latest *on-dit* of the day, but there was not a thing she could do to prevent it. She loathed gossip and sought to avoid it, in spite of what her aunts often feared.

Trying to block that disturbing man, St. Quinton, from her view, she concentrated on the target to the exclusion of everything, even the voices that murmured about the betting. She must get these shots all perfect, for it was a horrendous amount of money!

Sara closed her eyes a moment, then took a deep breath. She again notched the arrow, drew, and aimed. The arrow flew to the center area, as she wished. With a sigh of relief, she repeated her actions, again aiming true.

She couldn't refrain from sending St. Quinton a look of triumph that she had now hit five of her arrows to the center portion of the target. Now all she had to do was to send that last arrow where she wanted it. She tilted her chin in defiance, then turned her attention to the task at hand.

Had she looked at Lord Inglis, she would have seen a puzzled expression on his face at the intimate look shared between Myles and herself. Instead, she took a steadying breath and composed herself to face the target once more. She heard one of the ladies giggle. There was a murmuring of voices. Glancing at Lord Inglis, Sara resolved that she would hit the target one more time. She simply must hit it, for his sake. Such a stupid amount of money to wager on a foolish notion.

Moistening her lips, she swallowed nervously before raising the bow, notching the arrow with fingers that trembled a tiny bit, drawing, and aiming carefully at the target that seemed strangely far away. She must not allow her fears to send the arrow astray. She held the bow steady, the bowstring taut. The muscles in her shoulders and back ached with tension.

Closing her eyes a second in a fleeting prayer, Sara then fixed her gaze on the target and relaxed her fingers, letting the bowstring roll off them. Her hand moved back against her jaw as the arrow soared up in the blue sky. Her breath was released on a sigh as the final arrow sank home true in the center of the target.

Turning to Lord Inglis, she discovered him with the others, collecting on his bet. He was laughing with a jubilance she hadn't observed before, and it chilled her.

"Well done, Lady Sara. You would have made a fine Maid Marion for Robin Hood, I believe."

Sara glanced sharply at Lord St. Quinton, expecting to discover sarcasm or perhaps a sneer on that handsome face. Rather, she found what appeared to be sincere admiration. It was most disconcerting.

"I do enjoy archery very much. One gets tired of endless embroidery work and watercolor painting, you know."

The spring sun was slipping lower in the sky. Lacy clouds were forming in the distance and the day seemed cooler to Sara. She shivered as she watched Lord Inglis being congratulated by his friends and slapped on the back by Lord Langholm. Sourly she thought it was as though *he* was the one who had shot the arrows, not her. It was a sight which certainly gave her pause to reflect upon her choice of suitors.

Music could be heard in the dancing tent. Sara drifted in that direction, St. Quinton remaining discreetly at her side, yet never actually touching her. Catherine flitted past them, waggling her fingers at Sara in passing. "Clever girl," she warbled enthusiastically. "Your deed will make history."

"For at least a week," Sara murmured.

"You sound as though you are not best pleased with your efforts." Myles guided Sara into the dancing tent with nonchalant skill. As there were others forming a country dance, Sara allowed Myles to draw her into the group.

"I am pleased I was able to help Lord Ingles win that foolish wager, but I confess I would rather not have been part of it. I have no love for gaming, unlike most." She glanced around at the others in the tent. The bet had ceased to be the topic of conversation, but she doubted it would be forgoten as easily.

"But, my lady, there is little harm in a simple wager." Myles was separated from Sara in the pattern of the dance, but he could see her face, and it seemed she felt disturbed about the gaming.

When they came together in the next movement, Sara replied to his earlier remark. "I imagine little is harmful unless it is done to excess. That is what I fear. I had no idea Lord Inglis was so fond of wagering." The last was said half to herself, and was barely caught by Myles. Yet he heard it and smiled in self-congratulation. What would the fair Lady Sara do now that her scheme was coming to ruin?

Curiously enough, his feeling of elation was short-lived. That peculiarly hollow sensation inside him must be from the lack of food. He hunted up his hostess and hinted that the "breakfast" should be served at once.

"I vow you gentlemen are the most impatient of creatures." Catherine shrugged, then drifted off to instruct the servants.

Aunt Milly sought out Sara while the food was being served, plumping herself down on a chair next to her niece with a satisfied air. "Well, we shall have quite a story to tell when we get home. How do you feel about your triumph, dear?"

"I do not know for certain, aunt." Sara looked thoughtfully to where Lord Inglis spoke with his brother-in-law. Sara had scarcely had a word with him since their walk to the bridge. How grateful she was that St. Quinton had interrupted them before fateful words could be uttered. Now she knew that she must forget Lord Inglis and look elsewhere. "How odd it is that Lord Inglis has shown himself to be just what I most dislike. I fear I must turn to the next on my list. Heavens knows what Aunt Tilly will say when we tell her, yet I pray she will understand."

Sara sent her aunt a pleading look, begging for reassurance. She was given a tender pat on the hand as a small comfort. Sara bit into a succulent tidbit of roast fowl and tried to satisfy an unspecified hunger that food didn't seem to appease.

# 7

It was beginning to look as though it might rain. Sara hunted through the throng of guests for the gentleman who had brought her. How awkward, to say the least, to have to ask Lord Inglis to escort her home. Even with Aunt Milly along to act as a shield, Sara was not happy with the thought. Would he allude to the thwarted proposal on the bridge? Sara doubted such a thing, but she was wary when at last Lord Inglis approached her.

"Ah, there is my lucky lady. Your skill brought me a handsome sum today. You may have anything you wish . . . that I can provide, of course."

Sara glanced down at the ground, painfully aware that to some it was a nice thing to say. She did not appreciate it in the least. "I was wondering if we might take our leave now? The weather appears to be scowling upon us, and I would hate to have my bonnet ruined." As a request it probably left a great deal to be desired. It was hardly the thing to wish for, she supposed.

As they had driven out in an open carriage, Lord Inglis had no more relish for a soaking than the ladies. "I will have the carriage brought around in a trice. Let me give the order, then we can bid my sister good-bye."

Sara signaled to Aunt Milly and before long the three rode along the neatly raked gravel drive toward the London road.

Sara was relieved that St. Quinton had not been in evidence; she was spared facing his mocking pair of eyes.

The gloom that now descended upon the countryside was equally prevalent in the carriage. The silence among the three was as stifling as the air.

Oliver sensed that something had gone terribly wrong. Since the episode at the archery range, when—according to his calculations—Sara ought to have been ecstatic at his winning, there had been a change in her attitude. She had drifted away from him in more ways than one. He had hoped to return to the bridge, where he intended to ask her to marry him. Now he was of the impression that marriage to Lady Sara was out of the question. What had happened?

She had danced with St. Quinton. Oliver had seen them together when he entered the tent looking for her. Before he could make his way to her side at the end of that dance, another claimed her as a partner and Oliver hadn't been able to get near her until it was time to leave. It seemed everyone wanted to touch the lucky lady.

Her aunt had neatly cut him out when it came time to eat. Catherine had nudged him into looking after an heiress, pretty and featherheaded, and enough to drive any man from home in two days' time. Though he had sought to catch Sara's attention, he had failed. Now he wondered if he had failed in every respect, and was beyond hope.

Sara slanted a glance at the silent man at her side. What a pity he had turned out to be the wrong man. She thought of her first suitor, now off to Turkey, as far as she knew. Lord Inglis was the second. Would the third time prove lucky, as some insisted? She pulled her shawl more closely about her, shivering at the damp bite to the breeze. The pretty market gardens were ignored as the trio rode with naught but polite remarks among them.

By the time Lord Inglis set the ladies down at their door, it was misting. In spite of the wind, Sara had kept her dainty parasol unfurled. Her aunt had snuggled close to her so they could share what scant protection it offered.

The ladies hurried into the house. Sara lingered at the door to sadly watch his carriage disappear down the street, then slowly made her way up the stairs to join her aunts in the salon. As she straggled around the corner, she heard Aunt Milly telling the others about the eventful day.

"Wagered on her archery?" Tilly said in horrified accents.

"Never say they did such a thing." Eudora cast a scandalized look at her niece. It was one thing to collect gossip. It was quite another to cause it.

"I very much fear they did. It is unclear to me quite how it happened. I only know that Lord Inglis bet an awesome amount on a skill he was not certain I possessed. Corisande babbled to St. Quinton about my archery, and he wished me to show him my ability. Then came the bet. I could not believe my eyes and ears. All the gentlemen and quite a number of the ladies were wagering on me as though I was some kind of filly in a horse race. It was utterly horried. Lord Inglis is, I have decided, not the man for me." Sara stood by the warmth of the nicely blazing fire to take the chill from her body. She gave a tired shake of her head, then turned to face the one whose words she dreaded the most.

"Aunt Tilly, I do not care to hear one word about second best or third best or even fourth best. I am heartily sick of this entire scheme and I wish I had never thought of it." When those words had tumbled forth, Sara burst into tears and rushed from the salon, running up the stairs toward the sanctuary of her room.

The three ladies in the salon stared at each other for several minutes before Eudora said, "I believe our Sara is overwrought. A good night's sleep will set her right as a trivet."

Matilda, shaken to the core at the flow of words from her dear niece, shook her head. "I had no idea she felt like that. Clearly we shall have to proceed with caution. That she must marry, we have decided. Now it seems we must persuade her to start again. I shall not utter one word about second best. Poor dear, to undergo such an ordeal."

Millicent Garvagh rose, deciding it was best to take off her damp gown now that the worst had been revealed, inquired before she left the fire, "How severe will the gossip be, do you suppose?"

"Difficult to say," replied Eudora. "It is well St. Quinton is not her game. He is one who values his private life and loathes tittle-tattle. Do you recall how his sister was married by special license at their home to avoid publicity? He wished to escape the public spectacle of a fashionable wedding. I still remember the scandal his mother caused when she took off for Paris with that Frenchman, Comte Le Blanc. Drove St. Quinton's father to an early grave and set St. Quinton against women forever, I suspect."

Matilda nodded sagely, adding, "It would take someone quite special to overcome his revulsion. Of course, that does not mean he would not accept a private wedding in a church noted for such special ceremonies. I had hoped our Sara might succeed with him, for I feel he is a fine man in spite of what Milly says."

Milly sniffed, hoping the damp was not going to go to her lungs. "I merely said he was a scamp, and that was with affection. However, if I had married that father of his, I probably would have run off with a *comte* as well." Milly turned to leave the comfort of the fire, to discover Sara standing in the doorway, her face most astonished.

"I returned to apologize to Aunt Tilly for my outburst," said the bemused Sara. "I fear I overheard what you said about Lord St. Quinton. I had no idea of his unhappy background. Why did you suggest him as my first choice if you knew it was unlikely he would ask for my hand?"

The three sisters exchanged looks. It was Eudora who elected to explain. "We have known him and his family for ages. In spite of minor troubles, there is nothing seriously amiss there. Strangely enough, we felt that the two of you had things in common. I suppose we are getting old and losing our acuity. Will you forgive three meddling old fools, my dear?"

Sara shook her head. "If you think to gammon me with that nonsense, you are off the mark. First of all, you are sharper than most ever are, and second, I *asked* you to meddle—if that is what you choose to call helping." She held out her hand to Tilly, who graciously accepted it. "I came to apologize for hasty words and I still wish to do that."

"Prettily said, my dear. Now"—she nodded briskly at Milly and Sara—"if you two will change out of those damp gowns, we can have a nibble of something to eat while we plan what next to do. Eudora always gets hungry, you know."

"Hot chocolate, as well, I believe." Sara slanted a mischievous look at Milly as they hurried out the door and up the stairs to their rooms.

The conclave of oracles, as Sara thought of it, was held over buttered fingers of toast and steaming cups of chocolate. Maurice had taken refuge in Milly's lap while Xenia quietly muttered curses in the corner.

"We must proceed with the plan, my dear. Surely you can see that. What would the other girls say?" Milly relished a sip of chocolate and edged a bit closer to the fire.

Sara sighed and nodded.

Eudora cleared her throat and commenced. "His name is Viscount Lambert. I know the Eames family to be a distinguished one, and Vere Eames, the Viscount Lambert, has done exceptionally well since taking over his title. It was a pity his father died so young. Inflammation of the lungs, you know."

At that, Milly wound her shawl a little higher around her neck and edged closer to the fire.

"I can only hope he does not gamble." Sara rose to place another shovel of coal on the fire after seeing how Aunt Milly seemed to huddle. Poor dear, since her own beloved husband had been taken with a fever, she had feared the same for herself, draping her form with shawls and avoiding drafts like the plague.

"Well, you are to shop with Amanda tomorrow," said

Eudora. "Best get a good night's sleep, Sara, dear. Who knows, you may encounter Lord Lambert at Ackermann's, should you chance to look in there. I understand he is afflicted with the current craze for collecting prints." Eudora rose to receive Sara's good-night salute. She watched her niece kiss the other aunts before leaving to go to her room, then spoke to her sisters. "With all due regard, I am concerned. Do you find it worrisome that our information regarding Baron Inglis should have been so vastly wrong? I can only pray that what I know about Lord Lambert is the truth. He is reckoned to be an exceedingly proper gentleman, and I know of nothing to give Sara a disgust of him."

The sisters walked to their rooms in deep thought, each mulling over the events of the day from various angles.

Amanda was in good spirits when Sara joined her to go shopping. "I have decided to indulge in a new bonnet and a dress with the very latest gored skirt. Brown sarcenet, I believe, with cream trimmings, perhaps a pink rose."

Shaking off her trace of melancholy, Sara agreed. "The very thing. I am a bit blue-deviled today, so do not expect me to bubble. However, the notion you set forth sounds very nice."

"You went with Lord Inglis yesterday to his sister's *fête champêtre*, did you not? I gather all did not go well." Amanda's soft voice was full of sympathy and she gently placed her gloved hand over Sara's as they rode along to the modiste's where Amanda planned her shopping indulgence. Across from them their maids pretended to hear nothing.

Sara gave a tiny shrug, saying, "I should have known something would go wrong. Why cannot my plan go as smoothly as yours?" She proceeded to tell Amanda all about the party and the infamous archery wager. "I still do not understand how it all came about. Most confusing. Somehow I sense Lord St. Quinton had a bit to do with it, yet it was not he who egged Lord Inglis on to the bet. That was done by the earl. At any rate, I am now on to the next on my list, Lord

Lambert. Aunt Eudora says the Eames family, the Viscount Lambert's, that is, are high sticklers for propriety, which is certainly more desirable than gaming."

The landau rolled to a halt, and the girls were assisted down. They remained silent until quite alone again. The maids waited discreetly by the door on two hard-as-rock chairs. Amanda tilted her head and said, "I shall do all I can to help. But please know I do not wish to flirt or upset Lord Rolfe in any way."

Sara chuckled at that bit of errant nonsense. "I would never think to ask it of you, though I appreciate your offer." The modiste returned bearing a length of delicate brown sarcenet with a hint of pink to it that would be perfect for Amanda's delicate coloring. Marriage plans were set aside as the girls fell to the delicious task of choosing the design of the gown and selecting an appropriate bonnet.

As they left the milliner's shop, Amanda touched Sara on the arm. "We shall go to Ackermann's now. I know you are anxious to see what new prints are there. Do your aunts approve your joining the gentlemen in the pursuit of the collecting?"

"They only desire me to be happy." The two entered Amanda's landau and set off for the Strand, where Ackermann's Repository of Arts was located. Though she would have loved to attend the shop's evening receptions, Sara dared not make the request. Even though the fashionable gathered there to view the latest in prints and converse in a quite unexceptionable way, Sara felt that her aunts would not approve, although they might have accompanied Sara, had she wished to ask it of them.

The shop bustled with the business of a goodly number of people. Sara walked to the first of the collection of folios holding the separate prints and began to leaf through them. Amanda drifted off to study some plates of the latest in furniture styles. She was content to browse, knowing it was good for Sara to indulge herself for a bit.

Sara forgot herself while admiring views of the River

Thames as done by Westall and Owen. She had been hoping for some time to find the complete issue of twenty-four prints. She counted carefully, her excitement rising as she realized all were there.

"Well, I see you recovered from the expedition of yesterday."

Sara stiffened. There was no need to turn around to discover the identity of the speaker. She recognized the voice of her nemesis. "Lord St. Quinton, what a surprise. I thought perhaps you might have stayed on at Richmond."

Myles cleared his throat. He was not accustomed to addressing the crown of a bonnet, even though it was modishly trimmed with roses and velvet ribands. "I had business in the city." He glanced at the prints Sara now collected and added, "*The Picturesque Tour of the Thames*? Westall and Owen did a fine job there, not to mention Reeve's aquatinting of the highest quality. But why are you selecting such a large number? Surely you do not join in the current craze?"

He reached out for the prints and Sara brought her face up to give him a stubborn look. If this man thought she was going to relinquish these much-sought-after prints, he could go whistle. "I find, sir, that I am most desirous of purchasing these prints. Please allow me to bring them to the counter."

Myles snapped his fingers and at once a clerk appeared.

Sara cast Lord St. Quinton a fulminating look, then graciously gave the clerk her precious collection of prints, thanking her stars she had brought a goodly sum of money with her, as she wished to take no risk that another might purchase these valuable finds.

Leaning against the counter, Myles studied the decidedly flustered Lady Sara. "Have you managed to acquire a set of *The Microcosm of London* yet? I suppose so. All three volumes? I imagine anyone dedicated enough to hunt out all twenty-four of the Thames prints would find the *Microcosm* as well. Marvelous work, isn't it? Expensive hobby, though, wouldn't you say? Rather like a gamble, wondering if the prints will appreciate in value."

Gritting her teeth, Sara gave him an acid smile and replied with great civility, "I do not consider my purchase in the nature of a gamble. Rather, I buy the prints for their charm and beauty." She broke off the conversation as she noted with a sinking heart that Lord Lambert was coming her way. Wouldn't you know the one man she most desired to see was approaching while she was in the company of the one man she wished at the ends of the earth?

"Ah, Lambert. Good to see you, old fellow."

Pleasure was evident as Lord Lambert greeted his friend St. Quinton. Raising his brows, he inquired with the nicest show of curiosity, "Is this the young woman who performed so well at archery yesterday? I might know you would garner such a prize."

Incensed that her archery disgrace would be brought up, Sara shifted uncomfortably. She wished she might think of a clever bit of talk that would lead Lord Lambert away from that awful subject.

Noting her lack of enthusiasm, St. Quinton charitably turned the conversation, though why he should accommodate the little sharp-tongued vixen was more than he could fathom. "She has beat me to the acquisition of a fine set of the Thames prints, the Westall and Owen ones. It would have to be a lady who did it. Can't even wager on them in the hope of winning them from her."

"Oh, I say," said Lambert, disapproval evident in his voice. "That wouldn't be in the least sporting, old boy. I don't hold with wagering with females. Not that I count you responsible for the archery business yesterday. I suspect that was out of your hands, if I know that crowd."

Sara smiled over this bit of information while Lord Lambert brought St. Quinton up-to-date on an item of mutual interest. She paid the clerk, then took her parcel, turning to look for Amanda.

Her friend fluttered up in her pale blue muslin, cheeks pink with pleasure. "Lord St. Quinton, how nice to see you. And you are Lord Lambert, are you not? I believe we met not long ago at Lady Sefton's. Such interesting things in this place. Have you come to search out treasures as Lady Sara does?" Her look had no hint of fliration, merely polite concern. Both gentlemen found it a unique experience to have two ladies of the *ton* who exhibited such delicacy of manners, rather than the more usual outrageous flirting and casting lures.

St. Quinton was amused. Sara Harland looked as though she could cheerfully throttle him. What a feisty creature she was. Did amazingly well at the archery yesterday. Myles had had no idea she was that good. Fortunately for him, his stratagem would have worked either way. Had she failed, Inglis would have lost the wager and money. She won, and that hadn't pleased her either. It revealed a side of Inglis, and his relatives, that was against what she perceived as desirable. Myles smiled, his eyes lighting up with that familiar devilish fire.

Her surreptitious peeks at Lambert aroused Myles's suspicions. Could Lambert be the next one on her infamous list? He frowned, ignoring the flow of talk about him. If this was indeed the case, it would present a problem, for Vere Eames was one his closer friends, and even though he might not be the right man for Lady Sara, Myles wondered if he ought to interfere.

The ladies began to drift toward the door and Myles went with them. He would return later to see if the prints he desired to add to his illustration of Pennant's *History of London* could be located. A fellow had to look sharp to beat the other collectors to the punch when a new or different drawing came to light. What had begun as a casual interest was fast becoming an engrossing pastime.

Lord Lambert held open the door, beaming a smile on the demure Lady Sara as she walked past him. "Would you ladies join us in savoring an ice at Gunter's?" He glanced at Myles to note the look of abstraction, and added, "We would be most honored for your company."

Seizing upon the opportunity to help Sara, Amanda rushed into speech. "Oh, that would be lovely. I vow that looking at all those prints has made me as dry as a desert." Her look at Lord St. Quinton lacked any flirtatious quality, and he recalled her interest in Rolfe.

"Your servants, ladies." Myles resigned himself to sitting across from the demure Lady Amanda while his friend Lambert made discreet eyes at Lady Sara. The maids in attendance followed in Lord Lambert's carriage, a treat not lost upon Lady Sara, who thought it prodigiously kind.

The four rode in the landau to Berkeley Square, where, under the trees on the opposite side from Gunter's shop, a waiter soon scurried to them with a tray of delectable ices.

Gunter's was the one place in London where a lady might be in the company of a gentleman without incurring censure of any kind. Sara was vexed that while she was with the attractive Lord Lambert, St. Quinton must needs tag along. Still, he paid nice attention to Amanda, and that freed Lord Lambert to converse with Sara.

A sudden stiffening of Amanda's slim figure caught Sara's attention. Striding across the square came Lord Rolfe, the very last person Amanda wished to see at this moment.

"Oh, mercy," murmured Sara.

St. Quinton, aware of nuances Lord Lambert couldn't possibly fathom, wondered how Lady Sara would wiggle out of this predicament.

"Lady Amanda, Lady Sara, how pleasant to see you." Lord Rolfe turned his gaze upon Lord Lambert, flicked it to St. Quinton, and frowned slightly. "Gentlemen." He sought the fair countenance of his love, Amanda, and took note of her pleading expression. Trusting she would not play him false, he decided to withhold judgment until apprised of the facts. "Lovely day."

With a warning look at St. Quinton, who seemed to have a very knowing expression on his face, Sara swallowed, then said, "We were at Ackermann's, looking at the prints there, and got excessively dry, what with all those musty prints and having been at the modiste's and the milliner's before. Lord

Lambert kindly invited us to partake of an ice, and Lord St. Quinton happened along as well."

She ignored the annoyed look on St. Quinton's handsome face. He deserved to be relegated to an add-on for being so forward as to join them. She hadn't wanted his company.

By this time St. Quinton had had quite enough of being treated in this manner. He felt rather ill-used, piqued at being placed in such an invidious position. Lady Sara looked a cross between smug and annoyed. Well, Myles had no relish to thwart the sweet Lady Amanda, so he decided to leave, and quickly. Easing himself from the landau, he bowed to Lord Rolfe.

"Now that you are here to see to things"—Myles gestured vaguely—"I have an appointment I am obliged to meet. Sirs. Ladies. I shall see you later, Vere." He tipped his curly-rimmed beaver to the occupants of the carriage, then marched off in no particular direction, the memory of those dancing violet eyes haunting every step he took. Sara Harland seemed to occupy far too many of his thoughts of late.

The following Saturday, Amanda waited impatiently for Sara to arrive at the Fenwick library.

"Thank heaven you are come," she sighed as Sara whirled around the door, shutting it carefully behind her.

"Yes, do tell us what has been going on," demanded Fiona. "Amanda has babbled something about your saving her from disaster with Lord Rolfe, and we must hear all about the famous archery event. However did you permit such a thing?"

An infectious giggle bubbled up from Corisande. "I thought I was the only who who got into such pickles. Do tell us all about it, Sara. Was my cousin there, by chance?"

Groaning with dismay, Sara cast herself down upon a dainty chair and looked daggers-drawn at Corisande. "When is your cousin not in evidence? Actually, I cannot fault him this time. At least, I do not think I can. He did ask to see me use the bow, but it was not his fault that the others persisted in making such a thing of it. And he certainly did not force Lord Inglis to make such a shocking wager. I vow, I hope I do not hear of betting again. It was most lowering to have people discussing my ability as though I were a filly in a horse race."

"How distressing! You poor dear. You see, I told you Myles is the kindest of creatures. He would never embarrass you in any manner," Corisande said soothingly. She poured out the steaming tea into delicate cups, then passed around a heaping plate of lemon wafers.

Fiona bit into a wafer, savored the crisp lemony taste, then asked, "What now? I gather Lord Inglis is a thing of the past?"

"Well . . ." Amanda hesitated to relate the episode at Gunter's.

Sara had no qualms. "We met Lord Lambert—he's the next on my list, you know—quite by accident at Ackermann's while I was purchasing a set of prints. Lord Lambert was so kind as to invite Amanda and me to partake of an ice at Gunter's. Of course, your abominable cousin would take it in his head to come along, Corisande, thus complicating things. Then whom should we see but Lord Rolfe!"

"Well, Lord St. Quinton did excuse himself and leave so Jason could join us. I thought that most accommodating." Amanda was surprised to find herself defending St. Quinton. But he had shown sensibilities she hadn't expected of him.

"How did your Aunt Tilly take this development?" Fiona gave Sara a worried look. She was well aware how much Sara disliked getting a tongue-lashing from her dear aunt.

"Not as bad as expected. We had a sort of discussion." Sara thought of the snippet of family history she had overheard regarding St. Quinton, and decided not to discuss it, even with her best friends. There was no need to rake poor St. Quinton over the coals once more. Doubtless he'd had sufficient of it, even though he wouldn't know of her efforts on his behalf. If he were that private a person, she could respect it. Sara had no pleasure in being the subject of scandal-broth either. "I believe Aunt Tilly is quite resigned to Lord Lambert. He is most handsome and quite the kindest of gentlemen. You must know his family are all sticklers for propriety. And after all I have been through, I will appreciate that, you may be certain."

They leisurely consumed the tea and lemon wafers, chatting about their respective interests, wondering aloud about the latest designs for wedding dresses and what kind of ceremony each would have.

Sara thought of St. Quinton's sister and her very private wedding away from prying eyes. She wondered if he would ever marry, and hoped, strangely enough, that he would find someone nice.

"I think I shall ask Lord Lambert, supposing he comes up to scratch, to get a special license so we can get married privately," confided Sara. "I think that would be very romantic."

"Not me," declared Fiona. "I want all the pomp and ceremony St. George's has to offer. A wedding is to remember all the days of your life."

Sara nodded. She gave a wistful sigh and hoped St. Quinton wouldn't turn up to complicate her life again.

# 8

Myles stared out of the window in his room at his aunt's home. It was a deucedly difficult spot to be in, knowing that Lady Sara was interested in his good friend Vere Eames. He was bound to thwart the ambitions of that pert miss. Still, he didn't want to offend his friend.

Vere was a nice enough fellow, a bit starched-up, but not really what you might call high in the instep. They had gone hunting together a goodly number of times and Myles had fond memories of these events. Ah, yes, Vere was a good fellow. A jolly good fellow.

Dashed if it didn't present a coil.

But on the other hand, was Lady Sara the right one for Vere? Could he handle all that spirit Myles had had occasion to observe firsthand on more than one instance? She was such a fiery bit of womanhood, those beautiful violet eyes flashing up at him with such feeling. Myles shook his head. He could just see Vere's mother in a face-to-face confrontation with Lady Sara. Gads, the primness and propriety would be stifling for the young woman.

Yet, what had she said in the meeting this afternoon? That she welcomed the sobriety offered by Lady Lambert? Did she really know what she was getting into? Vere was a good sort of fellow, right enough. But Lady Lambert?

Myles began to pace back and forth as he considered the

formidable old lady and her views of the modern miss. He had heard them prattled about from Sally Jersey, she being much amused by them. Lady Lambert would take that lovely, vivacious Sara Harland and depress her into a colorless carbon of herself, the old grouch. Never would Sara be allowed to use her bow and arrows again!

Myles chuckled as he recalled that pretty little chin Sara had raised in defiance just before she shot those six arrows home to center. Incredible! What a woman. She had such spirit. She was devoted too, fussing over those aunts as she did. Unusual woman. But, he remembered, sobering as he did, she had called him *boring*! That an elegant, vividly alive woman like Lady Sara should call him boring, when he knew very well he was nothing of the kind, should bring a suitable retribution down upon her head.

He ceased his pacing and paused to check his watch. Time to head out to White's, then on to Carlton House, where he was promised. Lambert was certain to be there tonight. Myles would begin his little campaign. Judging from the intrigued expression on Lambert's face, there was no time to lose. No time at all.

After Myles had changed attire for the evening, he set off. Kit was leaving his room as Myles walked down the hall. He greeted Myles with affection. "Headed out?" Kit wore a faintly wistful expression on his face. His mother was trying to dragoon him into attending a musicale at Lady Huntley's and he knew it would be a dead bore.

Judging Kit to be desirous of a bit of company, Myles took pity on him. "How about joining me at White's for a bird and bottle?"

"Just the thing, old boy." Kit beamed with relief, as he knew his dear mother would not deny him the exalted company of his elder cousin. They sauntered down the stairs in affable harmony.

At the club, Myles looked about for his quarry, but saw not a sign of Lord Lambert. Well, the night was early yet. Myles would remain vigilant. Lambert was bound to come here eventually.

"Any more problems with the female contingent, Kit?" Myles lazily noted the flush that crept over Kit's cheeks. What was the lad up to now?

" 'Tis nothing much. You haven't noticed the Rolleston chit, have you? She's a dainty blond with cornflower eyes. Dashed fine gel. Looks so fragile, yet she can ride like the wind." Kit sighed, toying with his roast partridge while he stared off into space.

The last thing Myles wanted was to listen to a moonstruck lad. Yet he recalled his own salad days and held his tongue. "Admire her, do you? Thinking of tossing your handkerchief in her direction?"

Startled, Kit dropped his fork, ignoring the clatter of silver against china as he stared at his cousin. "Do you think she'd have me? Not that I'm sure I want to get leg-shackled just now. Young, y'know, and all that." Kit thought a moment, then added, "You don't suppose her mother has put her up to flirting with me, thinking I'm your heir? I know I *am* your heir, but you might get married and have your own sprouts, y'know." Kit studied his cousin with a suddenly astute eye. "Think y'might marry? Soon?"

Myles frowned at his glass of claret. It was entirely possible that Lady Rolleston might do just as Kit suggested. It was known that Kit was Lord St. Quinton's heir. No one had hidden the fact. Perhaps it would be wise to test the waters. To make it believable, he would have to keep the truth from Kit; the boy was as open as his sister. Myles didn't want someone to marry Kit just upon expectations. After all, even though Myles had no immediate plans to wed, he knew what was expected of him and planned to do just that someday. Eventually. Plenty of time yet.

"Well, you have caught me out there, my boy. Keep it to yourself, unless you think it wise to mention it to the Rolleston girl, just to see her reaction. Mind you, I don't care to have it bruited about."

"I ain't such a flat that I don't know you like your business kept quiet, coz. I don't suppose you'd care to mention a name?" Kit doubted Myles would tell him the fair lady of his choice, but, nothing ventured . . .

A wry smile twisted Myles's lips as he considered the total lack of desirable candidates. For no apparent reason, a piquant face framed in ebony curls, violet eyes flashing up at him with sparkling defiance, popped into his mind. He dismissed that face at once. Never would he wed such a woman. She would drive him mad in no time with her dramatic behavior. Yet she certainly possessed a natural poise. He couldn't help but admire the dignity she had wrapped about herself when confronted with the archery wager. She had come through that with flying colors. But her dignity was coupled with disdain for him.

Earlier Corisande had mentioned the mystery of the violets that Sara still received every morning. Myles had listened with apparent disinterest to the rapturous account of the romantic gallant who quite intrigued Sara. A *boring* man would never do such a thing. If the lady only knew she was weaving dreams about *him*. In a way, it was frustrating not to be able to tell her *he* was her mysterious gallant.

"St. Quinton. Been lookng for you, old man."

Myles glanced up from his abstraction to see the very man he had searched for earlier, Vere Eames, Viscount Lambert.

"Join us, won't you?" Myles gestured to the vacant chair at the table.

Lord Lambert glanced at the suddenly hurried consumption of food by Kit, smiled, then took the other chair to begin a desultory conversation with his friend.

Kit had returned to his neglected partridge with greater enthusiasm. He intended to seek out the charming Miss Rolleston to discover the truth of her affections without delay. Corisande would be attending that musicale this evening. Like as not, Miss Rolleston would be there as well. Come to think on it, Lady Sara would likely attend too. Because of her all-knowing aunts, maybe she might know whom his cousin intended to wed. He glanced toward St. Quinton, wondering if it were right to make inquiries. It was an invasion of St. Quinton's private life, but dash it all, Kit was curious, and a fellow ought to be able to know about his own cousin.

Soon finishing his meal, Kit made his apologies to Myles and Lord Lambert. Kit could see they desired to be private, and to tell the truth, Kit wished to be gone.

The musicale at Lady Huntley's looked to be quite as dull as Kit had feared. The Italian soprano screeched loud enough to jar the dead from their graves. He had never understood Italian and was now certain he never wished to, either.

Surveying the room, he located his sister seated with his mother, Lady Sara, and one of her aunts. Not far away from them was Lady Rolleston and the petite Miss Rolleston. Her blond curls were bound up in a blue riband that precisely matched her gown and those enchanting eyes.

Fortunately he had missed a great part of the program. This he discovered as the soprano bowed—an admirable feat, considering her girth—and retired for an intermission. He made his way to the side of his charmer, murmuring some nonsense over her hesitantly extended hand. He glanced at the mother. Did she think he might be worthy of her daughter simply because of St. Quinton? As he offered to escort the fair young lady to the light supper being presented, he formulated his plan.

Corisande exclaimed as she saw her brother with Miss Rolleston, "Well, now I know why you did not wish to come with us, Christopher Fenwick. Will you not join us?" She beamed an amiable smile in the direction of Miss Daphne Rolleston. "Sir Percy has gone ahead to secure us a table."

Lady Rolleston nodded her assent to their plans while moving to join Lady Fenwick and Aunt Tilly. The elder ladies assembled at a table with two other friends to enjoy the surprisingly tasty supper as they discussed the members of the *ton* not present.

Kit maneuvered around so that when all were seated, he was between Lady Sara and Miss Rolleston. He rushed to the table to heap two plates with food, then returned, noting that he was the first of the men to make it back.

He was careful to pay assiduous attention to Miss Rolleston, and was rewarded with shy smiles and gentle comments. Kit finally took the chance to question Lady Sara while Miss Rolleston was answering a question from Corisande. "I say, do you have any notion who the lady is that m'cousin is planning to wed?"

Startled, Sara nearly tipped out the contents of her glass. Searching for composure as well as words, she merely shook her head. When she had gathered her poise, carefully placing her glass on the table once more, she said, "What gave you that idea?" Her heart seemed to have sunk somewhere in the vicinity of her toes. There was no reason at all for her to feel so bereft.

"Had dinner with him at White's this evening. He said I might tell Miss Rolleston, as I wished to know if she cared for me or my expectations. Thought you might have heard something from your aunts." He popped a morsel of food into his mouth and chewed slowly while waiting for Sara to answer. He was sorry his words seemed to have distressed her. She'd become quite pale.

"I am certain Miss Rolleston cares for you, Kit, not just for those expectations you mention. Surely she is not that type of young woman. I doubt Lady Rolleston even considers the matter. She knows Lord St. Quinton is still a young man, and he could marry at any time." But Sara knew only too well that Lady Rolleston might contemplate a permanent bachelorhood for St. Quinton. He had been the most elusive of males, carefully avoiding the marriage mart and each year's buds of society. She wondered who his chosen lady might be. Frowning, she considered all the possibilities, and could think of no one he had shown marked attention to, other than herself, and that was vexing nonsense. "I fear I have no idea who she might be."

Kit shook his head in disappointment. "Well, I know you will be silent about it. You ain't no gabble-grinder. Y'know St. Quinton and his dislike for public notice." He cheerfully forked another piece of lobster salad before returning his attention to Miss Daphne Rolleston.

There was no point in trying to catch Corisande's eye, for that young lady would neither know who was St. Quinton's intended nor be able to contain the information that he was seriously involved. Sara searched the room for her aunt. Perhaps she might know. Excusing herself from the table of friends, she made her way to where her aunt sat.

Beckoning to Aunt Tilly, whose turn it had been to chaperone Sara, she whispered, "Do you have any inkling who might be the woman St. Quinton has asked to wed?"

Tilly gave her a shocked look and shook her head. "I have no idea, love. Fancy that, St. Quinton about to be leg-shackled." Though she spoke in a soft tone, her words were overheard by Lady Rolleston, who stored them away for later reference.

When supper was over, Lady Rolleston returned to her daughter's side, drawing her away from the others to ask a vital question. "Has young Fenwick said anything to you about his cousin getting married?"

Miss Rolleston blushed and nodded shyly. "Yes, Mama. He mentioned it to me while we were at supper. His sister was most kind to me, and all his friends are so nice. I vow, I felt quite welcomed." As Kit had not pledged her to secrecy, Miss Rolleston didn't bother to tell her mother to keep silent. Which would have been pointless, at any rate. Lady Rolleston was not a prattle-box who went about with nothing but gossip on her tongue, but this was different. St. Quinton was not your ordinary young man.

Sailing ahead like a ship into home port, Lady Rolleston reclaimed her chair for the remainder of the musicale. Miss Rolleston meekly followed, smiling demurely as Kit Fenwick took the chair next to hers. The gentleman who had been sitting there breathed a sigh of relief and stayed in the back of the room, glad for the reprieve.

For Sara the evening seemed unending. She wanted to be off by herself. Making a slight motion to her aunt, she slipped from her chair, tiptoeing toward the ladies' retiring room. Before she got there, she observed a pleasant little anteroom done up in her favorite shade of blue. She stepped inside and walked to the window to stare out at the muted glow of the city.

"Sara, are you all right?" Corisande entered the room to join Sara at the window a few minutes later. "That woman is perfectly horrid. How they can call that singing is more than I am able to see. Is that why you left? You were very quiet at supper. Something is bothering you, I fear. Is there anything I can do?" Corisande patted Sara on the shoulder, then sat down on a nearby sofa. "It certainly is peaceful in here."

"Ah, the elusive beauty." An apparently foxed young sprig of fashion entered the room. He paused to drink in the delicate beauty of the young woman seated on the sofa, seemingly alone. Then he lurched forward to make a dead set at Corisande. Before Sara could move, he stumbled on the carpet and sprawled over Corisande, tearing her dress and spilling a glass of wine across her skirt.

"Sara, help me!" Corisande begged, mindful that she dared not make a scene, lest she ruin her reputation.

The young man didn't budge, evidently having become unconscious from excessive wine. Before Sara could take action, a sound alerted her. Someone was coming.

"What is going on here?" Sir Percy entered the room, took a horrified look at what seemed to be a passionate encounter, and prepared to leave.

"It isn't what you might think, Sir Percy," pleaded Sara, stepping forward from the shadow of the draperies. "This, ah, person accosted Corisande. Such a terrible thing to have happen! I vow I was quite stunned by the suddenness of it. Please, you must help us."

"Perhaps I may be of assistance." St. Quinton entered the

anteroom, took one glance at his cousin's dishevelment, and turned to Sir Percy. "I'll get young de Lacey out of here while you help Lady Sara with Corisande." He looked at Sara. "Get her cloak. Borrow one if you must, say she has had an accident if anyone asks."

The three set to work. After St. Quinton lifted the limp young man from where he sprawled, Sir Percy assisted Corisande to her feet while Sara hurried to find the cloak Corisande had worn. Sara walked as fast as she dared without arousing suspicion. The curious must be kept away in all events.

When she returned to the anteroom, she found the obnoxious person gone, St. Quinton as well. Sir Percy was comforting Corisande in a most romantic way. Sara was loath to intrude, when Corisande caught sight of her and gave her a radiant smile.

"You may wish us happy, Sara. Sir Percy has asked me to marry him." Her face was illuminated with joy.

Knowing how Corisande loved Sir Percy, Sara beamed her delight. "Congratulations, my dears. I am very pleased for you both." Sara hurried forward with the cloak to wrap around her friend. As she enfolded Corisande in the soft fabric, she whispered, "How fortunate this has ended so very well."

"I told you my cousin is a wonderful person," whispered Corisande. "I can always count on Myles to do the right thing. Think of it, Sara, dear. You cannot now say he is boring. He has helped save me from disgrace! I shall always be grateful to him."

Casting a glance to Sir Percy, who drew closer to guard his love from any stray viewer who might pass the room, Sara shook her head. "I shall think about it," was her only answer.

"What is going on now, if I may ask?"

Sara turned to discover St. Quinton standing at the doorway, not a hair out of place. Her heart did a strange lurch, and she reached out to a table to steady herself. "Your cousin has a happy announcement."

Bubbling with delight, Corisande echoed her news to St.

Quinton, who then assumed a properly pleased expression.

"My best to you both. Lady Sara, if I might have a word with you?" He motioned to the hall, and Sara reluctantly joined him.

"I should not leave them alone." Her excuse was feeble at best, now that Corisande and Sir Percy were engaged. They would have no trouble in keeping occupied while waiting for Corisande's mama. Though soft whispers and gentle looks would be all they dared share for the moment.

"You will be relieved to know that Mr. de Lacey has been ushered from the house. Perhaps you could explain how this situation came about?" He fought a desire to kiss that sweet mouth. She looked so elegant and remote this evening. His fingers wanted to feel the silk of those black curls, touch the satin of her cheek. Her chin tilted up in audacious defiance, a very ladylike defiance, he granted.

Suppressing a desire to flee, Sara stood her ground, striving to be as cool as possible. "I wished to get a breath of air—the room was a bit stuffy."

"Not to mention the caterwauling of the soprano," murmured Myles, amused at her betraying flush.

"Yes, well, Corisande grew worried about me and followed me in here to see if there was a problem. That odious young man came in, foxed, as you no doubt observed. He thought Corisande was there alone, as I was concealed by the draperies. I gather he planned to make most improper advances to her. He tripped as he made his way across the room, and the rest you know."

She backed away from his intimidating presence. Not that she wished to let him know how he affected her. She certainly did *not* want that. Now that he was to declare for some woman, she must bury all those frightening sensations that clamored to be released when he got too close to her. She longed to ask him who the woman was who had won his hand and possibly his heart. Convention would not permit such curiosity, at least not from her. She turned to leave him.

"You enjoyed the evening—before young de Lacey intruded?" He found an absurd desire to keep her at his side, though he knew it was not well done of him to be alone, even in the hallway, with her.

She paused, turning again to face him. "I am certain the soprano is most gifted. My ears simply are not trained to appreciate her talents. Aunt Tilly wished me to attend."

"No doubt thinking Lord Lambert might make an appearance?" His brow lifted in amused awareness.

Sara flushed, for that was precisely the reason Aunt Tilly had given her when Sara stated she had no desire to listen to the Italian singing sensation.

He continued, "I saw him while at Carlton House. The Prince's reception was brilliant. The rooms were overheated, overcrowded, and the food overly rich. Much as usual, I fear."

"I have not attended a gathering at the palace as yet, so I would not know about that."

"Pity his princess is so unworthy of the title."

Curiosity nudged her to ask, "Is it really so beautiful? I hear many stories of the palace's magnificence."

"Well"—Myles chuckled at the thought—"it seems that every time I go, the furniture has undergone a change. You know what an avid collector he is, and he daily accumulates more. I get accustomed to one decor, and the next time I come, there is a different theme."

"I think I should like to see it." Her voice grew wistful as she considered who might have the *entrée* to take her to such an event. Not that her aunts could not manage it if they chose.

There was a muted sound of steps, and when Sara turned, she could see Lord Lambert coming up the broad stairs. It was just as guests began to filter out from the salon, where the concert appeared to be over.

"Slipped away from Prinny, did you?" Lord Lambert crossed the hall to join them. "I got involved with him on a discussion of Oriental wall coverings. He has such great curiosity." Lord Lambert glanced at Sara, then looked at his friend. What was this elegant young woman to St. Quinton?

"That is what you get for being so deucedly clever, my friend." St. Quinton bowed slightly, then added, "I believe I must go and assist my cousin. She is about to inform her mother of her engagement to Sir Percy Wolrige."

Lord Lambert frowned in puzzlement. "Rather odd, St. Quinton stepping into family matters, what?"

Sara wondered if St. Quinton might not be getting in a bit of practice. Engagements must have been far removed from his experience to this point in time, with the possible exception of his sister's. "I believe he is fond of his cousin. She is a delightful girl, you know, and my dearest friend."

Lord Lambert gave her a genial look at her obvious pleasure in her friend's happiness. He bowed politely when her aunt joined them. "I wonder if I might have the pleasure of your company for a ride in the park tomorrow? I believe you are acquainted with Lord York and Miss Egerton, are you not? If it is acceptable with you, we could join them."

Blushing faintly with pleasure and conscious that St. Quinton was within hearing of her conversation as he shepherded a cloaked Corisande toward the stairs, she replied with quiet enthusiasm. Ignoring that flash from St. Quinton's expressive eyes, she said, "I would be very happy to accept your kind invitation. Miss Egerton is a particular friend of mine."

With that, they all drifted down the stairs, bidding the hostess a polite good evening before sorting out the carriages and heading homeward.

"Now perhaps you can tell me what was going on all that time, young lady." Aunt Tilly folded her arms across her thin bosom and stared at Sara with curious, but not censorious eyes.

"It is such a muddle. I wanted to escape a moment, to think, you know. Corisande joined me, then this young Mr. de Lacey entered the room. He was very, very foxed, dear aunt. An accident occurred and Sir Percy and Lord St. Quinton took care of everything so Corisande's reputation would not be ruined. I shall explain more fully once we get home, for you must know Aunt Eudora will want every detail."

"And Corisande is engaged to Sir Percy?"

Sara chuckled. "True. Something good came out of disaster. I doubt she will mind her gown being ruined for such a worthy cause."

"Dear heaven!" Her horrified gasp brought forth giggles from Sara, who then found she must make further explanations. By the time the carriage arrived at No. 23 Brook Street, both ladies were in high spirits.

Aunt Milly pronounced St. Quinton a hero for his gallant efforts to save his cousin from social ruin.

"And," added Aunt Tilly, "Sara is to go riding in the park with Lord Lambert, Fiona, and Lord York tomorrow. It ought to be a most agreeable party."

"How true," Eudora said. "We cannot afford to have another episode such as the archery one. A lady does not behave in such a way as to cause gossip."

Sara wasn't so certain about this. It seemed to her that any number of so-called ladies were the source of much gossip. Married ones, usually. But then, as Aunt Endora frequently stated, this seemed to be the age of scandal. However, Sara need have no worry for the morrow. No scandal could possibly arise from an innocent ride in the park, thank goodness.

# 9

Sara rose early the following morning. Restless and absurdly ill-at-ease, she went down to breakfast hoping to find her Aunt Milly. Millicent Garvagh was the most cheerful of persons. If Sara couldn't find comfort in her, things were in a bad way indeed.

In the breakfast room, Sara found Maurice established in Aunt Milly's lap. The older woman was wiping her fingers on a damask napkin after offering a tidbit of kipper to the cat. She gave Sara a guilty look, then took a dainty sip of her morning chocolate.

"No need to worry, aunt. That cat may eat all the kippers in the kingdom for all I care." Sara filled her plate, then joined her aunt at the table. Smedley entered with another rack of toast for Sara before discreetly withdrawing.

"You seem a bit on edge this morning. May I inquire what might be your problem?" Aunt Milly took another slice of toast from the rack, spread blackberry jam on it, then nibbled at it with an appetite not usually seen in society ladies. "I should think you would be in alt in anticipation of an outing with the Viscount Lambert and your friends this morning. This is what you desire, an opportunity to get to know the viscount better."

"I had the most ridiculous dream. Or ought I rather say a nightmare? You know how much I enjoy riding. In my dream, something terrible happened, though I do not know precisely what. I vow it left me feeling blue-deviled."

"Best get over it before you leave the house. You know that a horse can sense if you are troubled." Aunt Milly studied her niece with a piercing look. "Somehow I doubt that is all there is to the matter."

"I worry about Lord Lambert. What if I fail? He is the third, no, the fourth, if you count St. Quinton. I am beginning to feel that either our choices were wrong or that I am under a spell of bad luck. 'Tis a blessing I do not believe in witches, or I might begin looking for one."

"Eat your food. 'Tis useless to speculate on luck, good or bad. The important thing is to look your best and ride as you have been taught. You are noted to have a good seat, which is more than a great many women can claim. I vow I have observed more bad riders in the park of late. Did you happen to notice Lady Bagshawe last week? Now, there is a woman who looks as though she is ready for a toss. Terrible seat. Not much else to recommend her either, come to think of it. She has a face that far too strongly resembles that of her mount." One of Aunt Milly's shawls slipped down from her shoulder and she valiantly attempted to pull it up while not dislodging Maurice from her lap. Sara rose from her chair to assist her aunt, giving Maurice a fond pat on his head before resuming her place at the table.

Sara chuckled. Her aunt's nonsense had lightened her mood. "That may be, but I cannot refrain from apprehension."

"Pish tush. Utter nonsense, my dear girl." Milly readjusted her shawl, then began to scratch Maurice under his chin. The cat gave a blissful smile, then settled more comfortably on her lap. "Be an angel now, finish your toast, then go up to get dressed for your ride. Which habit are you going to wear?"

"The black, I think. I have a new hat, one that looks much like the Spanish fashion. It should be easy to keep on my head."

Milly simply murmured a few incomprehensible words

while keeping an eye on her niece. Maurice begged another piece of kipper, and as Milly fed him, Sara finished her breakfast, took leave of her aunt, then returned to her room.

Fresh violets now sat upon her dresser, nestled in an exquisite silver vase, a new addition to the order of things. "When did these arrive?" Sara glanced at her abigail, wishing the young woman could answer all the questions buzzing about in Sara's head.

"They came a bit after you went down to breakfast, milady," Mary Gates replied, while laying out the black riding habit. She placed the new Spanish-style hat on the dressing table. The white cambric habit shirt that went beneath lay on the bed, looking crisp and neat.

Sara had thought perhaps the mystery was at an end when she dressed to go to breakfast and no flowers had arrived. As she slipped from her morning dress and began the ritual of preparing for her ride in Hyde Park, she tried to call up a vision of the man who sent the violets. None came to mind. The only face that persistently haunted her was one lightly tanned, with nearly black eyes and thick black hair. It was a face that all too often looked at her with a glint of sardonic merriment in those dark eyes. What thoughts went through St. Quinton's head when he looked at her thus? If he knew how his presence affected her, he would smile all the more. Wicked smiles, they were. At least, that was the only description Sara could think of for them. She found those smiles as unsettling as the man.

She drew on her boots, then allowed her abigail to position the new hat on her head with precise care. It looked well with her hair brushed up and away from her face. The stock that wound around her neck above the habit shirt she had recently ordered contrasted sharply with the black of her riding habit. Elegant, restrained. She couldn't help but wish—just for a moment, mind you—that St. Quinton could see her thus.

There was no need to pace up and down the hall while waiting for Lord Lambert to arrive. By the time Sara was dressed and had her dainty whip in hand, Smedley had ushered in the viscount with all the ceremony he deserved.

Sara smoothed her York tan gloves over her hands as she walked down the last of the stairs. Her rare bout of nerves assailed her once again. He seemed a nice man. She must not fail this time. Her aunts had faith in her ability, and this persistent lack of success was more than a little disheartening.

Lord Lambert bowed as Sara reached the foot of the stairs. "Good morning, fair lady. What a pleasure to see you are ready to depart. I can see you do not believe in keeping your hack or escort waiting."

He politely extended his arm. Sara looped her riding skirt up in the prescribed manner, placed her other hand on his arm, and they left the house.

Walking over to her mount, she reacquainted herself with the horse, crooning soft words so that he might know her voice, recognize her touch. Having to hire a horse was a bother, but her aunts did not keep a stable in town. Their carriages were kept in what was once the stable, horses hired when needed. Aunt Eudora arranged that they rent the same pair for the carriage for the entire Season. Truth be known, more and more families were finding a stable a burden that could not be sustained. Sara had ridden this hack before and felt pleasure that he seemed to know her.

She turned to Lord Lambert, nodding graciously when he offered to help her. Sara felt no reaction to Lord Lambert's polite assistance, though he stood very close to her as he helped her mount. The thought entered her mind that it was well that she had never gone riding with St. Quinton. Her horse would surely have sensed how wary and ruffled she felt in St. Quinton's company.

Lord Lambert mounted and had paused to speak before assuming the lead. "It seems we have a lovely morning for our outing. We are to meet the others at the entrance to the park."

With the carts and drays, not to mention the people out and about this early in the morning, they made no attempt to converse while they rode to the park entrance. The three clattered over the cobbles in single file for the most part,

Lambert going first to pave the way for Sara, her groom following behind at a discreet distance.

The driver of a cart came much too close for Sara's comfort, and she had difficulty in controlling her mount. It did not augur well for the ride. She glanced back at her groom and he shrugged his shoulders, signaling all would be well once she had a chance to run the fidgets out of her hack. Sara patted the beautiful chestnut, crooning soft words to assure him she understood his feelings regarding cart drivers who had no respect for blood horses, and he seemed to settle down once more.

At the entrance to Hyde Park, Fiona and Lord York waited patiently for them. Fiona looked dashing in her pomona-green habit of fine broadcloth trimmed in smart black braid. She wore a jaunty black hat with a small green plume clipped to one side.

"Good morning." Fiona glanced with charming affection at her companion, Lord York, then back to Sara. Her inspection of Lord Lambert was surreptitious, yet complete. Fiona would check to see if he rode well. A man who had a poor seat on his horse got no approval from her. From the expression on her face, Sara decided Lord Lambert had passed. Not by a wide margin, Sara could see, but he had passed.

By unspoken agreement, the four all urged their horses to a hand-gallop, the fastest pace permitted in the park. It was good to let the spirited mounts have a run before settling down to a pleasant canter along Rotten Row.

The morning mist was beginning to lift. The leaves in their spring-green dress stirred with a rising breeze. Not many people were in the park this early, which was ideal as far as Sara was concerned. The uneasiness she had experienced upon rising still clung to her like a limpet, refusing to go away.

Lord Lambert rode to Sara's right, as was proper. Fiona and Lord York rode ahead, Fiona engaging him in a spirited discussion as to the best method of training horses for women riders.

Sara looked at Lord Lambert and saw a faint frown. "Is something the matter, milord?" She decided to fall back a wee bit so that there was no danger of their words being overheard.

He turned from his critical inspection of the couple ahead of them to give Sara a benign smile. "You ride very well, Lady Sara. You have that willowy grace and relaxed, yet upright carriage seen in so few women." He glanced ahead once more, then continued, "Tell me, does Miss Egerton always argue with her escort like that?"

Sara firmed her chin, glancing at her companion with a hint of disfavor. "She really is not arguing, you know. She and Lord York quite enjoy a spirited discussion." Relenting a little, she added in a kindly manner, "I feel they are in a way of reaching an accord, if you follow my meaning. If ever two people were of a kind, it is Fiona and Lord York."

Ahead of them, Fiona decided to give Lord York a demonstration of what she meant by schooling a horse intended for ladies' use in what she felt to be the proper method.

Sara was not a little alarmed to see her take off thus. No dull slug for Fiona; she rode a chestnut gelding of fine temper who needed a firm hand at all times. At first Fiona walked the horse, apparently showing Lord York something to do with the handling of the reins; then she brought the horse to a halt before breaking into a trot. As always, her seat was perfect.

"I must admit she rides well."

Lord Lambert's words seemed grudging to Sara, and she gave him a sharp look. Sara felt his words were hardly adequate to describe her friend's abilities, but she allowed that many men felt that no woman truly rode as she ought. "That she does," was all Sara said in reply. She wished her feeling of unease would disappear. It was a glorious morning. The sun was burning off the haze so that a pale blue sky was in view and the air was scented with the essence of spring. It was cool, but perfect for a ride.

They cantered on in harmony. Having fallen behind, they

were in no hurry to catch up with the others. Sara felt that she was reaching an agreeable rapport with Lord Lambert, or at least the beginning of such. He seemed pleased with her company.

Suddenly, up ahead, Fiona's horse stretched into a gallop while Sara watched in horrified silence. This time there was nothing she could say to defend Fiona. Sara reined up in consternation. Was there anything she might do to help her friend?

"I say . . ." Lord Lambert also drew his horse to a halt, then exclaimed, "Do you suppose she has a runaway?"

Sara was about to say Fiona always had her horse under control, before she thought better of it. "That is a possibility. Lord York is going after her now, so it could be so." She knew her words failed to hold the conviction they needed to be believed. She spurred her horse forward, joining Lord Lambert in an anxious ride to catch up with Lord York as he raced after Fiona.

In the distance, another rider approached from the opposite direction. He reached Fiona first, grasped her reins—though Sara wondered how anyone dared to do such a thing—turning Fiona's horse in a wide circle, very gradually bringing the horse to a stop.

Sara and Lord Lambert rode up to them. Sara was amazed to discover the gentleman who had come to Fiona's apparent rescue was none other than Lord St. Quinton. Lord York and Lord St. Quinton were deep in conversation, while Fiona looked as though she devoutly wished she were at a distant point—China, preferably.

She looked at Sara, then past her to where Lord Lambert sat in solemn silence. Her face was a study in chagrin and defiance.

Sara wondered just how prone Lord Lambert was to gossip, then chided herself. She ought not think ill of the man simply because he did not know Fiona as Sara did, and could not accept her for what she was, a horse-mad woman who probably forgot she was not to indulge in a full gallop in the park because she was involved in an explanation of some fine point with Lord York.

"Lucky Lord St. Quinton happened along when he did. I had no idea Miss Egerton was in real trouble. Thought she was simply demonstrating something for me." It seemed to Sara that Lord York gave Fiona a look that pleaded for understanding and cooperation.

"I was happy to be of service to Miss Egerton." Lord St. Quinton shifted on his horse, as though to leave.

A look of such patent relief crossed Fiona's face that Sara almost laughed. The dashing redhead looked a bit wilted but unbowed as she nodded to St. Quinton. "I am most grateful to you for your timely rescue. If anyone, such as those people over there, had seen me at a full gallop in the park, it would not have set well, especially with my mama."

A large party came riding across the green directly toward where the five were gathered, curiosity and concern clearly displayed on the various faces. Among the group were two Sara knew to be the greatest gossips in London. Several she knew to be the highest sticklers of propriety.

One, a Lord Twiggenbotham, rode up to inquire, "The little lady all right?" He bowed to Fiona, then Sara, starchily correct. Turning to Lord St. Quinton, he said, "That was a fine bit of work there, St. Quinton, catching that blood as you did. If my wife had been on that horse, she'd be in a fit of the vapors at the very least. You're a brave young woman," he added to Fiona, who blushed a fiery red. So saying, he saluted Fiona with his hat and rode off with the group, several of whom gave Fiona approving nods.

"Good heavens," murmured Sara. She motioned to Fiona and the two walked their horses off to one side while the men rode on ahead, content to allow the women a private chat.

Fiona gave Sara a disgusted look. "My horse did not run away from me, as you undoubtedly must know. I was so taken up with the discussion on training that I completely forgot myself and I galloped! Lord St. Quinton caught me, and we walked as we waited for you to arrive. He suggested it best to permit everyone to think he had rescued me from a runaway rather than let the truth be known. Oh, Sara, he saved my life! Or at the very least, my reputation. How I could be so stupid as to forget what my mama has drummed into my head since before we came up to the city, I cannot imagine."

"I expect you were lost in conversation," replied Sara.

Fiona shook her head, then continued, "If this does not give Lord York a disgust of me, it will be a miracle. I saw the expression on Lord Lambert's face, polite but condemning. I wanted to sink, then and there."

"But Lord Twiggenbotham thought St. Quinton a hero for saving you from your runaway. There is no problem with those people. I doubt there will be any gossip. And as for Lord Lambert, he had just mentioned what an excellent rider he thought you to be. I feel he will not say anything. Surely he has more compassion than you give him credit for, dear." Sara glanced ahead to where Lord Lambert rode, seeming rather stiff next to the relaxed grace of St. Quinton.

"St. Quinton *is* a hero as far as I am concerned." Fiona studied Sara for a minute, then asked, "Sara . . . why do you have this dislike for Lord St. Quinton? What really happened at Christmas?"

Sara shook her head. "I would rather not discuss it now, Fiona. Maybe later. One never knows how our words might carry."

Fiona looked abashed, then grinned, quite unrepentant. "I do hope Lord York asks me to wed him soon, or I shall probably do something terrible." With those words, she urged her horse forward to join Lord York.

St. Quinton dropped back. "The ruse meets with your approval?" That devilish gleam was in his eyes again and made Sara want to scream with vexation.

"Miss Egerton is most fortunate to have you as her champion. It appears Lord York did not realize she was in trouble." Sara frowned, wondering just how Lord York accepted all this deception. "Lord York—how does he feel about it?"

"York knows how it is with her. I believe she has him around her finger. Has she always been this horse-mad?"

"I have known her since we started school, and I cannot recall a time when horses didn't come first with her, if you gather my point." Sara tossed St. Quinton an arch look that made him laugh. She wished he hadn't. It made him seem likable, and she didn't want that.

"You are having a pleasant morning?" He studied her glowing face a moment, then, recalling her scheme, added,

*"Gather ye rosebuds while ye may,*
*Old Time is still a-flying."*

He gave a pointed look to where Lord Lambert rode, engrossed in a conversation with Lord York.

"Quoting Herrick at this hour of the day, milord? As to gathering rosebuds, I fear I have no idea what you mean. There certainly are none in view." Horrid man, was he intimating she was to cast out lures for Lord Lambert?

"You understand very well what I mean, my dear." Before he could explain any further, if indeed he intended to do such, another party rode up to join them and Sara found Lord Inglis approaching her. An anguished glance to Fiona was no help, and St. Quinton appeared to be chuckling.

Lord Inglis maneuvered to Sara's right, displacing St. Quinton with practiced ease. His expression was guarded as he studied Sara's face. "Good morning, my lady. I have been denied the sight of you for some time. You are looking in fine form today."

Giving him the most civil nod she could manage while conscious of St. Quinton's proximity, Sara searched for Lord Lambert while seeming to survey the scene. "Thank you, Lord Inglis." Her tone bordered on frosty, and it would have taken someone who was utterly dense to be unaware he had fallen from favor with the lady.

Lord Inglis was quite sharp. He looked to his friend St.

Quinton, who merely shrugged and began a conversation about a race that was to be held in two days' time.

Falling back, thus permitting Lord Inglis to ride on with St. Quinton, Sara hoped Lambert would seek her side. He did. She tried to feel pleased. What actually went through her was an odd sense of disquiet as she observed St. Quinton chatting with Lord Inglis while they rode on ahead.

The two men trotted to the park gate, then rode through the cobbled streets until they reached St. Quinton's mews. A groom ran forward to hold both horses. They dismounted, then strode through the stable area until they reached an entrance to the house. In the study, St. Quinton poured out two glasses of madeira, offering one to Oliver.

"So . . . she spurned you, eh? Well, there are enough other women around. A man like you can have his pick." Myles gestured to a high-back chair by the fireplace, now with a low fire burning to take a chill off the room.

Oliver seated himself, crossing one booted leg over the other as he leaned back to study Myles. "I had come to believe I not only wanted her, but that she cared for me as well. What happened, Myles?"

A prickle of guilt assailed Myles and he looked away from his friend. "How should I know? There is no accounting for females, you know that."

"You seemed at ease with her today."

Myles avoided Oliver's searching gaze. Dash it all, the man saw too much, and asked questions Myles would rather not answer. "I believe she has turned her attentions to Lambert."

Frowning, Oliver said slowly, "How odd. I would stake my fortune that Lambert is no gambler."

"But then, perhaps Lady Sara is. He does have a higher rank than you." Myles felt like a dog, impugning Lady Sara's character like this. He honestly did not feel that rank mattered that much to Lady Sara. After all, he ranked higher than all the men on her list so far, and she had passed him over.

Oliver rose, setting down his empty glass with a loud clink.

"I find that hard to accept of Lady Sara, Myles. I have the strangest feeling that not all is revealed." He studied Myles with narrow eyes, then shrugged. Myles was as close as a clam, no answers to be found there.

"How about joining me for a spot of nuncheon?" Myles also rose, urging his friend toward the door and down the hall to the small dining room. He mentioned the race coming up and the two gentlemen fell into a discussion of jockeys and horses and other races of the past.

Sara returned to the house, inviting Lord Lambert to come in with her. He declined.

"I shall see you this evening, fair lady. It is a distinct pleasure to know I shall escort you and your lovely aunt to the Hertford rout. You intend to go on from there to the Inglesby ball?"

"You know how it is during the Season. There are so many invitations that come. Aunt Eudora desires to attend as many functions as time permits. She knows so many people, you see."

He did see what she meant, and knew his own mother felt the same, as indeed did every society woman. He had never understood why one couldn't simply attend a ball, or rout, or soiree of an evening, and let it go at that. This pursuit of the social life seemed a bit frenzied to him, but if Lady Sara wished his company, he would offer it to her.

He rode off toward his home wondering what Inglis had had to say to her. The lady did not lack for gallants, to be sure. He resolved to cut out the others. Aside from her sizable portion—one he really did not require, mind you—she seemed a proper young woman, one his mother might approve. In fact, if his mother were to be present this evening, he might be able to introduce the two women . . . no, three with Lady Bellew along. He was feeling quite pleased with himself as he left his horse with his groom and entered the family home.

* * *

At No. 23 Brook Street Sara ran up the stairs to greet her aunts in the salon, where they appeared to be waiting for her.

"How did the morning go, dear?" Aunt Tilly looked up from the newspaper she studied so carefully for any financial tidbits.

"Well enough. You may as well know that Fiona was involved in one of her scrapes. She was explaining something to Lord York and got carried away . . . and galloped!"

"Merciful heaven!" gasped Aunt Milly. "Never in Hyde Park! Did anyone see her?"

Eudora took a calmer view of the situation. "And?"

"Lord St. Quinton rode up to become 'hero' again. Honestly, dear aunts, the man is a positive gadfly, always coming to some maiden's rescue." Sara paused, and, hands on hips, continued, "First he more or less helped Amanda out of a coil when Lord Rolfe saw her in the carriage with us having ices at Gunter's. Then he came to the aid of Corisande at the musicale when that awful creature threw himself at her and tore her dress, spilling wine across it. And today he rescued Fiona." She pulled off her gloves, slapping them with impatience against her thigh as she strode around the room in agitation.

"That seems rather nice, Sara, dear." Milly gave her niece a tentative smile, then exchanged questioning glances with her sisters.

"Lord Twiggenbotham came riding up, praising St. Quinton to the skies. Bah! The man gives me a pain."

"I always felt Lord Twiggenbotham a bit starchy, but I cannot ever say he gave me a pain," said Aunt Milly, clearly bewildered.

"Not him . . . St. Quinton. The man is disgustingly heroic. Rides like a master horseman. He is so polite it makes me ill. I will never see why you thought the two of us might suit!"

With that, Sara marched off to her room. In the salon, three ladies exchanged wondering looks.

# 10

It was Eudora's turn to accompany her niece for the evening. She dressed in an elegant gray silk taffeta trimmed around the neck with cream lace. Eudora patted the delicate oversleeve of rose-pink gauze with a gloved hand as she peered into the salon mirror. The pink-satin-covered buttons looked dainty, not overdone, as she had feared. She had just checked the pink satin cuff of the sleeve to make sure the tiny button had not come undone when Sara entered the room.

"Oh, how elegant, dear aunt. I do like your new gown." Sara smiled at her aunt's vanity. Never would Eudora admit it was important to her to look fashionable. She muttered comments about Milly and her shopping, but when it came time for Eudora to make a public appearance, she wore the very latest mode.

"I approve your gown as well," Eudora pronounced, as though she hadn't decided what Sara ought to wear this evening.

Brushing out an imaginary wrinkle, Sara gave Eudora a mischievous glance. "It is well that deep pink becomes me, as it goes so well with your gown." Indeed, the deep rose pink of Sara's sarcenet evening dress with its scalloped hem border of cream and tiny pink silk rosebuds looked as though made to accompany Eudora's gown. Sara chuckled when her aunt actually blushed.

Flustered, Eudora vaguely waved her hand. "I wished us to look especially nice."

"Well, you certainly do," replied Sara warmly.

"Lord Lambert is coming to escort us. What a thoughtful young man, to be sure," said Eudora, giving Sara an uneasy look. "Has he mentioned his mother to you?"

Sara, flipping through a copy of the *Ladies' Monthly Museum*, missed that look. "Yes. As a matter of fact, he indicated he hoped to be able to introduce me to her this evening." Then, realizing there had been an odd tone in her aunt's voice, Sara dropped the magazine and turned her head to study Eudora's face. "Why do you mention Lady Lambert, Aunt Eudora?"

"I hope I did the right thing when I placed Vere Eames's name on that list—Lord Lambert, that is. I hoped, rather, I expected that his mother might cock up her toes long before this, and . . . she still might do so." Eudora's voice died away on this thin note of encouragement.

Sara walked closer to where her aunt stood fidgeting with the cords of her reticule. "Why do I have the feeling that all is not what I expect? What should I know about Lord Lambert's mother?"

Smedley appeared at the door to the salon with Lord Lambert close behind him. Sara took note of the expression of extreme relief on her dear aunt's face and began to wonder. And worry. There was no opportunity to question Eudora during the ride to Hertford House.

The carriage stood in line for some time until it rolled up the curving drive to the entrance of the stately home on Manchester Square. Eudora was not her usual serene self. Sara grew more apprehensive as the minutes passed. Only Lord Lambert seemed relaxed and quite at ease.

"Lovely evening for the rout. Lady Hertford is known to be a charming hostess." Lord Lambert assisted Sara from the carriage after the groom attended to Aunt Eudora.

Sara shivered from a slight breeze, then tried to shake off this peculiar sensation that all was not as it ought to be. She smiled up at Lord Lambert (could she ever learn to call him Vere, if they wed?). "Aunt says that not only is Lady Hertford dignified and intelligent, but also that she has such wide interests. It is known the Prince Regent consults her frequently when purchasing furniture, porcelain, or such treasures."

"He does seem to prefer older women," murmured Lord Lambert as they slowly made their way up the entry steps and into the house. "My mother wondered that your aunt should permit you to attend here. After all, there is Lady Hertford's connection with the Prince."

Sara shot him a withering glance. "Surely you do not believe that there is anything improper in the friendship between the Prince and Lady Hertford?" He raised a brow at her fierce whisper, and Sara hoped she wasn't overheard.

They moved forward in the line until Sara stood before the fortyish woman dressed in the highest stare of fashion. It was well-known the lady was passionately fond of dress. Sara discreetly studied her. She had lovely eyes and a pretty mouth—for a woman her age. Even her figure was nicely curved, and she had a youthful air about her, in spite of her years. Beside her, her husband smiled with absent gaze until he saw Lord Lambert, whom he greeted with pleasure, commenting to him on his own son, Lord Yarmouth, who was supposed to be around somewhere.

"I hope we do not find him." Lord Lambert spoke softly into Sara's ear as they left the receiving line to mingle with the other guests.

There was the usual crush found in a successful rout, but owing to the size of the house and the wide double staircase, people were able to move with a modicum of ease.

Sara was in complete agreement with his sentiments. "I find I do not care for the gentleman." Sara had heard stories about Lord Yarmouth, only son of the Marquis of Hertford and his second wife. Aunt Milly called him a *roué* of the worst type, which was quite damning in Sara's eyes. It was no surprise that

Lord Yarmouth didn't seem the least upset at his mother's intimate relations with the Prince.

Normally a young woman like Sara would not have known a thing about the affair, but living with her aunts brought tittle-tattle to her ears that was denied most young misses. Of course, she must at least pretend to know nothing of the more intimate side of the friendship. It seemed that although gentlemen knew every seamy detail of society life, an unmarried woman must needs be deaf and blind to it.

As Lord Lambert turned aside to converse with a friend, Sara found a chance to quiz her aunt. "Now, tell me what you meant by your words about the Viscountess Lambert."

Eudora looked uncomfortable, then shrugged as they were approached by a plainly dressed woman of middle years. Her hair was arranged in a severe bun beneath an evening cap of black lace. Her black twill sarcenet mourning gown was simply styled, not a dress the Marchioness of Hertford would be caught in, for certain. She extended her hand to Lord Lambert, stating her good-evenings in a high, rather piercing voice.

"Husband's been dead five years," Eudora whispered in an undertone Sara barely caught. "Lives in the house on South Audley with her son in attendance. Has a weak heart—she says. She was a fine woman—once. You may judge for yourself." Eudora nodded with great civility to the other woman, but said little while Lady Lambert continued to speak.

Eudora's eyes busily absorbed the details others might have missed as she permitted her gaze to wander about the rooms. However, once home she would note who was now being seen with whom, and delicious items of incipient scandal. But only to her leather-bound volume, and perhaps to her sisters. Fortunately for all, Eudora was not one of those who went from salon to salon with the latest *on-dits* slipping maliciously off her tongue.

Sara curtsied to Lady Lambert with charming grace.

"I am so pleased to make your acquaintance, my dear," gushed Lady Lambert with what appeared to Sara to be genuine sincerity. "I had not meant to attend the Hertfords' little do this evening until Vere mentioned you might be here. It is such a pleasure to see a young lady who has had such excellent training. So many of these modern misses have no concept of how to behave to their elders, don't you know."

She favored Eudora with a benign smile, reminding Sara of her son as she did so. "You are to be praised. I understand your niece not only lives with you but also assists in the running of the household to ease the burden from your shoulders. How I envy you. I hope when the day comes that Vere weds, he shall find such a lady. Though he quite depends on me to run his house now, don't you know. Yes, I shall look forward to sharing that responsibility with some fortunate young lady."

Lord Lambert looked uncomfortable at those words. Sara knew she couldn't control the blush that swept over her face, yet took pity on Lord Lambert. "I am certain your son would do all he could to please so caring a mother."

Lady Lambert beamed a self-satisfied smile on Sara at those kind words, then clutched at her ample bosom and turned an anxious face to her son. "Oh, dear. My heart! My vinaigrette—you have it, do you not?" There was a cunning sharpness to her look. "I do hope this is not to be a really bad spasm," she said faintly.

"I shall take care of everything, Mother." Lord Lambert shot Sara an apologetic look, then solicitously tended Lady Lambert. Sara watched as he moved away from where she stood, with his mother clinging to his arm, the vinaigrette held high in her son's hands if she needed it.

"Observe how a man treats his mother and you shall see how you will be treated as his wife. Or is it that he will favor the mother and neglect the wife? I can never recall."

Sara spun around to find St. Quinton laughing down in her face. "What are you doing here?" she demanded. "I might have known you would attend." That she was not best pleased by his appearance at her side was evident.

He grimaced, shaking his head at her with mock woe. "I am

desolated, my lady. I thought my pearls of wisdom would be most welcome. Or are your dainty ears numb from the accents of Lady Lambert's voice?"

"She is a very pleasant person." Sara glared up at him, wondering how he had managed to find her in this mass of people, and when, or if, Lord Lambert might return to rescue her.

"I am told there are poisons that are quite sweet." He bestowed upon Sara that smile she termed wicked. How merciful that he had no idea of its effect.

"And how do you treat your mother, milord? I cannot think it could be with greater kindness." Sara found his nearness in the press of the crowd to be overwhelming, and she had rushed into hasty speech.

A shadow crossed his handsome face. "Alas, I have not seen my mother for many years. I understand she is settled on the Continent with her second husband."

Stricken at her thoughtless words, Sara impulsively placed her hand on his arm. "Forgive me, St. Quinton. I would never knowingly cause pain to you . . . or anyone."

He looked down at the dainty hand resting so trustingly on his sleeve. What odd powers Lady Sara had over him. He felt as though he wanted to clasp her to him for the comfort she offered, hold her close to him, not in a passionate embrace, but one of solace. Shaking the peculiar sensation off, he gave her another mocking smile. "The lady makes a mistake. My mother is none of my concern."

Just as Sara sought to find rebuttal to these cynical words, Lord Lambert quietly walked up to them, smiling with genuine affection at his friend. He then observed the offended glint in Sara's eyes, and his smile faded. Behind them, Eudora moved closer, concerned. Seeing Lambert's unease, St. Quinton bowed and soon left them.

Like her sister Matilda, Eudora still felt Myles Fenwick to be the better choice for her niece. She sighed with a sense of defeat. If only the two didn't come to cuffs every time they got within touching distance. Her own husband, the Earl of

Bellew, had made no such shilly-shally when it came to choosing the one he wanted. What a pity he had been lost at sea. They had rubbed along together tolerably well for the years of their marriage.

Lord Lambert explained to Sara in detail about his mother's problem and how he solved it. "The doctor urges her to live quietly, but Mother will insist upon getting about." After another look at Sara, he went on, "Since we do not desire to play cards, perhaps we should think about making our way to the Inglesbys' ball." He searched Sara's face for a clue to her feelings toward St. Quinton. She revealed nothing.

"Youngest gel is making her come-out, as I recall." Eudora breathed a sigh of relief as they wove their way through the throng of people, bade the Hertfords farewell, and escaped into the pleasant evening air.

Sara didn't mind the wait on the front steps of Hertford House. Through the tall columns of the entry she could see Lord Lambert's coach slowly making its way to where they waited.

It was a blessing to be free of the place where St. Quinton had once again confronted her. Though she wished she had not made that unkind remark about his mother. Why couldn't she have remembered in time the story Aunt told about his mother having run away with some French *comte*? Though St. Quinton mouthed indifferent words regarding his mother, Sara sensed an inner pain, undoubtedly of some degree. Perhaps it was buried deep within, and he didn't realize how affected he had been. Her hostility softened toward him. He must have been very young when his mother left for the Continent, never to return. Sara sensed it was a subject never broached by any, given the unyielding reserve he presented to the world when one got too close for his comfort. And *she* had had the temerity to mention it.

"Here we are. Daydreaming, Sara, dear?" Eudora roused Sara from her abstraction, reminding her subtly that she was not paying proper attention to her escort.

The Inglesbys' ball was a delight in silver and pink. The walls were draped with silver tissue and pink silk roses were massed in the corners. Sara was entranced with the dainty silver-and-pink cakes piled high on the supper table when they joined the others in the light repast. She sat with Lord Lambert, Fiona, and Lord York, while at a nearby table Eudora listened to the latest tale from one of the dowagers in attendance.

Sara found her mind repeatedly straying to St. Quinton. Had his attitude to women been affected to any high degree by his mother's rejection (for that was what it must have seemed like to a little boy)? Then, scolding herself for ignoring the nice Lord Lambert, she applauded his choice of delicacies from the supper table, and gave herself up to the enjoyment of the evening.

Fiona sidled up to her after they had eaten and were returning to the ballroom. "How was the Hertford rout? Mama would not allow me to go."

"Lady Hertford looked charming and the house was well enough, what I could see of it. Aunt Eudora seemed happy to leave, if that makes you feel better." Sara exchanged an amused look with Fiona.

"May I see you tomorrow? I must return some books to the lending library and would welcome your company."

Sara nodded. "Very well. Shall you collect me?" Fiona's parents kept a stable and Sara enjoyed riding in their smart landau of dark gray with green accents.

"I will call for you late morning." Fiona wiggled her fingers in farewell as the couples were separated by the crush of people.

Aunt Eudora gave a prodigious yawn as they entered the house at No. 23 Brook Street in the wee hours of the morning. While not as late as Sara had remained out before, it was probably later than Eudora liked. Neither Millicent nor Matilda had waited up for them, a sure sign of the lateness of the hour.

As they walked up the stairs to their respective rooms, Aunt Eudora inquired, "What did you think of Lord Lambert's mama?"

"She appeared to be most amiable," Sara said carefully. "It was a pity she was overcome with the crowd and Lord Lambert had to help her from the house. He said she never knows when her heart will act up."

Before she turned to enter her room, Eudora gave Sara a searching look, then said, "It is to be hoped that Lambert intends to set up a separate house once he weds. I have a strong feeling that woman will lead his wife a merry dance should they all reside together."

Sara merely nodded, then went on to her own room. Closing the door behind her, she slipped from her gown rather than rouse her abigail, draping the pink silk carefully over a chair. She pulled on her soft muslin nightdress and crawled between the scented sheets.

Why was nothing simple? Why couldn't she feel that powerful attraction for Lord Lambert that Amanda, Fiona, and Corisande seemed to feel for their gentlemen? Instead, she discovered that there were complexities involved that it would take King Solomon to solve. Resolution was required. She could do anything necessary, and she really did not feel that the Viscountess Lambert was so terribly formidable.

Breakfast was a time of questions from all directions.

In a quiet moment Eudora slyly thrust in her little note of news. "St. Quinton was in attendance at the Hertfords'. Surprised to see him there. He spoke to Sara while Lord Lambert was attending to his mother. She had one of her spells. I keep wondering how her heart can withstand all the strain of her social engagements, for you must know she is ever on the go. Those spasms seem to occur at selected moments."

"Hmpf." Aunt Tilly sniffed loudly. "That woman has never wanted to let go the reins of the fortune left her by her nodcock of a husband. Naturally a great deal went to Vere Eames, but his mother controls enough to make life tedious for him. He must have the patience of a saint."

"I think it quite lovely that Lord Lambert is so considerate of his mother. Goodness knows I wish my Ivor would lean that direction a little." No one commented, as all knew Milly's disappointment in her only son.

Sara was pleased when Smedley entered the breakfast room to announce the arrival of Fiona. The redhead walked with an unusually demure air and she greeted the aunts with quiet affection. Sara feared the aunts might return to the subject of St. Quinton. It seemed to her he took up far too many of her thoughts lately as it was. She kissed each aunt on a soft, scented cheek, then left the house with relief, stepping into the gray landau as though afraid someone might call her back.

"You look so pretty today, Sara. Did Aunt Milly select your carriage dress?" Fiona settled back against the green velvet squabs as she studied Sara.

Knowing a faint blush must be stealing over her cheeks, Sara shrugged. "I suppose I cannot hide it from you, dear friend. I succumbed to the shade because it precisely matches the violets that still arrive each morn. Madame Meradan did a fine job of creating it, I believe."

"And well she ought, for she must be the premier of modistes, and frightfully dear," replied Fiona without a trace of envy. She was quite happy with the gowns her mother chose for her, although sometimes she did get weary of green. As long as Lord York kept looking at her with adoration in his eyes, Fiona wouldn't fuss at anything to do with dresses. She added in an afterthought, "You still do not know who sends the flowers each day?"

"No," said Sara repressively. Then she relented. "I wish I did, for it puzzles me greatly. If you have any ideas, please tell me."

They arrived at Hookham's library in Bond Street at a proper hour, before the street became the exclusive domain of the gentlemen. The groom assisted them down, then set off with the landau, for he knew Miss Fiona would be a spell making up her mind. He always returned in good time. The maid followed her ladies at a discreet distance, close enough to lend propriety, and far enough away so that the girls could talk.

Strolling about the wide-planked wooden floor, Sara sought to find a good book to read. Perhaps it would take her mind off the various and sundry things she would rather not think about.

"Here is one by Miss Austen, Sara. Have you read *Emma*?" Fiona tapped Sara on the shoulder just as a stout lady Sara recognized all too well entered the library.

The older lady sailed toward them with a prim smile on her broad face. "My dears," announced Mrs. Twiggenbotham, "how good to see you. And you, miss?" she said to Fiona. "You have recovered from that horrid runaway?"

Fiona turned an embarrassed shade of pink. "Quite well, thank you."

"How fortunate you had a nonpareil like St. Quinton to come to your aid." She uttered a few more remarks, then took herself off to where the latest gothic novels were to be found.

Sara hastily took the copy of *Emma*, then waited while Fiona selected her volumes and checked them out at the desk. Once free of the library and the presence of Mrs. Twiggenbotham, Sara breathed a sigh of relief.

"I vow that man's name must always come up," Sara complained, vexed that she couldn't shake her nemesis even in conversation.

"You were going to explain why you felt as you do about him," Fiona reminded her.

"I wish I knew." Sara joined Fiona in the landau, then requested they make a stop at Ackermann's. As the carriage rolled along over the cobblestones, she glanced at her friend, then away. "It isn't a simple thing, I fear. Perhaps someday I can talk about it. Not now, in a carriage going down Bond Street." She thought she glimpsed St. Quinton exiting a tailor's shop and looked the other direction. He was like a plague, she thought. He haunted her no matter how she tried to put him out of her mind. What was to be done?

At Ackermann's, Sara went straight to the folios of prints while Fiona wandered about to look at the many other things to be found on display in the print shop. Engrossed in perusing the variety of topographical prints to be found, Sara debated between an elegant print of the Tower of London and a charming one of the Buckingham Water Gate, Strand, by Thomas Shepherd.

"Take the Shepherd one, by all means. 'Tis the better quality work and will probably appreciate more." The voice continued in an aggrieved tone, "Though why I should encourage you to buy up the finest prints in London is more than I can figure. I shall have to turn to collecting prints of Shropshire, I believe."

With great resignation and not a little forebearance, Sara looked up into St. Quinton's face. "How is it you happen here at this moment, milord? I thought I saw you on Bond Street." As soon as the words left her mouth, Sara could have pinched herself for her stupidity. She had admitted not only that she was interested in how he came to be here but also that she had been aware of him earlier.

The twinkle in those dark, dark eyes allowed her to know that he was well aware of her chagrin. "I was certain I had observed you passing in the Egerton landau." At her momentary confusion, he smiled kindly, adding, "The gray-and-green carriage with the distinctive figure clad always in a shade of green is a familiar sight about London." His glance roved over the lovely violet gown, and that knowing smile broadened. "May I say I find your dress to be particularly fetching? Reminds me of the spring violets that grew on my country estate when I was a lad."

"Ah, er, well, it is a favorite color of mine." She bit her lip in aggravation that he had caused her to stutter like a Bath miss.

He glanced at the posy of violets Sara had carried with her this morning, as she so enjoyed the fragrance. The streets of London were often malodorous. Earlier she had defended her behavior to herself as a wise precaution against the miasmas and smells of the city.

"And flowers to match your gown." He took the violets from where she had placed them while searching through the folio to sniff the delicate scent. "That seems to be a predilection of yours. Are you thinking to start a new fashion? I should think that being one of the very select women who collect these prints would satisfy you."

"Each of us has his little follies, milord. Though I confess I have not sought to set a new fashion in posies to match a dress . . . exactly." Being an honest girl, she amended her statement, as she certainly had sought to match her new carriage dress. "The violets are a mystery, being delivered early each morning from an unknown gallant." Why she felt it necessary to explain to St. Quinton, Sara didn't know.

"A mystery! How intriguing. And do you like mysteries?" He handed her the violets and watched with eagle-keen acuity as she searched for an answer.

Sara took refuge in burying her nose in the violets. "Of course. Does not every woman enjoy a touch of intrigue? How dull life would be without it." She flashed him an amused look, curtsied, then picked up both of the prints—to St. Quinton's dismay—and marched to the counter, where she placed them before the clerk.

"What a pity," he said as he watched the clerk make note of the sale of the Buckingham Water Gate print St. Quinton had particularly wanted for his own, "that we do not get along better. Then I might have a chance to throw myself on your mercy." At her glance of inquiry, he added, "To get the print, naturally."

"I find it difficult to believe you have ever thrown yourself on a woman's . . . mercy." A faint pink crept into her cheeks as she considered what she had just uttered. What was there about this man that caused her to forget to mind her tongue?

A discreet coughing spell concealed St. Quinton's reaction to her hasty words.

"Cheer up, milord. There is a fine print of St. George's, Hanover Square, in the folio. 'Tis such an elegant building, although you probably have little acquaintance with it. You could even begin a collection solely of the fine churches to be found in London. After all, there are fifty structures from the reign of Queen Anne alone. Do not despair. As you said, you could always turn to Shropshire or even Devonshire for collecting. Perhaps I ought to do that as well. I have such a large number of prints on London now.''

She gave him a wicked little smile, collected her precious prints, and beckoned to Fiona, who had watched this interchange with fascination. Sara had decided she would return later and buy up every church print to be found, just to thwart St. Quinton should he lean that way.

The ladies seated themselves in the well-cushioned landau, pulling away as St. Quinton gave an ironic bow from the doorway of Ackermann's.

''Would you kindly explain why I felt as though the building might go up in flames just now? The sparks set off between you two are mighty interesting, dear Sara.'' Fiona repressed the urge to laugh at the set expression on Sara's face.

''Oh, pooh. The man is the greatest bother on earth. I hope never to see him again.'' At which lie Sara wondered that the sky didn't fall upon her.

# 11

"I vow he is quite the nicest man," declared Sara, while wondering why she couldn't think of a more eloquent word than "nice" to describe the man she hoped to marry.

Amanda gave her a speculative look, then met Fiona's gaze. Eyebrows were discreetly raised. "That is most, ah, charming. And his mother?"

Sara smoothed out the silk of her dainty lavender gloves and shrugged. "I do not see why my aunt fears her presence in the household. She seems genial enough to me."

"You believe she will live with you in the same house?" Corisande frowned in alarm.

" 'Tis done, you know. Lady Melbourne gave the first floor of their mansion to Caroline and William Lamb." Sara pulled off her gloves and set them aside. She picked up the cup of steaming tea Corisande poured for her and sipped, thankful to be silent again.

Amanda cleared her throat. "That was not perhaps the best illustration you could have found, Sara."

"Well, we are nothing like that pair. If you have read her novel, *Glenarvon*, you would know I could certainly never write such drivel," Sara declared fervently.

Corisande sighed. "I thought it vastly romantic."

"And containing utter nonsense—assassins, specters, manacled maniacs, and children changed at birth," refuted

Amanda. "Why she included all those devastating portraits of society members, I will never understand. It might not have been so serious had she not included Lady Jersey. I believe the first thing that good lady did was to cross Caroline's name off Almack's list."

Shuddering, Corisande reconsidered. "I suppose she would better have left it in a drawer."

"Or unwritten," said Amanda severely.

Giving a solemn "Ahem," Fiona interrupted. "I would like to change the subject, if I may." Once she had the attention of the others, she smiled with a triumphant twinkle in her eyes. "Lord York has told me how very much I will like his home and especially his stables. He has even given me details about the horses he feels I will admire the most. I suspect he believes he had better take me under his wing before I do something drastic—like gallop in the park again." She gave them a prim smile, totally ruined by an infectious giggle. "He plans to speak with Papa tomorrow when he returns from the country."

"Wonderful!" exclaimed Sara with genuine enthusiasm. "Two of us have achieved our goal. And he is perfect for you, dear friend. What about you, Amanda?"

With modest charm Amanda set down her teacup and said, "I feel it will not be long before Lord Rolfe seeks an interview with my father. We have found we suit on every point."

"And Sara likes Lord Lambert," pronounced Corisande with childlike pleasure.

"He is extremely . . . proper, you know. I shall never have to be concerned that he will disgrace me in his behavior. And *he* does not gamble. So many men are given to rakish leanings." The image of sparkling dark eyes below a thatch of black hair flitted through her mind until banished with great determination. "Yes, it will be a distinct joy to have a husband such as he."

"And his nice mother," muttered Fiona with a side glance at Amanda.

Bored to flinders with the talk about Lady Lambert and son,

Corisande asked, "Have you read the descriptions of Princess Charlotte's wedding dress? I have a desire to have a dress something like hers. After all, I am a blond as well," she added with a modicum of pride.

"It is difficult to imagine the dress from mere words. Surely your modiste will have an attractive solution." Amanda gave Sara a confident look. "What do you plan, Sara? We are quite certain you will succeed."

Sara wished she felt as strongly that her plans would turn out well. "Something simple for me. I think I should like to be married privately." For some reason, the quiet wedding of St. Quinton's sister popped into her mind. "Lord Lambert could get a special license. I sense a kindred soul in him. He has little care for society fuss. His sense of propriety is quite nice."

"Mama has booked St. George's for my wedding ceremony. Gunter's will cater the breakfast," said Corisande with a dreamy expression. "I cannot wait until the drawing of Princess Charlotte's gown appears in *La Belle Assemblée*. They promised to print it."

"I wonder how many others will have the same idea?" Amanda had a vision of dozens of duplicate dresses marching down the various aisles of London's churches.

"Oh," said Corisande in a disappointed voice, "I had not considered that. Perhaps I had best strive to be an original."

Laughing gently, Fiona said, "You already are an original, dear girl."

The Saturday meeting had been a leisurely one, and now Amanda rose, placed her teacup on the tray, and reached for her reticule. "This had been lovely. Who would have foreseen it would turn out so well when we began?"

Fiona joined her, looking at Sara with a half-frown on her brow. "Well, we had better not crow until all rings are in place, if you follow my meaning."

Resolute in her determination to give Lord Lambert a nudge in the proper direction, Sara also rose. "I agree. I would not wish to face Aunt Tilly with another failure." She thanked

Corisande for the tea and for permitting them to congregate all these weeks. "It shan't be much longer and we will all be married ladies." They strolled from the Fenwick library in complete harmony. If Sara knew a moment of unease, it was well-concealed.

The house settled into its usual state of Saturday-afternoon quiet. From the chair by the window, St. Quinton arose to prowl about slowly, having first assured himself the library door was securely closed. So Lady Sara thought Lambert a proper gentleman. Well, and so he was. Which presented a distinct problem for Myles. How the devil was he to find a weak spot in a proper gentleman? Why, the man never put a foot wrong. Which was not to be wondered at when you stopped to consider how Lambert remained tied to his mother by her incessant demands. Yet he was a nice fellow. Odd, Lady Sara had used that very word to describe Vere.

St. Quinton shook his head in distaste. Surely each of the persons involved deserved better? Vere needed a wife who understood his mother and could handle her with delicate skill. Myles somehow doubted Sara was right for the position. Dealing with three doting aunts on a daily basis was quite different from coddling a manipulative mother-in-law. Vere needed a wife whom he could mold into an obedient, willing helpmate. Myles totally ignored the notion that Vere Eames, the Viscount Lambert, might know better what appealed to him.

St. Quinton's pensive stance by the fireplace was undisturbed until that naughty gleam lit his eyes once more and he snapped his fingers. "Aha, I have the solution! She said that Lambert was proper, didn't she?" With that enigmatic statement he left the library, only to run into Kit in the hallway. The young man looked as though a dozen devils hounded him. Taking pity on his cousin, Myles slung an arm around Kit's hunched shoulders. "Come with me and we can discuss what is troubling you."

"That plain, eh? Dashed good of you, Myles."

The two strolled down along the quiet streets, St. Quinton having decided it might be wiser to stretch his legs while he listened to what was likely to be a tale of woe.

"Y'see 'tis this way. Miss Rolleston is a lovely creature, but she must have the schemingest mama in town. I wish you hadn't made me promise to keep your coming marriage a secret. Her mama ain't convinced you mean to wed. Dashed if she don't keep nattering on about my being your heir. Makes me fair ill to listen to the old lady. I wager she has enough tongue for two sets of teeth."

Myles murmured a suitably sympathetic reply. "I fear I cannot oblige you regarding the marriage yet, as I have not formally asked the young lady."

Kit's head sank further in despair. "Perhaps my fortune might not be as large as yours, but 'tis respectable enough. With a wife like Miss Rolleston, I could make it even greater. She is very economizing."

Not wanting to ask precisely how Kit came about this fascinating facet to the lovely Rolleston chit, Myles gave him a hearty clap on the back, then commiserated, "You'll come about, my boy. You're a Fenwick, after all, and we Fenwicks always do well with our choice of ladies."

Kit brightened considerably. "If that's the case, you won't have to worry about being turned down when you apply for your intended's hand."

Having forgotten for a moment that he was supposed to be contemplating matrimony, Myles almost ruined everything by asking what Kit meant by that remark. Catching himself just in time, he coughed, then ushered his cousin into White's.

With the fortune, title, and countenance Myles possessed, he doubted, with all due modesty, that any father in town would turn him down as a prospective son-in-law. But he was wise enough not to utter one word of these thoughts out loud. Instead he comforted Kit, urging him to try his luck at winning his fair lady's hand, if that was what he truly wanted.

An hour or more passed before Myles sighted his quarry. He

gave a lazy wave of his hand as Lambert paused in the doorway.

"St. Quinton." Lord Lambert approached Myles, seated at a
quiet table in the corner.

"Won't you join me?" There was no indication on St.
Quinton's face that he was plotting again. Indeed, he looked as
usual—faintly bored, slightly reserved, and excessively elegant.

Lambert seated himself, then studied Myles over the rim of
his glass of Madeira. "Rumor has it you are about to become
leg-shackled, old friend." He had scarcely credited the news
when passed along by his mother. She claimed to have had it
straight from his heir's intended, Kit Fenwick, via Lady
Rolleston. Now, as he watched the guarded expression on
Myles's face, he found he knew no more than he had before.

"Well, you know how rumors are. I sometimes believe half
are invented just to see if they might prove to be true." Myles
cursed Lady Rolleston and her flapping tongue. "For instance,
I heard this very day that you are about to be congratulated
soon. The lovely lady you have been escorting about of late
seems to approve your suit."

Lambert shifted about as though uncomfortable. "If you
mean the Lady Sara, yes, I am serious about her. She seems
elusive at times, difficult to fathom. You appear to have more
than a passing acquaintance with her. Any suggestions, old
friend?"

That persistent twinge of conscience assailed Myles again,
and he seemed to shake it off with greater difficulty than
before. Dash it all, he *liked* Lambert. Did he have the right to
interfere in Lambert's selection of a wife? Then Myles thought
of what Lady Sara had said. She thought Lambert nice. Merely
nice. The other young women had gone into raptures over
their chosen mates. Not Lady Sara Harland. She was as cool as
an ice from Gunter's.

He thought passion simmered beneath the elegant surface
she presented to the world, and wondered what it might be like
to explore beyond that outward reserve of hers.

"She is a delightful lady from what I have observed. Quite proper, of course. Not the sort to get involved in anything out of line. I heard from my cousin Corisande that Lady Sara admires propriety above all virtues. Indeed, if you wish to win her hand, that might be the path to take. Mind you, I cannot say for certain, as I am not inclined in that direction, despite what you may have heard from Kit."

Since Lambert had never mentioned his source of the rumor, it confirmed the truth of the matter in his mind. He knew how reserved St. Quinton was when it came to his personal life. It would be torture to a man of his reserved nature to have his affairs bruited about town.

They parted, Lambert to seek out the Lady Sara, and St. Quinton to visit the lovely Olivia.

Hailing a hackney, and rather sorry he had given in to the impulse to forgo his own phaeton, he set out. From the front of her discreet little place on Wigmore Street he could see candles lit in the small salon. It amused him that he provided her with a nest not far from the celebrated Hertford House.

The memory of his scene with Lady Sara not so long ago in that vast and faintly decadent mansion returned. Blast the woman, she haunted him. For instance, why had he told her to purchase that print of the Buckingham Water Gate when he had wanted it for himself? She couldn't possibly know how few had been printed, nor what a prize it was to find. If he had kept his mouth closed, it would have been his.

He sauntered up the steps, handed his hat into the care of Olivia's vigilant French maid, then went on up the stairs to the salon. Olivia was lounging on a divan, occupied in idly paging through a copy of the *Gentleman's Magazine*. The thought crossed his mind that it was an odd piece to find in her salon, and he wondered how it got there.

At the sight of him, she rose from her backless divan of the very latest mode to greet him with pleasure. Yet something disturbed Myles. How much emotion was genuine? How much was assumed? He protested he didn't care. He didn't keep her here to provide the kind of affection one might find from one's true love. He extended his hands and waited to be cosseted and attended to as she well knew how to do.

"I have missed you, my lord," Olivia chided. "I could die of ennui in this little place with nothing to keep me occupied."

Olivia Smythe-Jones (originally just plain Olive Jones before she became ambitious) was determined to so ensnare Lord St. Quinton that he would put aside his scruples and marry her. That her delusion revealed a total lack of understanding of his character was indicative of her own lack of mental abilities. It occurred to her that she attracted him because she was strikingly lovely. She failed to realize that that, plus her ability in bed, was the only appeal she had for his lordship.

Myles reached in his pocket to remove a small package. He gave a cynical smile as she trilled her delight.

Opening it, she discovered a ruby brooch edged with seed pearls set in gold filigree. Not appreciating the delicate beauty and exquisite quality, noting only the dainty size, when she wanted gaudy ostentation, she gave him a polite smile and a kiss of thanks.

Myles was not fooled for a moment by her feigned show of pleasure. Why the devil had he bought Olivia such a gift? He knew the sort of jewel she craved. The answer came unbidden from a dark recess in his mind: you were thinking of another raven-haired beauty, who has sparkling violet eyes instead of petulant blue.

He shook off that disturbing thought and permitted Olivia to practice her clinging charm. But he was abstracted at best, and left the house far earlier than usual.

The maid took note of his early departure and began to prepare for tantrums. The English lord had the look of a man in love, and it most assuredly was not with her mistress!

---

Sara looked around the charming Havell-Beaumont ballroom, where her aunts had decreed she attend the ball given by the Countess of Havell-Beaumont. The name was an alteration, as so many had come to be.

Aunt Tilly explained in soft tones, "When the Earl of Beaumont married Georgianna Havell, he also acquired a considerable fortune from her banker father. To do honor to his wealthy father-in-law, and perhaps assuage the lack of an heir, the earl has added 'Havell' to his own name. It cost him little and has pleased his wealthy relative no end. I wonder how Georgianna feels about it? Seems most kind."

She guided Sara across the room to where a friend who always knew the latest *on-dit* was seated. Tilly sat herself down and prepared for a lovely visit.

Sara tapped her fan against her wrist in impatient boredom. Though she was well aware that anyone who was anyone at all considered it the only place on earth to be at this time of year, she did not agree. It would be a welcome relief to get married to Lord Lambert and get away from the press of the London Season.

The sparkle had gone out of her life.

At that moment she observed Lord Lambert enter the room. She smiled, thinking what a perfect gentleman he was. She walked toward him, Aunt Tilly now right behind her, to greet him with polite enthusiasm.

He was chillingly correct. Sara wondered if he was angry with her. "Have you had a pleasant day, milord? The weather has grown quite delightful, has it not? I understand many have been at Newmarket to take in the races."

He smiled, at least she supposed that was what it was, and commented in a formal manner, "I do not approve of the turf, Lady Sara. Such a waste of time and money. Far better to spend one's time in improving one's mind, wouldn't you say?"

She gave him a startled look and agreed with a bemused nod. "Of course."

"You are looking most agreeable this evening, Lady Sara," Lambert said with stilted respect. "I had hoped the roses I sent you would find a match in your gown."

Flushing guiltily, Sara recalled how she had almost carried the violets, then decided at the very last to take the posy of pale pink rosebuds. She wore the same deep pink dress she had worn when last out with Aunt Eudora, and the posy went well with it. Though most young women would have died rather than wear the same dress twice, Sara felt it silly, and since she loved the dress, she wore it.

Lambert turned to Aunt Tilly, intoning, "It is so refreshing to find a woman who blushes with such charm."

It was as though he had been bewitched, thought Sara. What had happened to the nicely correct man who had been such pleasant company? Rather, here was a pompous model of perfection who bestowed a sort of frigid approval on her, as though she were some bud in a rose garden. She glanced with confusion at Aunt Tilly.

Aunt Tilly gave a tiny shrug, then continued on until she found a place with the other dowagers, leaving Sara to the mercy of this extremely civil gentleman. There would be nothing to worry about this evening, unless Sara decided she wanted a flesh-and-blood man instead of this pattern-card of respectability.

His dancing was sedate. They performed the first set of country dances with all the enthusiasm of a funeral, she decided. He was correct in every detail. At the conclusion of the dance, rather than drawing her aside to whisper compliments in her ear, he promptly returned her to her aunt. Sara didn't know whether to be grateful or not. The only bright sign was that he sought her hand for a third dance, with Aunt Tilly's permission, naturally.

Amanda looked radiant this evening. Sara caught a glimpse of her early on, then persuaded Lord Lambert to join Amanda and Lord Rolfe at supper. The countess might have a fortune, but her supper was for those who had done nothing more strenuous than sit in a chair all evening. It was thin of food, and what was there was not very appetizing. It did nothing to improve Sara's temper.

The talk during supper was thin as well. Sara decided that she would have to wait for any visiting until the morrow. It seemed the excessive civility of Lord Lambert placed a damper on the others. One by one they fell silent, until Sara indicated to Lambert she wished to leave. As they left the supper room the sound of giggles and chatter followed.

Nothing appeared to be going right this evening. The hour was late and Sara devoutly hoped they might be able to depart soon.

Standing close to where her aunt sat chatting to one of her bosom bows, Sara failed at first to notice the arrival of St. Quinton. Not so their hostess, who was delighted to snare the elusive gentleman. Watching St. Quinton adroitly detach himself from her cloying attentions, Sara had to admire his finesse. Resolutely she turned from the sight.

He took out his quizzing glass and noted the spot where Sara stood before casually wandering in her direction.

"Good evening, fair ladies."

Sara froze at the well-remembered voice, then turned to greet him. "Lord St. Quinton." She inclined her head as he bowed most correctly over her hand. The wicked glance he gave her wasn't seen by anyone else—she hoped.

He looked to where Lord Lambert was performing a rather stiff gavotte, then back to her. "Gathering rosebuds this evening?"

Knowing instantly to what he referred, Sara feigned ignorance, and rather held out her flowers. "How astute of you, milord. These match my dress well, do they not?"

He studied them much like a painting one isn't quite certain about, then shrugged. "I rather prefer the violets. You will honor me with a dance?"

It was a waltz. Sara felt like an awkward piece of pasteboard in his arms at first. Then he gave her that lazy smile. "You remind me of a garden this evening."

Amused, and a bit intrigued, Sara tilted her head and forgot to be stiff. "A garden, milord?"

"Let me see. Strawberries for your lips, or ought it to be cherries? Peaches for your cheeks, of course. But what could I say for your eyes? Plums? Grapes? Never!"

Sara chuckled at the ridiculous nonsense of it all. She sparkled. She was as radiant and vivacious as Amanda and all the other women rolled up in one. She was like one come from a cold, cheerless night into the warmth of home and hearth. And love.

"No," he mused, "I shall have to turn to a different kind of garden—violets for eyes, of course, apple blossoms for your cheeks, and . . . fuchsia for your mouth, I believe."

Feeling more alive than she had for days, Sara laughed engagingly. "According to Aunt Millicent and her language of flowers, that would be faithfulness, preference, and . . . taste." Her voice faded away at the intense look from those so very dark eyes. Sara trembled at that look. It was as though she actually experienced the hard pressure of that well-shaped, dangerous mouth against hers. For a moment she had the utterly wanton desire to lean against that marvelously broad chest and know the sensation of his kiss. There was a warmth flowing through her she certainly had never known before.

Totally confused by the warring emotions that whirled within her, Sara looked away to encounter the disapproving gaze of Lord Lambert. All of a sudden the thrill was gone, the happiness she had known at the silliness of St. Quinton's little game as well.

Following the direction of her look, St. Quinton commented, "I believe your Lord Lambert is not best pleased at the moment."

"So it would seem."

The dance ended.

St. Quinton quite properly returned Sara to the side of her aunt, where Lord Lambert also waited. He gave Myles a hard stare. "Playing the gallant this evening, St. Quinton?"

Myles still retained Sara's hand, and he lightly pressed it, saying, "Being courteous and attentive to a lady such as Lady Sara is a distinct pleasure, as you must know. However, if you desire to moralize, please excuse me. I fear I am not up to that." He gave Lambert a knowing look, then left them.

Shortly after, Sara saw him leave the room. The candlelight seemed dimmer, and she was certain someone must have opened the doors, for the warmth she had known before had gone. She sent Lord Lambert on a quest for a glass of lemonade to have a moment to assess her confused feelings.

Across the room, Lady Rolleston had watched the entire scene with the concentration of a matchmaking mama. When St. Quinton left, and Lady Sara looked as though she had lost her last friend, Lady Rolleston went into action. Sailing around the perimeter of the room, Kit and Daphne trailing behind her, she pounced.

"Dear Lady Kerr, Lady Sara. You both appear in first form this evening. But then, having the attentions of such a gentleman as St. Quinton, I am not surprised."

Startled at this assault, Sara murmured something about Lord Lambert.

"But," countered Lady Rolleston, "we are on to your little secret. Dear Christopher told us—in strictest secrecy, of course—that St. Quinton is getting married. Since you are the only woman in the room who had his attention, we knew it must be you." Her keen-eyed gaze never left Sara's face. "Dear girl—so fortunate—all that wealth and such a handsome man. I vow he quite makes my heart flutter."

Sara steeled herself to reply. "How kind of you, ma'am. But I fear you mistake the matter. I am not pledged to St. Quinton in any way." Nor likely to be, she added to herself. She cast a beseeching look at her aunt.

Lord Lambert arrived with the no-longer-wanted lemonade. "Here you are, Lady Sara."

He proffered the glass with a stiff dignity that quite undid Sara. She drank as much as she could, then turned to her aunt. "Shall we take our leave now?"

The ride home was another of those silent ones, Aunt Tilly wondering if her hopes might be realized after all. Sara wondering what it would be like to become a spinster.

# 12

It was a perplexed gathering of ladies. Sara sat stiffly before the fireplace while her aunts discussed the results of the evening.

"I declare, I was vastly disappointed in that young man," stated Aunt Tilly in no uncertain terms. "He seemed like such a promising candidate, in spite of that mother of his."

"Lord Lambert did nothing improper, aunt." Sara felt obliged to defend the nice man who had been her escort.

"I knew he was refined and straight-arrow, but his dignity bordered on the excessive." Aunt Tilly's complaint met with an arrested look from Eudora.

"In other words, Lambert was a dull dog," said Aunt Milly with evident dissatisfaction.

Sara mused that Aunt Milly had described Lord Lambert to perfection. On the other hand, Lord St. Quinton had been delightful fun, with his nonsense about gardens. She had waltzed with him more than any other gentleman. That was undoubtedly a mere coincidence, made notable by Corisande's insistence on how beautifully he waltzed. She was correct, too. He waltzed extremely well, Sara remembered with disturbing pleasure.

"Well," Sara said, "I believe Amanda shall have happy news for our next Saturday meeting, from the looks of things tonight. That means three of our four have succeeded." Sara gave them a valiant smile that well concealed her inner sense of loss. "I believe I shall prefer to be a spinster. I do appreciate all you have done for me. However, it seems the gentlemen change once I get to know them. I fear my judgment is no longer trustworthy. What I thought I wanted, turned out to be all wrong." She gave a great gust of a sigh, then rose from her chair. "If you do not mind, I believe I shall wander on up to my bed."

The three aunts watched Sara as she listlessly strolled from the room. They turned to face each other, frowns on every brow. Eudora demanded, "Now, Matilda, tell us what really happened."

Matilda Kerr leaned forward, speaking in the soft voice of one who intrigues. "There is a factor here we have ignored. I believe it is one we must now consider. And that, my dears, is St. Quinton."

Eudora nodded. "He is of the very highest *ton*. Family goes back to the ark. I wish Sara had not taken him into dislike."

Tilly shook her head. "I am not convinced that our Sara does dislike him. I watched most carefully while she danced with him." She glanced at Milly, pleased to see she'd perked up. "St. Quinton again asked her to waltz this evening. *And*, as Lady Rolleston carefully pointed out to us when she walked over to chat, Sara was the only woman he partnered at the ball. Sara looks very different when in his arms. Quite vivacious. I must say," Tilly added with a coy smile, "they do look well together, both tall and slender, with that black hair. Most striking."

Eudora got to the heart of the matter at once. "What shall we do?"

"Well," said Tilly, "Lady Rolleston informed us she had it from Kit Fenwick that his cousin intends to wed. Since we know the only woman St. Quinton has paid the least attention to is our Sara . . ."

"How exciting," bubbled Milly. "But how are we to bring this about?" She also leaned forward, ready to conspire for her dear niece's happiness. "I do not trust those young people to get it right. Something happened at Christmas that quite put Sara in the dismals. That must not occur again."

"I have a notion or two." Tilly rapidly offered her suggestions to the others, who nodded their agreement.

Milly giggled like a schoolgirl as they concluded. "Oh, this will be famous. It makes me feel so young."

When they walked up to their beds, they were tired but extremely pleased with their scheme.

When Lord Lambert took Sara out for their drive the next day, she decided to be as stiffly proper as he. It was not the most pleasant ride she had ever made through Hyde Park. If anything, it confirmed her decision to gently disengage his interest in her.

Corisande and Sir Percy were observed strolling along beneath the trees. Sara impulsively waved, then begged Lord Lambert to stop so she might greet her friends. He frowned, but complied.

"I vow 'tis the most agreeable of days." Corisande gave a tiny bounce, with a glance at her fond love, Sir Percy. "Percy and I have been planning our future home together. I believe it is so nice to look forward to a place with just the two of us. At least for a time, you know." She blushed a delightful shade of rose. "Percy's mother is a lamb, but she prefers to live by herself. Does your mother intend to reside with you when you marry, Lord Lambert?" It was a highly improper question, and none but an irrepressible peagoose like Corisande could have brought it off. Corisande was not convinced this rigidly disapproving man was right for her dear Sara. No chance to expose Lord Lambert's true character should be allowed to slip by.

"My mother will remain in my home." Lord Lambert allowed himself a smile, and Corisande wavered in her feelings about him. "Mother is exceedingly frail. I should count myself the most unnatural of sons to suggest she remove herself from the place where she has spent so many happy years."

Corisande firmed her mouth, meeting Sara's gaze and raising an eyebrow as though to say, "You see?"

Sara gave a barely perceptible nod, thinking that his mother was happy because she was allowed to rule unchallenged. All Sara said was, "Most proper sentiments, milord."

They chatted a bit longer, then left with Corisande's bubbly words ringing in their ears. "I shall see you Saturday, Sara, dear."

"You see Lady Corisande often?"

"We are bosom friends. She is a dear, dear person, and I am quite devoted to her."

"Hardly the sort of woman to cultivate, my dear Lady Sara," said Lord Lambert with cool disdain.

There was no mistaking the proprietary sound in his voice. Sara decided the sooner she spoke, the better it would be for all concerned. "Lady Corisande will remain a dear friend. I would not wish to associate with anyone who found her objectionable in any respect. Perhaps you ought to return me to Brook Street, my lord. I have found in your conversation that which quite disturbs me. You see, I have no desire to share my home with a mother-in-law, for example, nor would I ever countenance having my oldest and dearest friend turned off. Our viewpoints seem to be rather divergent."

In unyielding silence he bowed to her request, and shortly thereafter they left the park. At Brook Street, Sara accepted the hand of the footman who rushed out to assist her.

"Perhaps it is best if you not call again, my lord. I find we have little in common." Her voice was steady and as polite as possible under the circumstances.

Unlike the departure of Lord Inglis, Sara did not linger to watch Lord Lambert set forth down the street.

On Saturday afternoon Sara arrived at the Fenwicks' the same time as Fiona. The footman, James, informed them Lady Corisande would be home soon, then ushered them into the library, where tea was waiting.

Fiona poured them each a steaming cup, took a lemon

biscuit, and perched on a chair to watch Sara restlessly pace about while mangling her reticule cords. "It all fell through?" she hazarded.

Sara laughed, a little bitterly, Fiona thought.

"Oh, yes, it all collapsed. I found the very idea of living with his mother rather daunting. And he wanted me to cut my friendship with Corisande. Can you imagine?"

Truly horrified at the prospect of a husband dictating to that degree, Fiona shook her head in dismay. "No. But then, my Brian is ever the most amiable of men. What shall you do now? Is not that the end of your list?"

"I suppose the thing to do is become a spinster and visit my friends when they have babies. I do love children so."

The wistfulness in Sara's voice tore at Fiona's loyal heart. "You have never explained what happened at Christmas between you and St. Quinton. Would you talk about it now?"

"Why not? 'Tis of no import at this point." Sara paused near the window and not far from the high-back chair. She turned to walk toward where Fiona sat. Placing her tea cup on the tray, she began in her clear, sweet voice.

"I never believed in love upon first sight until I saw Lord St. Quinton at the house party. But I took one glimpse of him and was lost. There was a large group, as you know. It was not difficult to manage to be in the same room or to partake in the same diversions."

Sara looked down at her hands, then faced her friend once more. "He was so handsome, so polished. I admired everything about him, his attire, speech, delightful sense of humor. Such nobility of address! I thought that he embodied everything I had ever dreamed of in a husband. And then I fancy I became a bit too obvious. Somehow he must have noticed my regard, though I vow I did try to conceal it."

"What happened?" breathed an engrossed Fiona.

"I was leaving the salon and tripped. It was quite by accident, I assure you. I am not so past praying for as to purposely contrive such a thing. And anyway, it never occurred to me. St. Quinton was nearby, and rescued me from a nasty fall, quite the hero as far as I was concerned. Oh, Fiona, his arms were so strong, and he so tenderly placed me on my feet again. I chanced to lean against him in a most shocking way, I fear. He seemed so manly and gallant. There was no one about, and for a moment I thought he might actually dare kiss me."

"And did he?" Fiona whispered, entranced with the tale.

"No. He gave me a look as though he suddenly recalled something rather nasty. He merely examined my ankle—in a most professional manner, mind you—then drew away from me as though I had the plague. The touch of his hands was such that I can never forget it, so very gentle and sensitive. After assuring himself I had not injured my ankle, he left, and made a point of avoiding me from then on. I felt like such a fool. And I had adored him." Sara's eyes misted, and she wiped them with a scrap of cambric from her reticule. "So you can well understand why I could not bear to deliberately set out to attract him now. My aunts prated to me about how fine he is, and how well we should suit. If they only knew the truth. St. Quinton despises me."

"That is not my impression. Only think on it. If he dislikes you"—Fiona refrained from using the more extreme word—"why has he sought you out so often? He waltzed with you at the *fête champêtre* and the ball. And he keeps popping up wherever you go. Remember, I was at Ackermann's that day he followed you from Bond Street. No, his behavior is not consistent with one who dislikes."

"Maybe he wants to persuade me to sell him a print I have that he covets." Sara's attempt at levity felt flat.

"That does not make sense. I think there is more to it than that," said a bewildered Fiona.

Then Corisande opened the door to enter with Amanda into the library. Corisande dazzled the footman with a smile while requesting a fresh pot of tea. Looking at Fiona and Sara, she said, "I am dreadfully sorry to be late. I was trying to select the fabric for my wedding dress and Mama and I were daggers-drawn between cream satin and ivory lace. We ended getting both. Well," she demanded of Sara, "what did you do yesterday after we parted?"

Sighing as her eyes met Amanda's, Sara replied, "I suggested that our views were far apart and he should not see me again."

"Good for you," declared a pleased Corisande. "That man declared his mother would live with him and his wife. If she was as darling as my Percy's mother, it would be no problem at all. But Lady Lambert hasn't an unselfish bone in her body!"

"I fear for once you have the right of it, Corisande. But what shall you do now, Sara?" As ever, the practical Amanda sought to find a solution.

"If my secret gallant would come forward and reveal himself, perhaps I could find happiness with him. I vow that anyone who enjoys mystery as much as he appears to would be an ideal mate for me. But he is undoubtedly too shy to declare himself, no doubt a worthy man of little means. Pity, that. I wonder if I shall ever know his identity." Then, desiring to move attention from her misfortunes, she turned to her friend. "Amanda, do I detect a ring on your finger?"

A delicate pink blush spead over Amanda's cheeks as she held out her hand for them to see.

"How lovely," murmured Sara, admiring the exquisite sapphire that graced Amanda's finger. Turning to the three, she said, "I refuse to say our scheme is a failure. I suspect I was doomed from the start. I fear I do not have what is appealing to gentlemen, or at least the gentlemen who appeal to me." Her laugh was almost convincing unless one knew her well—as her friends did.

"We shall not discuss it if it bothers you," the diplomatic Amanda assured her. "Rather, Corisande must describe the design of her dress, and then we shall hear the plans for Fiona's wedding which I know she is bursting to tell." Amanda cast a discreet look at Sara. Her friend was not as joyful as the others, but Amanda knew that Sara took great pleasure in the happiness of her friends. It was a shame that Lord St. Quinton had been declared out of bounds. He would have been so perfect, thought Amanda.

The footman, James, entered the library with fresh tea, cast a puzzled look toward the window, then withdrew after another glimpse of the greatly admired Lady Corisande.

The four women chatted on about wedding dresses and ceremonies, Corisande giving a dramatic rendition of what they all, except Sara, were to recite.

"I am impressed that you have memorized the words, Corisande," said Amanda with barely concealed amusement.

"I was afraid I might forget the lines and not hear the bishop. He is Percy's cousin, and rather old."

Before long, they drifted off to errands. Sara went with Fiona to find a suitable wedding gift for her Brian, while Amanda went straight home to rest for the evening.

Once more the house returned to quiet. Corisande curled up on the window seat in her room, daydreaming about her future.

For some time after the girls left, St. Quinton remained seated in the high-back chair, his chin resting on his hand. He was startled from his preoccupation when the young footman approached with a silver salver holding a bottle of excellent brandy and a glass. "Milord?"

St. Quinton accepted a glass of brandy, then sank back into reflection. "That will be all, James. Better leave the bottle here," he added as he shut his eyes in self-disgust.

Poor Lady Sara. That such an exquisite, elegant woman should be so disheartened by what he had done was terrible! He was beneath contempt! What had begun in a spirit of fun, now had turned horribly wrong. He downed the first glass of brandy and poured another. What could he do to make amends? He felt utterly rotten. The enormity of his actions was beginning to penetrate his mind. He had ruined her life! She had planned to marry, and now this vital, delicately lovely creature would deliberately remain on the shelf.

Rising from his place of concealment, he cursed the day he had fallen asleep in that chair, then listened to the scheme presented by Lady Sara. How roundly he had condemned her. But he had been no better with his own ill-begotten scheme. He had fixed things so that Lady Sara had lost three possible husbands. That they had been carefully investigated by her aunts made the matter even worse.

He felt a complete knave to have heard that declaration of love from her sweetly curved lips. That she had so esteemed him only to be served so badly cut Myles deeply. He felt quite unworthy of her regard. And she was such an appealing creature. Her hurt had been well concealed beneath that lovely exterior.

"A bit early in the day to be castaway, ain't it, coz?" Kit paused in the half-open door to survey his dismal-looking cousin.

"If I have my way, I'll be corned, pickled, and salted before the day is over." St. Quinton gave a derisive sniff.

"Drunk as an emperor? That's bloody drunk, old man. What brought this on, if I may ask?"

"I was a damn fool, Kit. Thought I could play a little joke, you see. Only the joke is on me. I hurt a fine person and I have no idea in the least how I can repair the damage I have done." He swallowed the last of his third glass of potent brandy and studied his young cousin. "How goes it with you?"

"Well enough. Decided to marry Daphne. Miss Rolleston, that is. Figured out we can get away from her mama somehow or other." Kit scratched his head as he tried to conceive of some manner of removing himself and Daphne from the Rolleston influence.

In a mood to be of help in any way he could, Myles thought a moment, then suggested, "Why don't you take over the estate in Kent? It isn't very large, but as I recall, it has a fine old house. Nice grounds."

Kit gazed at him with incredulous eyes. "You mean it? It ain't the brandy talking, now, is it? Dashed if that wouldn't solve the problem. Daphne will be in alt when she hears about this." Kit examined his cousin for signs of wavering. "You won't change your mind?"

Myles shrugged. "Glad to know I can do something right for once. I'll see to it, rest assured." He picked up the bottle, then replaced it as a thought struck him. "Come to think on it, I believe I'll go over to my town house now. My secretary ought to be there. I can have him draw up the papers for you while I see how things go on. The refurbishing ought to be about done. Should be out of your mama's hair any day."

"Been good to have you here, you know that."

"If you only knew the whole of it, dear boy," Myles responded in an abstracted manner. He set the glass down, then wandered out of the library and up to his room, where he found his beaver and cane. He murmured something to his long-suffering valet, Timbs, about moving soon, then left.

Hearing the front door close, Kit wondered about his cousin. Dashed if the old boy wasn't behaving in a mighty peculiar way. With more pressing things to hand, he turned his attention to his own future. His face lit up when he considered the neat little estate in Kent. If he recalled rightly, it had come into the family through an heiress in the seventeenth century.

Dear little Daphne must know about their good fortune right away. Kit grabbed his curly-rimmed beaver, hurried out the door and off down the street, joy giving his steps an added spring.

On Monday morning at No. 23 Brook Street Sara meditated on the matter of violets and elusive strangers and what in the world she was going to do about getting away from London. Her aunts were strangely uncooperative about leaving town. Of course Sara understood, in one respect. The Season was lifeblood to them, especially Eudora. When they repaired to the country estate willed to Eudora after her husband was lost at sea, life had become utterly bucolic and dreadfully quiet.

Tilly appeared in the door of Sara's room, giving her niece a severe look. "The world has not ceased to spin simply because you have had a slight reversal. I would like you to go with me on an errand or two. It will do you good to get out of the house. We refuse to permit you to pine away like one of those Minerva Press heroines."

"I was not aware you knew what was in those books. You've implied they are naught but drivel." Sara grinned at the vexed expression that crept across her aunt's face.

Aunt Tilly actually blushed, shrugging. "Sometimes I cannot sleep, and they are an excellent soporific."

"Why, you sly lady." Sara laughed, finding it impossible to remain in her room and brood when her aunt was bent on cheering her up.

The air was mild and the sun most pleasant as the two ladies rode to a draper's shop on Pall Mall. "Howard and Harding have excellent quality. You cannot find such as this in the country, you know. The styles are so slow to filter to the rural communities."

Sara watched as her aunt selected a length of India gauze in a most becoming dark red print for an afternoon dress. "I have missed the silks and muslins my dear Osbert used to send me from India. If he had not died of that dreadful disease he would be with me now. I sadly miss him." She gave directions to the clerk for delivery of the parcel, then beckoned Sara to follow her to the carriage.

Cholera was a danger the East India merchants chanced when working in that far-off country, Sara reflected. Tilly had been brave about her loss, never complaining. She adored the pretty patterns of the paisleys and India mulls, and wore them often, claiming they brought back happy memories of her husband.

"Milly wants some new plumes. I wish I dared buy her something other than purple."

"Violet?"

They shared comfortable laughter and Sara began to appreciate the purpose of the outing. Her aunt was reminding her in a most subtle way that life continued on regardless of the blows dealt to you. How you handled adversity was the measure of your character. Either you had backbone or you faded away.

They shortly left Oxford Street and the interesting establishment of Nicolay's Fur and Feather Manufactory, where a marvelous shade of violet had been produced in elegant ostrich feathers. Tilly directed the carriage across the city to the Strand. The warmth of the day had brought out not only carriages full of ladies on shopping expeditions but also, unfortunately, the unpleasant smells of the city streets.

Sara placed her cambric handkerchief drenched in heliotrope scent up to her nose. Catching sight of an elegant blue whiskey, she recalled precisely where she had seen such a vehicle before, and who had occupied it. She tried to study it as discreetly as possible. This time, the lady was not alone, nor did a maid sit with her on that plush velvet seat. If that wasn't the back of St. Quinton's head, Sara would eat her handkerchief.

"The odors are unusually pervasive today, are they not?" Tilly inquired. "I believe we must stop by a jeweler's shop on our way home to see if they have one of those cunning fountain rings I saw Lady Havell-Beaumont wearing at her ball. To send up a spray of scent would be rather nice at times, do you not agree? Sara? Are you attending, dear girl?" Tilly glanced at her niece, then at the blue whiskey that sedately wove its way through the press of traffic, guided by a skilled hand at the reins.

"I see," said Tilly to herself, for Sara was otherwise absorbed. If the girl disliked St. Quinton, why should the sight of him with another woman, no matter if she was his mistress, upset her so? And Sara was upset, judging by the manner in which she was shredding that dainty handkerchief.

At Ackermann's, Sara was permitted to browse through the print collection in one of the large folios on display, while her aunt sat by the counter examining prints of the latest furnishings. Overhead, the windows permitted sunlight to flood the interior of the shop. Sara appeared engrossed in the topographical prints. But her aunt noted that they were turned over very slowly.

A muted sound at the door brought Sara's head up. She gave a sharp glance, then turned in such a way that the person entering could not be seen by her.

Curious, Tilly looked as well, a sly smile creasing her face as she observed St. Quinton, sans mistress, crossing the spacious shop floor. He headed straight for Sara.

"Lady Sara. I am pleased to see you this afternoon."

She lifted her gaze from her study of a print of the Mansion House to give him an indifferent look. "Good day, Lord St. Quinton."

Undaunted, for after all he knew she was disheartened, he persisted. "That is a fine example of Thomas Shepherd's work. Will you purchase it?"

"No." She waited with an air of exaggerated patience.

"Permit me to buy it for you." His mien of bonhomie grew strained.

"I already have one." She began to edge away from him, her air of dismissal quite evident to all but the most dense of persons.

"Dash it all, Sara, I want to pay a call. Will you allow me to come see you?"

She turned the full beauty of her extraordinary eyes on him, the drenched violet color deeper than ever in her distress. "If you wish, you may call tomorrow."

He gave her an oddly relieved smile, then bent to examine a nearby folio of similar prints.

Sara's head was whirling. She did not trust St. Quinton. What could he possibly want to see her about?

She scarcely remembered leaving Ackermann's and pausing at the jeweler's shop for the fountain rings, buying one for each of them. She absently agreed to stop at Floris' perfume shop, where Aunt Tilly bought a favorite perfume. Sara agreed to try a bottle of Vetivert, the popular "violet" scent from the mysterious East. Tilly was extremely pleased with her expedition. When they arrived home she left Sara, hurrying to the salon to report to her sisters.

In her room, Sara opened the Vetivert to gently inhale the exquisite scent of violets. On her dressing table sat the nosegay from her secret gallant. If only he would reveal himself, come to carry her off in some romantic manner. Replacing the stopper on the bottle, she set the perfume on the table, then sank down on her chaise longue to dream of the impossible.

# 13

Olivia had tried to be as inconspicuous as possible while she followed the Earl of St. Quinton to Ackermann's Repository in the Strand. It was not like St. Quinton to leave her as he had, right at the corner of Old Bond Street and Piccadilly. She wanted to know if there was another woman; her instincts told her there was. He had been around to visit at Wigmore Street less and less often, a certain sign of waning interest. She had thought the disordered state of his town house would bring him around more.

At Piccadilly he had entered a hackney and headed for the Strand. She was fortunate her tiger had handled the reins well so that she was able to keep St. Quinton's carriage in sight. Odd, how he never minded hiring transport on occasion. Most of the gentlemen she knew wouldn't dream of riding in anything but their own well-cared-for carriages.

But when he stopped on the Strand and strode with that long-limbed grace of his into Ackermann's print shop, she was stumped. She had lurked about in the nearby doorways, wondering what might be going on with St. Quinton. Well, not much, she knew that. What could a gent do in a shop in the middle of the day? Mind you, she had known one or two men who were pretty clever in getting their way. But she hadn't had to worry about that for some time. And she had no intention of going back. She wanted St. Quinton as her own and did not intend to lose him.

And then he had come out of the shop escorting a lady. Oh, it fair made her blood boil to see the look he bestowed on that miss. Her, with her fancy ways and elegant manner. Her bonnet had prevented Olivia from seeing much of her face and nothing at all of her hair. But her form had been trim and her manners very hoity-toity.

Olivia had returned to Wigmore Street in a fury. For a time she debated what she must do. At last she decided.

"Lisette," Olivia rapped out at her maid, "I want you to do a bit of looking around for me. There's something most peculiar about his lordship lately. See if you can get friendly with a maid at the house where he stays, the Fenwicks'. I suspect he is taken with some little miss. Find out who she is. I must know."

The maid curtsied and hurried from the house with a smug look on her face. Her instincts were right. Trouble was brewing and she had best step lively to prevent a disaster from falling over their heads.

Olivia restlessly paced about the room, then picked up the current issue of *The Gentleman's Magazine*. She had taught herself to read improving material. In the event she needed to find a new protector, she intended to be well up on the very latest. She had no problem finding gowns of the current mode, so there was no need to study the women's magazines. Her protector always took care of her bills, or had, she amended with rising ire. Those fashion journals didn't help a girl where it truly counted. And that was how to hold on to a man.

Sara had nibbled at her toast and sipped chocolate after pushing Maurice off her chair without so much as a pat on the head, much less a piece of kipper.

Aunt Milly made note of the odd behavior but said nothing. When Tilly entered the breakfast room, Milly cleared her throat and gave a discreet nod at Sara.

In turn, Tilly remarked to Eudora about the happy results of her shopping expedition yesterday, as though it hadn't been discussed backward and forward the evening before. The conspirators shared a knowing look.

Ignoring them all, absently stepping around Maurice as she drifted from the room, Sara wandered down the hall and up the stairs. She looked out the window of her bedroom, holding the sheer curtains back so she might see for a distance.

Why had she agreed to his visit? What could he possibly have to say to her that she would want to hear? "Gather ye rosebuds while ye may"? Somehow she doubted St. Quinton intended quoting poetry to her.

He had looked very handsome yesterday. She couldn't forget he had been with his mistress, however. She was well aware that nearly every man of the *ton* kept a woman, but it was not something she could tolerate.

Any man who won her hand would have to forgo such indulgences. Sara firmed her chin, resolutely deciding she would so captivate her husband he would not have time or inclination to look elsewhere. (The decision to remain a spinster was for the moment shelved.) Hadn't Aunt Milly said most women were silly fools to neglect their husbands, forcing them from the home? Of course, Aunt Tilly had stated that many women did so because once they produced an heir, they no longer wished to risk childbirth.

A child. What might it be like to have a child with St. Quinton? The forbidden thought whirled through Sara's head, leaving her quite dizzy. She turned from the window to pace about the salon.

Fool! Cork-brained ninny! Aunt Eudora would call her a cabbagehead. What made her think St. Quinton had anything like marriage on his mind? More than likely he would offer her a slip on the shoulder rather than something as honorable as a wedding.

Yet that lazy grin had promised something. She made an impatient spin to pace back to the window. Would he actually come? He had sounded almost angry yesterday when at last he announced that he wanted to call on her. She chuckled softly at that statement blurted out in a manner so unlike the polished lord.

Why? That was what teased her mind, had all night. Why? It didn't make any sense. He had made it so plain what his sentiments toward her were all these months. If he had shouted from the rooftops that he detested her, it couldn't have been more clear. True, he had waltzed with her. He had also sought her out on one or two occasions. Perhaps he had decided that her near-fall was a coy trick, and now he enjoyed toying with her at every social function. Ackermann's didn't count. She couldn't credit that he had followed her there, even if Fiona thought so. Something was not right.

She wandered to her dressing table, picking up yesterday's violets to study them with a curious eye. No flowers had been delivered today. What did that mean? Her sense of unease grew. Yes, something was not right.

Myles studied his reflection in the mirror. "Timbs, the cravat isn't right. Do you think this the proper pin to use? Sapphire?" He flicked an imaginary speck of lint from his blue coat as he frowned at the mirror.

Clearly affronted at being questioned on a matter of taste, Timbs merely said, "As sure as I can be, milord."

"We shall be moving as soon as you can gather my things. My aunt has placed her footmen at your disposal. I shall see you at my place later on today."

"Very good, milord." Timbs gave a discreet bow as he opened the door for his master. "If I may say so, milord, I hope the day goes well for you."

Startled, Myles glanced back to see the normally bland countenance of his valet wearing a slight smile. Myles relaxed and smiled in return. Timbs had been with him a donkey's age, but he couldn't possibly know what was afoot. Myles himself hadn't until last Saturday.

Kit lounged in his chair at the breakfast table. As Myles entered the room, he rose to salute him. "Devilish good of you to solve all my problems, coz. The fair Miss Rolleston, my Daphne, that is, was delighted to accept my offer of a snug estate in Kent. Her mama must have decided that my fortune plus the estate in Kent did the trick. The banns are to be read this Sunday. M'mother's right pleased. Said she couldn't believe I'd chosen so well. Turns out Daphne has a sizable dowry. Father in banking, you know, got the title for being so important."

"No, I didn't know." Myles chose an ample meal, then wondered if this was what a man was supposed to feel before he proposed marriage—condemned.

"Something on your mind? You look a bit blue-deviled. Heard the latest *on-dit* in the clubs? Dainley's back in town. Seems his wife died this past year and he is spreading his wings a bit."

"Hmm." Myles began to eat, figuring he would need strength for his day's work.

"Well, though you ain't the greatest one at conversation this morning, I don't mind telling you I am grateful to you. Dashed fine thing you did. Mother said so too. Much obliged to you. I'm willing to help you in any way I can, y'know. You got a problem, coz?"

Frowning, Myles glanced up at his younger cousin. "No. At least I don't think so. Not at the moment, at any rate." Knowing Sara would accept his offer, and that he would end the day nearly leg-shackled, Myles shifted in his seat. As uncomfortable as the thought made him, the girl was in love with him. She had admitted as much to her friend. Pretty as Sara might be, he disliked the feeling that he no longer controlled his future. He resented feeling obliged to marry, even one so lively and sweet as Sara.

His fork clattered to his plate as he suddenly rose. "Lost my appetite, Kit." His barely touched food ignored, he went to leave the room, oblivious of his cousin's surprise. At the door he paused. "By the by, I ordered my things taken back to my house today. The redecoration work has been completed. I must tell your mother how good it was of her to put me up for the nonce. I'll see her later." He strode from the house, leaving a bemused Kit at the table.

Having elected to use his phaeton, Myles took the reins and set off at a sedate—for him—pace. His groom raised his eyebrows but said nothing. The master was in a rare mood this morning. He had heard it from Timbs belowstairs. Something was afoot.

St. Quinton tooled along the cobbled streets, not happy about the interview with Sara. She was beautiful and showed rare spirit. They both enjoyed print collecting, something he doubted any other woman he knew liked to do. But she was a schemer. So was he, he admitted in a burst of honesty. But not like her. She had plotted to snare a husband, using every wile at her disposal. She showed a want of delicacy of principle that reminded him uncomfortably of his mother.

Where was his mother now? Had she been happy with her chosen path? His father had been a silent, clutch-fisted man, from all accounts. Not the sort to keep a lovely woman happily caged. From the Gainsborough painting in the salon, he had always known his mother possessed great beauty. Once she had produced an heir, she had fled from the gloom of the great country house, leaving Myles and his taciturn father behind.

Myles had probably been no more lonely than most children of the *ton*. Parents seemed only too eager to deposit their children with nannies and governesses, then later on tutors and schools. He had gone off to Eton with a heavy heart and then found he had kindred souls in abundance there.

The phaeton lurched as he drove over a gap in the cobbles, and he chided his ham-fisted driving. Best pay attention.

At No. 23 Brook Street he handed the reins to a relieved groom, then walked with deliberate tread up the final steps to the door. His tiger nipped past him to rap smartly with the knocker. By the time St. Quinton got to the top step, the door was open and he was being welcomed inside with a gratifyingly obsequious air.

"Lady Sara is expecting you, milord. Follow me to the salon, if you please."

Although he had been here before, at the time of her ball, he hadn't set foot in the house since. It was a nicely decorated place, he observed. Quite up to the minute.

He followed the butler up the curving stairs, noting how well-polished everything was, how neat things appeared. In the salon, graceful Empire chairs flanked a surprisingly comfortable-looking sofa. In the corner a rather moth-eaten macaw gazed at St. Quinton with a malicious eye.

With no desire to take his ease, Myles began to pace slowly back and forth, glancing out the window as though he longed to fly from the room across the rooftops to his own home. He carried the violets in one hand, the violets he normally had delivered to her each morning. Would he tell her he was her secret gallant?

Pausing in the doorway to the salon, Sara silently watched the man who waited for her to appear. Anyone less loverlike she could not conceive. Her eyes narrowed in speculation, she wondered for the hundredth time what it was he wanted.

"Good day, milord." If she wanted the satisfaction of seeing him caught off guard, she had it. Heavens, the man was as jumpy as a rabbit. It was Dutch comfort that he felt no more at ease than she did. This lion of society was not going to make a May-game of her. It took a lot to fool Sara Harland. "I will confess I was taken unawares at your request of yesterday."

Of a sudden, St. Quinton felt like some out-and-outer to be here, asking her to wed him. Yet he knew there were many marriages of convenience, bondings of a practical nature. He must remember that her vow to remain a spinster was all his fault. He was beginning to feel quite noble at his sacrifice for her sake. "Can you not imagine why I might wish to have a private talk with you?"

He groped for his quizzing glass, then recalled it had been left on the table in his room. Drat! He felt a desire for something in his hands. He was nervous, he realized with amazement. It was more difficult to toe the scratch than he anticipated. He held

out the nosegay of violets to Sara, and she accepted them with
a faint air of surprise.

"I seem to recall you have a fondness for these flowers. They
do reflect the lovely color of your eyes." He noted she did not
appear to be greatly impressed by his offering. Yet she had told
her friends how she adored these flowers. Undoubtedly she
wished to seem self-possessed.

Sara, with more pretense of serenity than she felt, glided
over to a chair, gesturing for St. Quinton to be seated as
well—on the sofa, at a comfortable distance. She studied the
violets in her hand rather than face him. "It promises to be a
lovely day, does it not?" He looked complete to a shade today.
Even without gazing at him directly, she could detail his
appearance. Not that she had ever seen him less than perfect,
come to think on it.

He seated himself as though afraid the article of furniture
might collapse beneath him. He glanced at Sara. She was as
fresh and sweet as an innocent babe. The color of her eyes
reminded him of a windflower, an anemone of rich violet.

Sara looked up to return his gaze with caution. How odd
that he should bring her the same sort of nosegay that usually
arrived every morning. Except today.

"What I should like . . . that is, my dear Lady Sara, surely
you must know . . . that is, I wish to seek . . . Sara, I wish us to
be married." He hadn't meant to be so blunt, but then, he'd
had little practice in this business. The final words had come
out with a rush, much as a schoolboy hurries over a recitation,
anxious to be done with the deed.

Sara bent her head to look at the violets once more. The
man was mad. He had to be. He was certainly not in love with
her. Why, she wasn't even certain he liked her.

"I hardly know what to say, my lord. Of all the proposals I
might have expected, yours was not one of them."

Myles frowned. "Daresay I surprised you. We certainly shall
get to know each other better. Don't give me an answer this
moment if you are in doubt, my dear. Allow a bit of time." He
had not the least notion why he was urging her like this. All he

had felt necessary was to make the offer. If she chose to deny him, that was her problem. But she wouldn't. He knew his worth far too well.

Sara held up the flowers to her nose and sniffed at them. She was foolish beyond permission to consider his proposal. Even for a moment.

In the corner Xenia let out a squawk, muttering a number of choice words her previous owner, a retired sea captain, had taught her. Sara blushed, wondering how she would ever survive this scene.

Casting a startled glance at the parrot, St. Quinton experienced the unusual feeling of a situation slipping out of hand. "Would you care to go for a drive with me this afternoon?" he asked with a sudden feeling of desperation.

"When?" she asked with surprise.

"Now." Good heavens! He was pleading. He had never pleaded for anything in his life.

Deciding she must find out what this was all about, Sara made up her mind to allow him full rein. He was no more inclined to marry her than fly to the moon. "I should like that, I believe."

Sara rose from her chair, then halted in mid-step as Xenia began again. With a dread born of familiarity with the parrot's repertoire, she braced herself.

"Neat but not gaudy, as the devil said when he painted his bottom pink and tied up his tail with a pea-green bow." The words were quite precise, without feeling, but horribly clear. It would be impossible to misunderstand them. Sara felt ready to sink.

"Good Lord," breathed St. Quinton.

Sara took one look at his elegant lordship standing in awed silence while he stared at the parrot, and she began to laugh. Soon tears were rolling down her cheeks and she searched desperately for a handkerchief. A soft piece of linen was thrust in her hand.

"Here." St. Quinton found his arm supporting her, rather

liking the feel of the fine-boned body so close to him. The scent of violets, more than might come from the flowers, enveloped him with a pleasing fragrance. Odd situation. It *was* funny, all right. Crazy old bird. Myles laughed as well.

St. Quinton glanced at the parrot, then back to Sara. Any other woman would have had the vapors. This miss simply laughed off what must be an embarrassment. St. Quinton could not help but be impressed with her *sangfroid*. The feeling of stiffness that had pervaded the air seemed to melt away. A sense of charity with Lady Sara began to grow.

"That phrase is the one thing of which that dratted bird seems quite proud. Aunt Eudora has tried to wipe it from its memory. As you can tell, she has not succeeded as yet." She sniffed, blew her nose with a delicate grace, then neatly folded up the handkerchief. "Thank you for your care, I shall return this to you once it has been washed."

"Our drive?" Suddenly the ride that had seemed like such a penance promised to be more appealing.

"If you like. Dare I leave you in here with that bird?" She chuckled at St. Quinton's expression.

"No one has wrung its neck yet. I gather I shall survive—if you do not keep me waiting for long." St. Quinton gave her a smile and Sara drew in a sharp breath. She had never realized what absurdly long eyelashes the man possessed, nor had that smile been directed at her in such a delightful manner. She slipped up to her room in a bemused state. This day was of a certainty proving to be anything but dull.

Sara had a few moments of trepidation when it came to St. Quinton's equipage. A high-perch phaeton was not her idea of a safe ride. Yet she knew him to be an excellent whip.

As though reading her fears, St. Quinton spoke softly in her ear. "I assure you it has been many years since I had an accident?"

Smiling at her silliness, Sara permitted him to help her up to the seat, a task which involved picking her up and placing her on the carriage. Preferring not to think about the touch of his hands on her body, she concentrated on settling herself. She held her breath while he walked around to the driver's side, then joined her in the phaeton. She was quite certain they must be nearly six feet above the ground, at the very least. It seemed fearfully high and she knew the dangers inherent in going around corners.

In moments she was riding along next to St. Quinton, the man she considered to be her nemesis, headed for Hyde Park at the hour when she was likely to see everyone. Her heart sank. She must have taken leave of her senses.

Barely aware of the beautiful day, she sat with rigid control, perched high in the air. The clip-clop of the horses rang loudly, it seemed to her. All the city sounds were magnified—the cries of the street hawkers, the rumble of delivery carts, the laughter of children playing in the park while stern nannies and governesses watched over them.

She was intensely aware of St. Quinton. As the carriage jounced over a rough spot when they entered the park, she felt his arm brush against her. His hand, so very strong and masculine, reached out to steady her.

"I have a couple of rare prints which might interest you. Allow me to present them to you as a gift."

Sara's eyes widened in surprise. She was well aware of the keenness of his hunt for unusual prints. "You need not feel it necessary, my lord. Indeed, after doing you out of that print of the Buckingham Water Gate, it is I who ought to share with you."

St. Quinton grinned at her. She really was not such a bad sort, now that her earlier stiffness had dissipated.

Nearby, Lady Jersey said to her companion, "I perceive that St. Quinton has Lady Sara Harland up with him. Can you ever recall seeing him with a woman in that phaeton? I wonder what this portends." She issued a directive to her coachman, then sat back to observe with eagle-eyed pleasure the occupants of the carriage that approached.

Her friend Lady Dorothea Harte smiled and made note of

the delicious *on-dit* to be repeated while at the opera that evening. One did not come on really good bits of gossip every hour.

Sara wondered what had possessed her to accept a ride with St. Quinton. As she scanned the restlessly moving throng, she recognized too many faces. She was aware of curious faces. Coming toward them, she saw Lord Palmerston astride his tall, sturdy horse. Not for him the manners, airs, and graces of the finely bred park hack. Other gentlemen of equal importance rode beneath the spreading branches of the trees along one side of Rotten Row. Their hacks were the finest specimens to be found in England. Impeccable attire, highly polished boots, and a mien of polite disdain for the rest of the world were found on most of the riders.

The *beau monde* was greatly in evidence, to Sara's dismay. Ahead of her were to be seen ladies in elegant carriages, attended by powdered footmen in magnificent liveries. Bewigged coachmen wearing three-cornered hats and French gloves paid careful attention to the high-stepping horses.

Sara was aware of the scrutiny from Lady Jersey, though she tried to ignore it. But when the lady hailed St. Quinton, it was no longer possible. The fat was in the fire, for certain.

"La, St. Quinton, I am surprised to see you with a passenger." Her voice purred with provocative intent.

Sara gave an uneasy glance at the man next to her. The best thing to do, she decided, was to eliminate gossip before it began. "Lady Jersey," she said with most demure propriety. "How clever of you to observe Lord St. Quinton's gallantry. He knew I had been simply perishing to take a ride in one of these daring phaetons, so he broke his custom. I believe that is the mark of a true gentleman. For him to set aside his preferences to accommodate a mere miss is to be greatly admired. Do you not agree?"

The smug look faded. "To be sure."

Lady Jersey chattered on, Sara felt, with an intent on discovering precisely why a man like St. Quinton would be paying attentions to Sara. At last Lady Jersey took another assessing look, then ordered her carriage to proceed.

Sara almost laughed aloud at the audible sigh of relief from St. Quinton. "I believe that is now that," she said.

"Quick thinking, my Lady Sara." He looked to where she sat, as prim-looking as a nun, eyes brimming with mischief.

"Since I have not given you an answer to your earlier question, I deemed it best to quash any speculation before it began."

St. Quinton discovered he rather looked forward to her answer, one he was certain would be favorable. Marriage might not be so unbearable after all, although he still felt quite noble at the thought of the sacrifice of his freedom he would make. "When may I expect a reply?"

"Would you think me a shilly-shallying sort of female if I begged a few days? Say, Saturday evening?" She bestowed a conspiratorial smile on him, and Lord St. Quinton fell under its spell.

An entire regiment of hussars could have charged through the collection of assembled society, and the couple in the high-perch phaeton would not have paid the least attention.

# 14

The intervening days and evenings were full of activity. St. Quinton kept to his bargain, with a deal of relief, unless Sara missed her estimate of his reaction. He agreed, with an unflattering degree of haste, to her suggestion that they assume a polite friendship before the members of the *ton*.

Why she hadn't given St. Quinton his answer and sent him on his way with a flea in his ear, she didn't understand. Was it because for a few delicious days she enjoyed contemplating the idea of being engaged to him? But he was such an odious man. Not top-lofty, just so sure of himself. That was another reason to keep him on a cliff edge. Far better to permit these days to pass than give him his *congé*.

Leaning back against the nicely padded squabs of her aunts' carriage, she pulled out her oft-referred-to copy of *The British Ladies' Diary* to check her engagements for the coming week. With St. Quinton no longer bothering her, she could enjoy what was left of the Season with reasonable pleasure. She paged past the engravings and small fashion illustrations for the year 1816 until she reached the portion of the book devoted to her listing of soirees, routs, and other delightful parties.

They were to attend the opera the next week, she noted. One of Mozart's creations, no doubt adapted for British taste. Lord and Lady Sefton had a soiree on Friday that she planned to attend. Closing the book with a snap, she tucked it into her reticule as the carriage drew up before the Fenwick residence.

Corisande had informed her in passing that St. Quinton no longer resided with them. Sara hadn't told her of Myles's proposal. It wasn't that she couldn't trust her bubble-headed friend. It was the mystery surrounding the proposal, plus the fact that Sara intended to turn him down. Sara wasn't usually quite so suspicious. But St. Quinton aroused in her suspicions of the greatest magnitude. It simply did not make sense that a bachelor of his long standing would declare for *her*. She was no antidote, and possessed a considerable dowry, but she recalled vividly his former disdain for her.

Before she let him go, she wanted to solve the hidden meaning behind that blurted-out offering for her hand. She giggled as she again considered his lack of address during what must have been, for him, an ordeal. Poor man. Well, it had been an unfortunate occasion, what with Xenia spouting off and Lady Jersey quizzing them both in Hyde Park.

She was still smiling when James, the footman, opened the door to let her in. By now he was quite accustomed to the ladies gathering on a Saturday afternoon.

"Lady Corisande will be down shortly, Lady Sara. If you will follow me to the library, there is fresh tea awaiting you." Feeling uncommonly chatty, he confided, "It is a pity Lord St. Quinton will not be able to join you today, as is his usual custom. He has returned to his house, and no doubt is busy with settling in there."

James poured a cup of tea for the elegant lady, then prepared to leave. He paused when he noted her dumbfounded expression. "Is anything amiss, my lady?" James had ambitions to be a butler. He wanted very much to impress this lady with his polish. If she married, she might well consider him for the position of butler in her new establishment.

"Forgive me . . . James, was it not? Did you say just now that Lord St. Quinton would not be able to join us to-day?"

"That is correct, my lady." James had been consumed with curiosity over the weeks, wondering what his lordship was doing in that room with those four ladies. Yet the few times when he had entered the room, there had been no sign of the gentleman at all.

"But he was here each time in the past?" The words were drawn out slowly, thoughtfully, as the past Saturdays paraded before her memory.

"Yes, my lady." James waited with proper condescension.

"That will be all, James," Sara said in a vague, faraway voice. "Oh, and, James, please say nothing of our conversation to his lordship."

Her odd request quickly granted, James left the library to dream of becoming a butler in a grander house than the Fenwick residence.

Sara ignored the steaming teacup on the tray. How? Why? "The man ought to be shot!"

"What on earth is the matter, Sara?" queried Fiona as she and Amanda entered to discover Sara pacing furiously about the room.

"That blackguard! That no-good, brass-faced knave!"

Alarmed at the furor displayed as Sara continued to pace, they turned with relief as Corisande slipped into the room, closing the door behind her.

"Corisande, love, will you please tell us what is amiss? Sara is utterly frantic." Amanda stood in the center of the library while Fiona dropped onto a chair in bewildered concern.

"How should I know? I just arrived." Corisande gave Sara a perplexed look, then reached out to touch her arm.

Sara paused, the red haze of her fury subsiding as she saw the anxious face of her friend. Brushing a trembling hand across her forehead, Sara said, "Forgive me. I have just received the most astounding news."

Giving a small bounce of excitement, Corisande squealed, "Oh, do tell us. I love surprises."

"Somehow I doubt you will like this one, my dear." Sara stood in the center of the Persian rug, hands on hips to declare, "It seems we have had an unseen audience these past Saturdays. Everything we have said while in this room has been overheard!"

"Everything? Dear heaven," said Fiona. Her gaze met Sara's, and when Sara gave her a significant nod, Fiona looked away in deepening concern. "How perfectly dreadful."

"But who would do such a thing?" Corisande stared around the room in bewilderment. "I vow I do not understand how anyone could be concealed in here. There is no secret compartment, nor a convenient screen to hide behind. Who, Sara? Tell us who would do such an odious thing."

Taking her hands from her hips, Sara began to walk about the room, examining everything from different vantage points as she went. "Who, you ask? Who has been teasing me and spoiling my plans? That insufferable cousin of yours, *that* is who."

"Myles? Why would St. Quinton bother with our little meetings? He most assuredly has no reason to do so." The dainty blond sank onto her favorite chintz-covered chair in total confusion.

"I cannot tell you that, I only know that the man heard everything we said over the past weeks." Sara paused to meet each pair of eyes with growing dismay. "And I fear that is not the worst of it. Last week I told Fiona what actually happened to make me remove St. Quinton from the list my aunts gave me. It was because I had foolishly fallen in love with the man at that Christmastime house party. He listened to my declaration of love and admiration while in this room . . . concealed! If that was not sufficiently wicked, the man later came to the house and actually offered for me." She gave a bitter laugh, adding, "And did a very bad job of it."

Sara began to stride about the room again, until she came upon the high-back chair near the window, where she saw a slim volume tucked along the cushion. "Corisande, do you sit here often to read?"

"I certainly do." The blond bounced up to declare, "It is the most famous chair, for I can hide from Mama if I choose. You see, if she looks in at the door, I am completely concealed. That way, I can avoid doing those horrid things I do not wish to do. Why?"

"Because I suspect St. Quinton discovered it too." She hit her fist against the top of the chair, then turned anguished eyes to Fiona. "He asked for my hand out of pity. He heard me say all those stupid things about how much I adored him, and felt sorry for me. Oh, I believe I shall die of mortification!"

"This is terrible," murmured Amanda, truly distressed for her dearest friend. "Something ought to be done."

"Well, listening is not a hanging offense," said Corisande, pouting slightly, for she found it difficult to censure her beloved cousin.

"I agree with Amanda," said Fiona in rising ire. "He cannot be permitted to simply walk away from this. What if he reveals our scheme?"

"Somehow I do not think he intends to do that, for he has asked for my hand." Sara returned to where the three sat, a considering look on her face. She recalled how nervous St. Quinton had been that day he proposed, jumping like a frightened bunny when she spoke to him. "Mind you, I should think being nibbled to death by rabbits far too kind for the man. I must repay him in kind. Perhaps we ought to seek the advice of wiser heads than ours."

"I thought you said you never wanted anyone else to know about our scheme." Corisande gave Sara a bewildered look, then sank back against her chair as she wondered if her dear Sir Percy would hear of the famous plan.

"My aunts, dear girl. I suggest we go to them and relate what has happened." Sara gazed at each of the girls, her resolve quite firm.

"Sensible idea," agreed Amanda. "The more heads we put together on this, the better it will be."

"I still say he ought to be punished," declared Fiona stoutly. "I could understand a woman eavesdropping, but a man . . ."

"Reprehensible!" agreed Sara. "Do not fear on that score, Fiona. My only concern is to see he gets his proper comeuppance. In short, he must be made to *pay*, and pay dearly. I intend to see that his punishment fits the crime . . . somehow. Let us all travel to Brook Street together.

The other carriages can follow behind later."

Sara ushered the others from the Fenwick house, James holding the door for them, a faintly puzzled look on his face. The quality were always hard to understand, these ladies a bit more than most.

"I fear my notion of a modern scheme to find good husbands for each of us has had a grave setback." Sara smoothed her pale violet gloves over her fingers as they rode along in depressed silence. A sudden thought brought a gasp to her lips. "The violets! That man gave me the violets. He knew about my gown, how much I loved those dratted flowers. He must have thought it vastly clever to tease me so, referring to the violets so often in that sly manner of his. I do not think I can bear it. St. Quinton, my secret gallant, all the while laughing at my expense!" Tears of frustration came to her eyes. Sara reached into her reticule for a handkerchief and dabbed at her tearstained cheeks. "This is too much. It is simply too much to be borne."

Even Corisande was upset at this turn of events. "It is really too bad of him to behave so. I cannot understand him in the least. But then, I do not claim to be much of a thinker."

Amanda and Fiona exchanged looks across the carriage, but said nothing. By the time they reached No. 23 Brook Street, Sara had dried her eyes and assumed a grim look.

"I still believe he would be a good husband for you, Sara. At least you both like to scheme." The total lack of guile on Corisande's face was the only thing that saved her from Sara's wrath.

"I refuse to dignify that notion with a reply," Sara declared firmly. She waited for the groom to assist them from the carriage, then led the way up the steps to where Smedley held the door open for them.

Inside the house a raucous squawk was heard, followed by hissing and frantic meowing. Sara cast an impatient look up toward the salon door, then turned to Smedley. "I can tell that my aunts are not in the salon. Pray, where may I find them?"

"Lady Garvagh is in her room, and Lady Kerr is in the sitting room with Lady Bellew." He bowed, prepared to do anything for the young woman who usually maintained peace and order among the sisters.

"I think Lady Garvagh ought to be summoned. We shall all be in the sitting room. Thank you, Smedley." With a gracious nod, Sara led the others down the hall to where Aunts Eudora and Tilly were deep in a discussion about the implications of the latest royal-family behavior.

"What has happened?" said Aunt Tilly, her sharp eyes noting the evidence of recent tears on her niece's pink cheeks and the worried faces of the other girls.

"Nothing good." Sara removed her bonnet and invited the others to make themselves comfortable. Placing the bonnet and her pale violet gloves on the table with exaggerated care, she studied her aunts.

"What would you say if I told you that someone had heard every Saturday conversation we four girls have had since the beginning of the scheme?" She stood, hands clasped tightly, while her gaze darted from one aunt to the other.

Aunt Tilly gasped in horror. "That is serious business indeed."

"You know this for a fact?" Aunt Eudora knew her niece was not given to flights of fancy, but one must be certain.

"I discovered the truth quite by accident this afternoon when I came early and the footman casually mentioned it was a pity that . . . that Lord St. Quinton could not be with us today." Sara had stumbled on the words, so very difficult were they to say.

The dramatic statement left the room in shocked silence. At the door, Aunt Milly stood shaking her head in puzzlement. It was she who broke the quiet. "It does not seem like the sort of thing he might do, even for a lark."

"Perhaps you were right when you called him a scoundrel," admitted Eudora. "I thought he had more *ton* than to behave in such fashion. Very bad *ton*, my dears. Very bad."

Sara faced the group with a brave facade. "He also heard me tell Fiona that I had fallen in love with him at the

Christmastime party." Lowering her gaze, she examined the damp handkerchief she had retained in her hand. "I had not told you, aunts, because I intended to refuse him, but he came here earlier this week to ask for my hand."

Eudora sent a significant look to her sisters. "We could not help but wonder just a little when he sought an audience with you alone."

Sara gave a reluctant laugh. "Hardly alone, with the door wide open and Smedley lurking about, not to mention Xenia in the corner spouting off that horrible nonsense of the pink bottom and the pea-green bow."

Milly gave her eldest sister a superior glance, challenging her to deny the awful behavior of her pet, before turning her attention to Sara's problem. "If only your secret gallant would come to your rescue. You could waltz off with him, leaving St. Quinton in the dust."

Seeing Sara's distress, Amanda spoke up. "That is just the trouble, Lady Garvagh. Sara believes St. Quinton to be the one who sent her the flowers."

"Oh, I quite forgot. A lovely posy arrived just before you came home. There is a small card attached, which we left for you to read." Aunt Milly rang for the footman, then quietly gave him her request.

A delicate arrangement of violets in an exquisite silver holder was soon brought to Sara. She withdrew the card from where it nestled deep in the blooms. " 'Your secret gallant awaits your decision,' " she read aloud. "St. Quinton" was scrawled across the bottom of the card in bold script. "This proves it." She handed the card to Aunt Milly to read, while wondering what to do with the flowers. It wasn't their fault a miserable blackguard had sent them to her.

"I still say," insisted Fiona, "the man must be punished."

"I was foolish beyond permission to think I could flirt with a man like him." Sara turned a sad gaze on the others. Then, as thoughts of the dreams she had nurtured about her secret gallant flooded her mind, she stamped her foot in anger. "I agree. The man must be punished, and more than just a rap on the knuckles." She gave a searching look at her friends and aunts. "It must be extremely clever, you know, for we do not wish to reveal to anyone else what we have done." At Corisande's blank expression, she added, "Our infamous scheme."

"Oh," sighed Corisande, comprehending. "I could not bear to lose Sir Percy, nor, for that matter, admission to Almack's."

"It will not come to that. We are all slated to attend the Calthorpes' ball this evening. I told St. Quinton I would be there to give him his answer. As I recall, they have a lovely, though small, garden just outside the ballroom. I believe that will be a suitable place to tell his lordship how I feel."

"Sara, you would never tell him all," exclaimed Aunt Eudora.

"No, of course not. I will merely refuse him." Sara gave them an earnest look. "He must not know that we know what he has been up to, agreed?"

Aunt Milly had been standing over by the window deep in thought. Her tender, romantic heart was deeply offended by the behavior of a man she had secretly admired. "He should be paid in kind."

"Beg pardon, ma'am?" Sara looked confused for a moment, until she followed her aunt's reasoning.

Milly walked to stand by her sisters, gazing at the four young women with patient eyes. "I said, I believe he should be paid in kind. What a pity he is not contemplating matrimony. We could make mice-feet of his plans."

"I begin to comprehend what Aunt means." Sara rubbed her chin thoughtfully. "I mentioned I detected the fine hand of St. Quinton when Lord Naesmyth decamped to Turkey. St. Quinton heard what I said, so he must have resolved to be more careful with the next prospect on the list. Since he knew the name, it was child's play to muddle that up good and well. Recall that St. Quinton was at the *fête champêtre*? He was right alongside," she mused aloud, "urging Lord Inglis to gamble. Not that that excuses Lord Inglis. If he had not been so inclined, he would have ignored the wager."

"How lowering to admit that St. Quinton may have done you a favor in that regard." Aunt Tilly frowned in concentration. "And Lord Lambert, not that I was not fond of him, you know. It was his mother. We could but pray that she cocked up her toes before she drove you to Crab Street. What about him?"

"I do not know for certain, but I suspect St. Quinton had a hand there as well. Remember, Aunt Eudora, he turned up at Hertford House? I believe it was proper of Lambert to leave me to attend to his mother. Though I do not know what St. Quinton could have to do with Lady Lambert's heart flutters," she reflected. "It was after that night that Lambert became such a starched-up prig. St. Quinton might have meddled there."

Sara recalled the disturbing sensations St. Quinton had the power to stir inside her, and firmed her resolve to do something utterly nasty to the man. "I disregard Lady Rolleston's implication that St. Quinton plans to wed. Sheer fustian."

"What I cannot understand is why he went to such trouble. What happened that made him so naughty?" Corisande flinched at the six glaring faces that turned in her direction. "Very well, more than naughty. Bad."

"I am vastly puzzled about that," admitted Sara. "He has made some odd remarks from time to time, but that hardly reveals his motive. Goodness knows, he ought to have recovered from my interest in him by the time we girls met in the Fenwick library. 'Tis most peculiar."

"To get back to the issue at hand, we must devise a means of retribution," said Eudora. She was more upset than she cared to admit, that the gentleman she had recommended had turned out to be such a blackguard. "Sara has had three perfectly good suitors—if one forgets about Lady Lambert—driven away."

"St. Quinton has the temerity to offer himself as a substitute," said Sara, still highly miffed.

"I say that proves he felt badly about his deeds and wished to make amends." Corisande pouted at the lack of agreement, but because her words made some sense, no one glared at her as before.

"He makes me feel like some vulgar scheming creature, with great want of conduct, casting out lures to ensnare my victims. All I desired was to use a sensible, methodical approach to marriage. What's wrong with concentrating one's efforts on the most likely candidate?" Sara swallowed with difficulty, then firmed her chin. "I vow, he will be all puffed up in consequence when he is set free."

In her pragmatic way, Eudora offered her thoughts on the matter. "St. Quinton is an extremely private person. Agreed? It would seem to me that what we must find is a way to embarrass the man."

"Possible. Quite possible." Aunt Tilly nodded in accord. A crafty look slipped over her face as she continued to ponder the situation. "I believe Milly told us you saw St. Quinton with his mistress. The very same one we saw in the blue whiskey that day we went to Ackermann's to look for more prints."

"I remember that. 'Twas the day you bought the fountain rings. I do enjoy mine so much. Sprays my favorite scent whenever I wish," sighed Aunt Milly.

"Yes, dear," said Tilly with great patience. Her needle-sharp mind sped along with her thoughts. "Why not use both points? Embarrass him in regard to his mistress?"

"But how, dear ma'am?" Sara thought her aunt had slipped a cog.

"Let me think. Eudora, how might we best accomplish this?"

Flattered to be so consulted by the sister who was considered the acute one, Eudora thought intently for a moment, then said, "We plan to attend the opera this coming week. With the special program, everyone will be there. It could work then, something to publicly mortify him before the entire *ton*."

Sara was angry with St. Quinton, but she also surmised the reason for his aloof behavior. "That seems a bit drastic, doesn't it?"

"Fiddle. I agree. Now what do we do?" Aunt Milly had

quite come down from the clouds in regard to the Earl of St. Quinton.

"Sara, one way or another, lost her suitors. Why not lure his mistress away?" said Fiona, blushing a fiery red at her boldness.

"The very thing, dear girl. How clever of you." Aunt Tilly beamed such a warm smile on Fiona that the blush rapidly faded from view.

"That is all well and good, but how, pray tell, does one accomplish such a thing?" asked the prudent Eudora.

"Well," offered Aunt Milly, "I could send one of the maids to get acquainted with the woman who serves Miss Smythe-Jones. Not having done this sort of thing before, we may have to fumble our way along." She tapped her cheek a moment, then added, "I suspect we will need another gentleman, a protector, I believe they call them."

Sara half-choked in amusement at her aunt's words. "Who?" was all she managed to say.

"I heard my brother tell Mother that Lord Dainley was in town. Did you not know him before he married, Sara?"

"You might say we were friends. I knew the girl he married. Why?" Sara waited for Corisande to puzzle out her thoughts.

Amanda replied instead. "I agree he would be a good one to approach, fresh on the scene, unaware of any undercurrents. No harm in trying." Her soft gray eyes were filled with concern.

Aunt Tilly stood up with an air of resolution. "So be it. Milly will take care of the maid. Sara will find a way to approach Dainley. And St. Quinton will be sorry he ever decided to tangle with the ladies of Brook Street, plus you three, of course." She smiled at all the girls, then rang for a lavish tea, saying, "Sustenance! All that brainwork has worn me to the bone."

As they poured out steaming cups of tea and selected dainty cakes, Sara wondered if they were all a bit daft. Miss Tilbury's School for Young Ladies had not prepared her for real life. However was she going to approach Lord Dainley with the offer of a mistress?

# 15

As Sara dressed for the Calthorpe ball, she was overly aware of the butterflies lodged in her stomach. How could she manage to keep the deep anger she felt from showing on her face? While studying her reflection in the cheval glass, she impatiently ran a hand through her ebony curls—to the horror of her abigail.

"Oh, dear, I fear I have disarranged your work. I am not myself tonight." Sara gave Gates a pleading look.

The abigail gave Sara a commiserating smile before reaching out to retouch the curls so carefully contrived to simulate casual simplicity. She set a dainty evening cap over the restored curls, then stood back to approve the effect.

"You look just lovely, my dear," said Aunt Tilly from the doorway, where she paused in admiration. "You shall drive the man simply mad with frustration when you oh-so-politely turn him down." She dismissed Gates with a wave of her hand, then entered the room.

"Well," replied Sara, "I do not wish to drive him mad, merely puzzled. Perhaps bewildered and confused?"

"I believe the delicate violet of your gown is an excellent choice." Tilly walked around her niece, her head at an angle as she continued her inspection. "It makes your eyes look so mysterious."

"I fear it is not the dress, but the lack of sleep. I vow I scarcely slept a wink last night, and could not doze earlier today either. Last night I worried how best to phrase my regrets. This afternoon I seethed with anger.''

Tilly walked to the four-poster to test the mattress, fearing it had developed lumps her niece had failed to report. "Your bed seems well enough. Is the down comforter getting thin? You ought to notify the housekeeper, dear.''

"You must know it is not that. My room has every comfort to be found in London. I loathe the confrontation with St. Quinton tonight." Sara paced back and forth in her distress.

"Oh, pooh. If that is not utter nonsense. Simply tell the man you greatly fear you would not suit, and be done with it." Tilly masked her concern with a carefully set face.

"If it is so easy, why do you wring your handkerchief? I am the one who must face the scoundrel." Sara gave a reluctant laugh as her aunt shrugged her thin shoulders.

"Take care you do not allow your anger to show, love," Tilly cautioned. "While we know him to be a naughty scoundrel, he is the darling of the *ton*. If anyone, anyone at all, suspects what is going on, I shudder to think of the scandal." Tilly wrapped her arms about her frame, a shiver of dread coiling down her spine at the total disgrace that could befall them if Sara failed in the plot. Yet St. Quinton could not be permitted to go unscathed. How often did a woman get a chance at retribution in today's world?

Sara nodded, then walked to where several posies of flowers sat on her dressing table. "The violets are here. Much as I adore them, I refuse to carry them tonight. I shall be an original and not bring any blooms this evening. The beautiful earrings you gave me are all the adornment I need.''

"I could wring his neck." Tilly stood in earnest concern at the sight of her brave niece fighting to retain her composure. Sara's sweet face had a valiant smile and the set of her shoulders above the line of her gown was resolute. Tilly approved the way the soft violet silk dipped to a rather daring décolletage above the high waist. She was well aware of the effect of such a view on a gentleman's senses. Since Sara must seek out Lord Dainley's help, so much the better. Tilly expressed a strong regret that St. Quinton had turned out to be such a scamp. She had held such high hopes in that direction.

"Oh, no," Sara insisted. "I was the veriest fool to think I could cast a lure his way." She gave a self-conscious little laugh. "I thought I was being so discreet, too. Blinded, I daresay. I confess to feeling a trifle overset at the time. Now, well, I am not convinced our latest scheme is the most suitable one, but since I have no other suggestions, I will do my best."

A rustle of silk at the door announced Aunt Milly's entrance. "Forgive the intrusion, but the door was open. Oh, dear girl, you look lovely. Simply lovely. Does she not, Eudora? I vow those new earrings are prodigiously charming. Not too long, a mere inch and a half, but the gold filigree setting vastly becomes the amethysts." She sighed with pleasure at the sight of her elegant niece attired in the very latest mode. Sara would do them all credit tonight.

"In my day a gel wore superior gems, not this cheaper stuff. Now I see peridot, topaz, even turquoise! I far prefer diamonds, rubies, and emeralds." Eudora smiled at her niece to take the edge off her words. "However, I do agree the earrings are becoming." She held up a small package, offering it to Sara. "I could not resist purchasing a trifle for you when I was at that new Soho Bazaar Tilly and I visited yesterday. Do you know there were simply lines of carriages drawn up outside? The young female who waited upon us was quite modest, and I feel it is a most worthy cause, to know our purchases help the widows and daughters of men lost in the war."

Sara was not fooled in the least. How like her aunt to cloak a gift in such a manner. She unwrapped the package to find a lovely amethyst pendant on the daintiest of chains. Sara exclaimed in delight, hugging her aunt before putting on the necklace. She caught her Aunt Eudora's look of satisfaction as Sara noted the manner in which it hung to accent the low dip of her neckline.

Milly cleared her throat and brought forth a small package

from behind her. "I found something too." She tucked it into Sara's hand as she gave the others a troubled look. "I was going past Rundell and Bridge's and decided to find something to cheer up Sara. I fear I saw St. Quinton in there as well. Oh, I took care he did not see me. He was buying diamonds."

The look shared by the three aunts did not escape Sara, even while in the act of opening the box from the jeweler's. The delicacy of fragile gold chains connecting a series of cameos to form a bracelet was lovely. But her pleasure in the exquisite jewelry was dimmed with the knowledge that St. Quinton had been making a purchase for his mistress.

Sara nicely said her thanks, then added tartly, "Do not worry, I well understand the significance of that business. Miss Smythe-Jones is to get another pretty."

"Now, Sara," Aunt Tilly said soothingly.

"It was a vulgar piece, my dear. Not the sort of thing a gentleman gives to a lady of quality, you know," offered Aunt Milly by way of comfort.

Sara firmed her lips to keep back the words that longed to be said, that she would never receive anything from St. Quinton—vulgar or otherwise—and that somehow it mattered very much indeed.

Aunt Milly gave a sage nod. "The ring on the finger is what matters the most, dear girl. Never forget that for a moment."

Sara shook her head in wry amusement, then gave Aunt Milly a hug as well. Turning to Aunt Tilly, she curtsied. "I gather time is still ticking by? We had best be on our way or the ball will be over and I shall have the dreadful task of facing St. Quinton tomorrow."

"You know," added Aunt Tilly, never giving up hope for her scheme for a moment, "gentlemen frequently present a mistress diamonds or some such gift when giving her her congé."

"We are going to the Calthorpes' ball. Now!" Sara stamped her slippered foot, then gathered up her Indian shawl. She tossed a defiant glance to Aunt Tilly, then marched down the hall.

"You will have your hands full tonight, sister dear," whispered a worried Eudora. "For once, I do not envy you. Millicent and I will attend the Greshams' musicale. If we are still up when you come home, we will hear the sum of it this evening. Otherwise we meet at breakfast."

Sara saw him the moment they entered the Calthorpes' ballroom. He was standing with a tall, slender woman who was rather overdressed, to Sara's eyes. A flaming redhead, she wore a pale green dress with at least six tiers of ruffles and three bracelets on each arm, not to mention a diamond tiara and outdated wide earrings—diamond as well. Sara tilted her delicate nose in the air and wished that her simple gown had at least one flounce to it.

Tilly murmured, "She looks to have on the contents of her entire jewelry chest."

Mortified that her sense of pique was showing, Sara abruptly turned from the sight of St. Quinton bestowing attention on another woman.

Although she might not have had much success with the men on her list—thanks to Lord St. Quinton—she fared well at the ball. Gratified by the number of gentlemen who sought her hand for a dance, Sara was flushed with pleasure when St. Quinton appeared at her side later in the evening.

"Good evening, my lord. I trust you are having a pleasant time?" Sara tossed him a flirtatious glance. Now that she knew the whole of it, she found she no longer cared what he thought of her. Tonight she would behave as she pleased with him; his scheming had abolished her awe. He was merely another man, albeit a devilishly handsome one. What a pity his dark hair gleamed with health and looked so well in the cropped wind-swept style currently popular. His snug-fitting pantaloons clung to a well-formed figure. He had no need of padding of any sort, she decided in what might be termed a miff.

Encouraged by Sara's air of coquetry, Myles offered her his arm. "It seems to have improved considerably just now."

"As to that, I am certain there are a number of opinions."

Sara glanced at the ruffled front of his shirt, visible just below his exquisitely tied neckcloth, and wondered what manner of heart beat beneath that cambric covering. She gave him a look of mock alarm when he drew her into the waltz just beginning. " 'Tis well I adore the waltz, is it not?" Her smile was deliberately coy.

Sara glanced across the room at the redhead, who now clung to Lord Inglis, and frowned. She supposed Lord Inglis might have been cured of his tendency to gamble, given help. The thing was, one never knew about those habits. They might grow worse.

"You promised to give me your answer this evening."

St. Quinton's voice was far too seductive to her senses, and she fought the effect he had on her. He whirled her about in a dizzying way, holding her much too close. She could see two of the tabbies whispering while staring at St. Quinton and herself. One way or another, it seemed she was destined to be talked about. With possible disgrace looming in the distance, the way she behaved this moment seemed to matter very little.

His reminder that she owed him her answer carried only polite enthusiasm, which made Sara grit her teeth. Earlier she had weakened for a moment, almost feeling sorry for him. She knew how he felt about publicity, how he detested stares and gossip. But with his obvious reluctance to wed her, even after offering for her hand, her pity fled. So he thought to atone for his deeds by marrying her, did he? His conscience must be plaguing him something fierce.

"So I did, my lord. Perhaps we might find a less public spot for our conversation. I detest people who make spectacles of themselves, do you not?" She dropped her lashes to conceal the discomfort she felt. It was one thing to encourage a gentleman you felt shared a number of interests and would make a suitable husband. It was quite another to lead a man on for the purpose of humiliating him. Sara discovered she had no relish for the task at hand.

Then she observed Lord Lambert—his mother nowhere in

view—escorting a prim-looking maiden in palest pink gauze. The delicate blond was one, Sara knew, who couldn't say boo to a goose. Poor thing, she would have to contend with that awful dragon, the Lady Lambert. Suddenly Sara wondered if St. Quinton hadn't done her a favor in that instance. She pushed the idea aside as she saw the tender regard bestowed by Lord Lambert on the young lady. *He* would never offer for a woman out of pity. Her spine stiffened and she raised her eyes to meet St. Quinton's.

Her clever scrap of an evening hat did little to conceal her carefully arranged hair. Myles whirled her about in the intimacy of the waltz as he wondered what might be going on beneath those black curls. What thoughts did she have? She had flirted with him, ignored him, then calmly announced they should have private conversation.

"I have been looking forward to this evening." That was a clanker if he ever said one. Yet he had to confess he dreaded her answer less now than before. He ought to marry; he found he desired an heir. Sara Harland was well-looking enough. Face it, man, he admitted, she was quite beautiful and possessed not only charm and grace but also a healthy dowry. She was eminently suited to be his countess. He frowned. His nobility of purpose suffered when he thought of her in this manner. Far better to consider how good it was of him to do this for her. Though he had to admit she hadn't appeared to be suffering in the least when he approached her. Every buck and dandy at the ball had been hovering over her from the time she arrived.

Sara wondered what made him frown. Was he worried she might accept his "worthy" offer? For a moment she was tempted to say yes, then change her mind later. But she couldn't do such a thing. Not only would he look a fool, she would seem a care-for-nobody. She wished for him to be paid in full, but she really didn't desire total abasement.

At last the waltz concluded. Sara stood a moment, reluctant to face what was to come next. Then she recalled how he had spoiled her future with his nasty little schemes and hardened her resolve. "Shall we, my lord?"

Fortunately there was a sufficient throng of people so that Sara and Myles were able to weave their way along without the gossips taking undue notice. As Myles had been careful to head in the direction of the supper room, Sara supposed this was a help. She gestured to the partially concealed door leading to the terrace and small garden.

"Are you warm? Or is this the privacy you spoke of earlier?" Myles raised his brows in surprise. The lady was indicating a *very* private conversation. Well, he certainly knew what was expected of him now.

Sara felt her face warming under that speculative gaze. He seemed to be misreading her, yet there was naught she could say just now to change his position. He would know soon enough what she thought of him.

"La, sir, I have no desire for anyone to know our business. Nor do you, I suspect." She turned away from him to inspect the neat terrace. It was empty. Hardly any sound reached them out here. There was soft light from a three-quarter moon filtering through the trees. How utterly romantic, she thought with disgust.

Myles slowly turned her about, studying her partly shadowed face as she raised those amazing eyes to look at him. So she was to be his wife.

Sara was puzzled at his silence. As he bent his head to seek her lips, she realized he had misread her intentions far more than she believed. "No," she whispered, wondering why he had to kiss her now when she didn't want it. She would have welcomed it with joy last Christmas.

His arms were strong and wonderfully insistent upon holding her as close to him as possible. The lips she had admired so many times were as deliciously intoxicating as she had feared. For a moment, a long moment, she gave herself up to his kiss. She even allowed her own desires to surface, clinging to him with a delicate response, returning that kiss with growing hunger. She knew regret when the kiss ended and he stared down into her face with a sort of waiting attitude.

Sara felt weak, with the strangest lassitude creeping over her. How odd. She groped for words, but none came. She wished he hadn't kissed her like that. It made her task far more difficult, now that she knew what she was giving up.

"I have the family betrothal ring with me." His voice was husky with the emotions that had surfaced during that kiss. Sara Harland was proving to be far from what he had expected. He was sure she had no idea what she stirred in him with her response. Untutored though she might be—he was certain of that—she would be easy to teach the lessons of loving.

The languor Sara felt dissipated at his words. How conceited could a man get . . . bringing along the family ring! She wished she knew what it looked like. Then she saw it in his hand, an elegant diamond cut with exquisite delicacy. Her stomach took a plunge into icy water.

"My lord, I hardly know what to say. I fear you have misunderstood my intent this evening. What I wished to say . . . that is, my reason for desiring privacy was to shield you as well as myself from any speculation. You see . . . I believe we should not suit, my lord." She rushed on, "I decline your *kind* offer of marriage."

Sara gently withdrew from his loosened clasp, then walked past him, the swish of her silk skirts the only sound in the night.

He was stunned. He ought to feel elated, for he had done the honorable thing in asking her to wed him, and her refusal freed him. Instead, he found himself perplexed and, curiously, disappointed. Had there been a slight emphasis on the word "*kind*" in her refusal? He shook his head. No, she couldn't possibly know the true reason for his offer. He tossed the ring in his hand, watching the glitter in the cold light of the moon. It would return to the safe tonight, and his staff, who were well aware the ring had been removed and cleaned, would wonder.

He had made a hash of the whole thing, he decided. This proposal business would take a bit of study to be done right and suddenly he knew he desired an affirmative answer. He pocketed the ring, then left the sudden chill and gloom of the terrace for the gaiety of the ball. Pausing long enough to see Sara chatting quietly with Lord Dainley, Myles took himself off to his club.

Sara knew precisely to the moment when St. Quinton left the ball. She had been carefully discreet, standing so she might unobtrusively maintain a watch on the terrace door.

The first step of the plan had passed without a hitch. So why did she have this horrid empty feeling inside? St. Quinton had appeared so shocked that she might have laughed had she been capable of such a thing. Instead she had fled from the terrace, signaling to her aunt that the evening's work was half over, before seeking out Lord Dainley.

"I believe supper awaits us, Lady Sara. Shall we join the others?" Lord Dainley's voice intruded on her morose thoughts, causing her to feel a bit foolish. Mooning over St. Quinton like a fool!

Flashing Dainley a grateful smile, Sara placed her hand on his proffered arm and strolled again in the direction of the supper room.

"It is pleasant to see you in town again, my lord. You have been missed." Sara beamed a genuine smile at him, for he was ever a kind and gentle man. From what Helene had written, he had been a good husband.

His returned smile was bemused. He had always enjoyed the delightful Lady Sara. "Everyone persuaded me it was time to come to London. Helene has been gone for over a year."

Sara sobered as she thought of her friend's death in child-birth. "I had hoped to visit the two of you, then with the passing of my parents it was not possible."

He gave her a distressed look, not quite certain how to reply to this. Seeking to cheer her, he said, "You would like our little girl. She looks a bit like Helene, more like me, I fear."

"Naughty man, looking for compliments. You must know you are the handsomest gentleman around." The saucy glance from Sara increased the harmony between them.

Lord Dainley laughed, feeling lighter than he had for some months. "As I am the only man close to you at the moment, I shall give that the disdain it deserves." He placed a nice amount of food on her plate, then his own, escorting her to a small out-of-the-way table.

"Tell me what has been going on in town. I feel vastly out of things after all my time in the country." He began to enjoy the light repast, feeling as though it might be easier to slip back into society than anticipated.

"This and that. I daresay I could tell you tales that would simply be a substitution of names for scandals you knew a few years ago." Sara attempted a gay laugh, which was more of a sigh when she thought of how dangerously close she walked to scandal herself.

She picked at her food, wondering how she might approach the subject of St. Quinton's mistress, Olivia Smythe-Jones. She had found the name, discovered by the sleuthing Aunt Milly, to be pretentious. She wondered if the woman had ambitions. From what Eudora said one time when she forgot Sara was in the room, rumor had it that Harriet Wilson, that cream of cyprians, had tried to marry into the peerage . . . and failed.

"Is something troubling you? You seem tense, unlike the Lady Sara I recall. Please consider me the older brother you declared me years ago. If there is anything I might do for you, you have but to ask." His voice was warm with concern and caring. It was nearly Sara's undoing.

Unexplainable tears started in her eyes, to be blinked away. " 'Tis silly of me, I know. Were you not someone I feel is a friend, I should pretend utter ignorance of what you mean. Truth is, I need your help and I have been searching for a way that I might ask for it."

"Ask, then, and I shall see if there is some manner in which I may serve you. I know Helene would wish me to help."

"She always did say you were her knight. Very well. I must

caution you that this will not be simple, and it requires a bit of daring."

He merely looked more intrigued. "Go on."

"Someone I know, a man—but not a kind gentleman such as you are—wounded me very deeply and I have a wish to pay him back. Not very principled of me, I suppose, but I will add that this scheme has the blessing of all three of my aunts. I desire that this blackguard get his just deserts."

"From your expression, I gather this is not something you consider lightly." Lord Dainley gave Sara a sympathetic look.

"No. It is awkward to explain. I feel a bit foolish. You see, I wish you to escort a certain lady to the opera, to the box that my aunt has arranged for you to occupy."

Lord Dainley tilted his head while studying Sara. He pursed his lips, then inquired, "Who is she?"

Sara knew she was blushing, she could feel her face simply glowing with heat. "Her name is Olivia Smythe-Jones and this is her address." Sara delved into her reticule to pull the slip of paper with the fatal address on it.

He gave a wry acknowledgement when he noted the woman's location and the deep blush on Sara's face. "It seems this *lady* is not a lady. Am I correct?"

"She is very lovely, my lord. I doubt if you will be disappointed in her company." Sara sat, her breath nearly suspended, while she waited for Lord Dainley to decide.

"It seems innocent enough as far as I am concerned. Or do I run the risk of being called out by some irate lover?"

Sara gasped in dismay. She had not considered such a possibility. Then, recalling St. Quinton's dislike of the public eye and gossip, she shook her head. "No. I am quite certain you will have no problem in that regard. The gentleman in question values his privacy far too much."

Lord Dainley nodded, deep in thought. "I will help you, though to achieve what ends, I can only wonder. I gather I am to ask Miss Smythe-Jones as soon as possible?"

"Aunt Milly said all the cyprians like to be seen at the opera, though I have observed they seldom pay attention to what is on the stage." Relieved that her mission was completed for the evening, Sara relaxed against her chair, sipping her lemonade.

Dainley choked on his wine, then shook his head, chuckling. "What those aunts of yours can be thinking of to permit you to hear such stuff is beyond me."

"I know," Sara said ruefully. "I am a sad rattle of a lady, I fear." She giggled at his expression and looked forward to the opera with more enthusiasm.

Across London, in the little house on Wigmore Street, the lady in question was vexed to the extreme. The sparkling bauble that rested around her throat compensated for days and nights of being left to her own devices. It did nothing to allay her fears. St. Quinton had stayed so briefly, said so little.

Turning to her maid, she pounced. "Well, tell me, what did you learn tonight?"

"It may be as you suspect. I made friends with ze leetle maid from Fenweek 'Ouse. She say St. Quinton tell his cousin he plan to marry soon. Per'aps it ees time to find ze new protector. No?" The maid dipped a curtsy, then backed toward the door. She didn't trust the woman who paid her wages in the least.

"Yes! Clever girl. What would I do without you? I will begin the hunt soon. Tomorrow I'll inspect the field when I go riding in that miserable carriage St. Quinton gave me. My next man will do me better. I shall have a carriage-and-two." Olivia thrust aside the ambitions she had held in regard to St. Quinton. There were other men, men with money, who might be cajoled into marrying her.

She retired to contemplate her next move. Yes, shortly she would be seen at the opera, no less, and on the arm of a handsome man. St. Quinton could go to the devil!

# 16

"I am a seesaw, up one moment, down the next," Sara declared to Fiona several days later. "At times I fairly gloat that St. Quinton will at last receive the set-down he deserves. Then I think of how private a man he is, how kind he has been to Corisande and that rattle of a brother of hers, and my heart tells me I am doing wrong. I do not know what to do at this point."

Fiona nodded agreement, then rose from the chaise where she had reclined during tea, to cross to the window in Sara's room. "I see Lord Dainley comes to visit. You knew Helene well. What feel you for him? I expect he is looking for a second wife, for he needs an heir. He might be a solution."

"He is kind and good, a fine man. Helene wrote me about her happy life with him." The intimacies of marriage were foreign to Sara, but Helene had implied that her dear husband treated her like a princess. The older girl's confidences had revealed that theirs was a loving match. "If he took a notion to seek my hand, I suppose I could do worse," Sara said with little enthusiasm. "Though I believe it would be almost like marrying a brother. He simply does not stir me in any way." Sara rose to check her appearance in the cheval glass, then moved toward the door.

"And what do you know about being stirred?" Fiona turned from the window to give Sara a hard look. In all the confidences about Lord Inglis and Lord Lambert, there had been nothing about stolen kisses—or any other kind. Lord Naesmyth she didn't bother to consider.

Flustered, Sara sought an evasion, when a gentle rap on the door saved her.

The maid entered and respectfully curtsied. "Lord Dainley has come to pay a call and has a message for you, my lady."

Sara nodded, dismissing the girl as she glanced at Fiona. "He has something to report. I'd best see what it is. Do you mind, my dear?"

"Mind? Not unless you fail to satisfy my curiosity later. Tell me about it at the opera tonight?" Fiona slipped from the room, hurrying down the stairs and past the salon, where Lord Dainley waited.

Sara paused before the salon door to compose herself an d still all those bothersome worries that plagued her. Smedley opened the door for her at her nod, and she studied Lord Dainley a moment. He was handsome in a nice way, with his sandy hair and green eyes, the sort of man one looks at a second time. When he rose from the chair she noted his tall, slender figure, the pleasant expression on his face. Certainly she could do worse. Of course, he was different from Lord St. Quinton. No devilment lurked in these eyes, which looked at her with admiration, not censure.

"Lady Sara, delightful to see you again."

Sara crossed the room to greet him with reserve. Fiona's words had put thoughts into her head that hadn't been there before. She studied the man who bowed over her hand. His manners were refined, and she knew he possessed a respectable income. There had never been talk of his gaming losses, nor was he an over-proper pomposity. And he had *never* mentioned antiquities. She gave him a tentative smile and hoped Xenia could be silent for once. The bird stirred restlessly on her perch.

"I thought to set your mind at ease regarding your scheme." He led her to the long sofa, seating himself at a proper distance, yet close enough to have a faint touch of intimacy.

"What has occurred?" Sara met his eyes, relaxing as she saw amusement in them.

"It was far easier to meet the person in question than I had thought. I went for a ride in the park on Sunday, and a friend of mine pointed her out to me. You failed to tell me she had been in the keeping of St. Quinton," he chided.

"I was under the impression I was not supposed to know about things like that." Her pose of primness brought a chuckle from him.

"Well, my friend introduced me, and when I invited her to attend the opera, she jumped at the opportunity. I have a feeling she sees me as her next protector."

"I ought to be shocked." Sara gave him a forgiving look. "But living with my aunts has opened my eyes and ears to more than the average miss knows."

He nodded. "Quite so. At any rate, I suspected you would feel more at rest if you knew the lady in question will be at my side this evening."

Sara closed her eyes a moment. "I had wished not to think about it until the very last moment. I confess I am full of misgivings about this scheme."

"I could sympathize if I knew more of what was afoot. She is, as you intimated, a lovely lady. In fact, she looks remarkably like you. Does this have any bearing on the matter?" His curiosity was scarcely restrained. He seemed to recall seeing Lady Sara waltzing with St. Quinton at the ball the other night, and they had appeared to be in intense conversation.

Startled, Sara shook her head. "I see I had best tell you some of it. Lord St. Quinton . . . Oh, it is all of a muddle!" she cried in exasperation. "Suffice it to say that I apparently said or did something to upset his lordship. I certainly do not know what it was." Her vexation regarding this point was obvious. "He retaliated in a most unkind manner. Now that I am aware of what he has done, I desire to repay him in kind, so to speak. Tit for tat, you might say."

"I still am in the dark in spite of your explanation. I hadn't expected to become part of an intrigue when I came to town. It certainly has livened up my return to society."

"Neat but not gaudy . . ." began Xenia.

Sara looked around to glare at the parrot, wishing she might strangle the moldy old bird, when her Aunt Eudora sailed into the room to drop the night cover over the stand.

Rising as she entered the room, Dainley watched in fascination as she performed this task, then turned to greet him as though nothing unusual had occurred.

"Good day, Lord Dainley." Eudora surveyed him with a kindly smile, graciously acknowledging his bow.

"A pleasure, Lady Bellew. I was unaware the parrot could talk. Interesting bird." He glanced at Sara to see her choke back a laugh.

"We are all quite fond of it." Lady Bellew's look defied Sara to so much as smile at that remark.

At that moment Maurice entered the room, immediately noted the bird was covered, then jumped up on the sofa to curl up for a snooze. The cat wore a remarkably smug expression on his face. "All but the cat, of course," Eudora added.

"Understandable. Well, I must bid you adieu for the nonce. I shall see you ladies at the opera this evening."

Eudora watched him leave the salon, then turned to Sara. "How much does he know?"

"I fear the explanation I gave him was so garbled that he knows little more than he did before. This is a very complicated situation, aunt, if you but realize it."

"We discussed it over breakfast." Eudora gave her niece a worried look. She had agreed with her sisters that there was far more to this than met the eye. Not being privy to what was going on in St. Quinton's mind or, for that matter, their niece's, the ladies were unsure which course to take. Eudora had been assigned to explore the subject with Sara.

Meeting her aunt's probing gaze, Sara dropped her own, then walked to the window, where she stood idly toying with the fringe of the drapery. "All is in readiness for this evening. Lord Dainley has kindly agreed to take Miss Smythe-Jones to the opera, and will occupy the box you arranged for his use." She paused, her throat suddenly constricted. " 'Tis not too late for us to stop this, is it?" Then she remembered that naughty gleam in St. Quinton's eyes and how much he knew of her intimate thoughts, especially of her love for him. Oh, the man deserved every bit of his come-down! "No." Her resolution was quite firm. "We shall proceed."

"Is your heart still engaged, my dear?" Eudora asked with great gentleness. She had to find out more, even if it meant probing into tender places.

Sara glanced back at her, sighing deeply. "I am as much of a muddle as this scheme is, I fear. Best not to consider how I feel or what I think at this point." To deflect further questioning, Sara changed the subject. "Have you decided what you will wear this evening?"

"My midnight blue, I believe, the one with the silver spangles. And you?" Eudora had found the blush that stained Sara's cheeks during the discussion of her feelings toward St. Quinton quite interesting.

"I will wear blue as well, the new one with the flounce of blond lace. Did my new toque arrive from the milliner?"

Sara tried to whip up her lost enthusiasm for the opera. She adored Mozart's music. However, she did not relish the scheme, however necessary it was to put St. Quinton in his place.

"The hat came this morning. Millicent desires you to wear her sapphire parure this evening. The earrings and necklace will set off the dress nicely."

"The neckline is cut very low and the waist very short." Sara cast a cautious glance at Eudora.

"You have the figure to set it off, dear girl," said Eudora with satisfaction at the thought of Sara's nicely full bosom enhanced by the lovely new dress.

Xenia's perch was uncovered before they left the room, and soon Sara heard the hissing of a teased cat.

* * *

"Stop fidgeting with your fan and smooth out your gloves." The sharp command revealed how tense Eudora was as the carriage rolled toward the Royal Italian Opera House.

Sara studied the toe of her white satin slipper as she again smoothed her white kid gloves for what must have been the tenth time. The carriage rolled to a halt, and the door was opened. They had arrived.

The blue satin slip rustled beneath the matching blue net as she walked up the steps to the entrance. Pausing while Eudora gathered her shawl and reticule, Sara noted with relief that she saw neither St. Quinton nor Dainley.

Sara and Eudora bustled through the entry and up to where their box was located. Eudora remarked on the size of the gathering audience. The opera house would be full.

"Catalani is singing tonight. I expect that all the *ton* will be here to hear her perform. One never knows when her temper will get the better of her. 'Tis said that her backstage performances outshine the ones on the stage." Eudora settled onto her seat in the second-tier box the sisters kept from year to year.

"As if we do not have sufficient to worry about, we must consider the singer's temper? Mercy!" Sara glanced to St. Quinton's box, stiffening when she observed him enter—alone.

"Ah, but Catalani smiles all the while. I daresay she would do so in the midst of a death scene." Eudora took note of St. Quinton, two boxes to the left and across from their own. The box arranged for Dainley and the Jones gel was directly opposite St. Quinton's, in the same tier. Eudora darted a look at a very pale Sara, admiring the firm resolve displayed.

Excited at the thought of a spectacle, the members of the *ton* thronged the five tiers. Sara carefully scanned the red-draped boxes, studying the faces revealed in the lights, faces avidly taking in the assemblage, searching for tidbits of gossip—who was wearing what, who was seen with whom.

Her aunts' box was directly above where the orchestra now tuned their instruments. Behind the musicians the dandies strolled about in the pit, ogling the occupants of the boxes most shamefully. That they wished to display their foppish dress was obvious to Sara. Only a few eyes were on the red curtain, awaiting the performance.

When a nearby rustle signaled the arrival of Lord Dainley and that woman, Sara held her breath, watching St. Quinton with avid intensity.

There was a light hung directly above Dainley's box. It acted as a beacon to call attention to the woman who seated herself with a flourish at the front. A diamond necklace sparkled—Aunt Milly was right, it *was* vulgar—from her amazingly ample bosom.

"They're here," Eudora whispered unnecessarily.

Apparently it was reasonably well-known that Jones, as Sara thought of the woman, was under St. Quinton's protection. Like an audience at a battledore-shuttlecock game, eager faces peered first at her, then to where St. Quinton sat in frozen dignity. In the pit, the dandies raised quizzing glasses to gape at the sight. The buzz of conversation seemed much louder than usual to Sara's sensitive ears. It was far worse than she had anticipated.

Enchanted with the attention, Miss Smythe-Jones preened herself, sending smiles to her admiring audience. Emboldened, she raised a dainty gloved hand and blew a well-aimed kiss to St. Quinton. Sara could almost hear the gossip that sailed through the assembly. Heads bent as whispers began. While plumes nodded vigorously, fans shielded gossiping tongues.

St. Quinton sat quite still, looking bored and remote. Sara wondered what was going through his mind. Down a little from his box, she espied Amanda and Corisande with their families and their betrothed.

Amanda waved her fan, a pleased expression on her face. Corisande merely looked blank. Sara could almost hear her asking Amanda why she was smiling so.

A rustle behind her warned her someone approached. Sara turned with relief to find Fiona at her side, Lord York behind her. "They are here," Fiona whispered. "The curtain has gone up, but I daresay no one is paying the least attention. Catalani may have one of her fits onstage if this keeps on. Everyone is dying of curiosity to see what St. Quinton will do."

"He won't do anything," Sara replied softly with sudden insight. "He will sit there and wonder, perhaps burn with anger, but he will never do a thing. Oh, Fiona, I know he must be mortified at this display."

"Just remember what he did to you, my dear. It is only what he deserves," Fiona whispered. She glanced to where Lord York conversed politely with Lady Bellew. "We shall see you later." Fiona pressed a comforting hand on Sara's arm before slipping from the box.

Sara sat in an agonized suspension. In the next box she could hear the chatter of the ladies as they not only discussed the latest *on-dit* but also recalled the decampment of Lord St. Quinton's mother years ago. Every aspect of his life was getting a raking over the coals.

At first intermission Sara sought out Amanda and Corisande. Fiona was quick to join them. The four put their heads together as discreetly as possible.

"It went off perfectly," exclaimed Corisande. "And the performance is not over, either. Amanda said she thinks there will be more. Did you notice you are both wearing blue, Sara? How dare she!"

"Shh," urged Sara. "Not so loud."

"No one could know a thing from my words," complained Corisande before getting a nudge in the ribs from Amanda, who had noticed how pale Sara was.

"I, for one, will be happy when I can leave here for home. This is the worst night of my life," declared Sara.

The gentle-hearted Amanda nodded. "I have heard it said that revenge is sweet, but I perceive it is not always so."

The gentlemen reminded their respective ladies that it was time to return to their boxes. Sara walked back to hers with that same seesaw of emotion in force. She had been aware that what she did would hurt St. Quinton, whereas he had not known her well enough to realize how wounded she would be. Yet how glad she was that St. Quinton could experience a bit of humiliation for once. She had had to bear a good deal with the defection of Naesmyth, the default of Inglis, and the disappointment of Lambert. Nevertheless a part of her heart felt pity for St. Quinton.

Was that how he had felt when he came to propose? Guilt, a desire to atone? Then what had stirred within him when he kissed her? For she was not so lost that she had failed to observe that he had been quite affected by that kiss.

Miss Smythe-Jones had not left the box at intermission, preferring to remain the cynosure of all eyes. When she seemed certain that enough of the *ton* had returned, she leaned over the rim to wave her handkerchief—most vulgarly, Sara thought—directly at St. Quinton. She blew another kiss, then pointedly turned to Lord Dainley, who had sat in amused silence through the entire performance. Her evening gown of Prussian blue sparkled with diamante, glittering like that vulgar diamond necklace whenever she moved, which she did often, with great animation.

The second act began. The audience settled into their respective seats with anticipation.

As the singers assumed their roles onstage, Sara turned to her aunt, wishing the lady might be persuaded to leave. "I believe we have achieved what we set out to do."

The older lady raised her hand to her brow, appearing distressed. "I seem to have developed a headache. Perhaps you would be good enough to call for our carriage?" Eudora, too, wished to leave. She knew her sisters would be glad the plan had gone off without a hitch. Now they could but hope.

Sara hopped up to instruct their footman, then returned to begin gathering up the shawls, reticules, and fans that seemed to have multiplied since their arrival. She carefully avoided looking toward St. Quinton. Eudora swept majestically from the box, murmuring instructions for Sara to follow when she found everything. Eudora was certain she had dropped her vinaigrette somewhere.

Sara stared at her aunt, mystified at her abrupt departure, then realized the headache could be very real. Eudora was at times given to the most awesome megrims. Sara knelt to search for the missing vinaigrette, found it at last beneath the chair in the corner, then rose to leave. Her arms were loaded with two shawls, two reticules, two fans, the vinaigrette, and her aunt's posies.

Below, on the stage, Catalani was pouring forth one of Sara's favorite arias. The audience was restless, still speculating about St. Quinton and his mistress, the hum of voices audible above the music. Sara slipped from the box, only to encounter a rather large body clothed in stark black and white and smelling most familiarly of costmary and another spicy scent.

"Going somewhere, Sara?"

She faltered, then tried to move around him. "Lord St. Quinton, I fail to see why you are here, or for what reason you bar my way. Please let me pass." The speech would have been more effective if her heart hadn't been pounding so madly that she sounded breathless and giddy.

He lounged against the wall, one lean, rather powerful hand resting heavily on her shoulder. She couldn't move.

"It has been a most instructive evening." His voice had the hard sound of steel.

"I do not see what it has to do with me." Her voice had a lamentable tendency to quaver. She cleared her throat and backed up slightly. He seemed to loom before her like an avenging dragon—about to breathe fire, she was sure.

"Corisande talked." This information was imparted in a most menacing way.

"Oh." Sara considered her scatterbrained friend, then added, "What about?"

"I think we should find a more private place to hold our conversation. Don't you?"

He asked this with the casualness of inviting her to tea, all the while propelling her down the now-empty corridor to the front entrance. Sara held wild thoughts about appealing to one of the footmen or coachmen wandering around in front of the building, then thought better of it. There had been quite enough sensation this evening. She had no desire to add to it.

"My aunt is waiting for me, sirrah. As far as I am concerned, we have nothing to say to one another, you . . . you blackguard." Head held high, Sara wrenched herself from his clasp, running the last of the distance toward the family coach with its rented horses, as though actually expecting to elude capture.

She never made the coach. Myles gathered the shawls, reticules, vinaigrette, and fans from her hands and tossed them inside to a startled Eudora, then swung Sara up in his arms. "We shall see you later, Lady Bellew."

The posies fell from Sara's hands to the ground, rolling beneath her aunt's departing carriage. The coachman had taken the unspoken command from St. Quinton as orders.

"Put me down this instant," Sara hissed, while wondering what this madman was going to do with her.

Myles simply held her closer and strode toward his elegant phaeton, where he dumped her on the seat and climbed up beside her while his tiger held the horses. "It would be utter folly even to think about jumping, my dear. I wish to talk with you, and talk we will." His tiger released the horses, then jumped up behind as they set off.

Sara took a fearful look at his grim countenance illuminated in the flambeaux held by linkboys in front of the Royal Italian Opera House and shut her mouth. She clung frantically to the phaeton as they racketed down the street, thinking that not a footpad in London would dare attempt to attack them tonight.

She longed to know where Myles was taking her, what he would do. In her wildest dreams, she had not anticipated this reaction. "This is . . . kidnapping, you know."

"No, it isn't. We are friends, or were. Friends no more, I think. And I doubt I'll ask a ransom for you."

Sara's terror grew as she heard the threat in his voice. The debonair darling of the *ton* had turned into a fiend!

No one could have been more amazed than Sara when they

drew to a halt before the Fenwick mansion. "Whatever a
doing here?" This didn't fit her idea of a horrid place to dis
of her body, or whatever he intended to do with her. T
Fenwicks were at the opera, except for Kit, and he w
probably dancing attendance on his Daphne.

"No one is at home. Why do you not simply let me go and I
shall attempt to forget this entire ghastly event." Sara bravely
met his eyes as he turned the reins over to his tiger, then pulled
her from the carriage. She wasn't allowed to walk; supposedly
she might dash free. He again swung her into his arms and
marched up to the door.

"We are here precisely because no one is at home. Consider
it a compromise between my house and a closed carriage.
More comfortable for you, I'm sure." His glance hinted at
things Sara would rather not consider at the moment.

James revealed not a flicker of surprise as he opened the
door, merely ushering them into the house. He disappeared
once the two were in the library.

Placed none too gently on her feet, Sara surveyed the library
with a bitter look. "Return to the scene of the crime, eh?" Fear
disappeared as her anger returned full force.

Myles frowned, then gestured toward a chair. "Why do you
say that?" Sara sat primly on the dainty chintz Corisande
favored when they had met each Saturday.

"Why? I know that you know everything." Sara crossed her
arms, giving him a defiant look. "You were in this room eavesdropping each Saturday, were you not?"

Her air of virtuous indignation was almost too much for
Myles. What a little fury she had turned out to be. He
coughed, then motioned for her to proceed. "Somehow you
have found me out. What has that to do with this evening?"

Sara glared at him. "You contrived to get Lord Naesmyth
off to Turkey. You prompted Lord Inglis to bet. You were
somehow behind the stuffy change in Lord Lambert, for I vow
he was quite normal when I first met him. You *knew* the men
on my list and you dispatched them, one by one. Why?" Her
final word was wrung from her heart.

His anger subsiding a bit, Myles took a deep breath, then

ead. "You should never have called me boring, my
. A man can take almost anything but that."

it?" she cried. "Boring? But you are never . . ." Her
faded away as she recalled that first morning when she
arched for a reason for her rejection of St. Quinton. "I
not tell the truth, you see," she added softly in a
ment of honesty.

"And that is?" His anger abated considerably as he watched
her discomfiture.

"Oh, come now, Lord St. Quinton," she temporized.

He interrupted her. " 'Myles,' I think. We have surely come
beyond such formality, Sara."

"Myles, you are the favorite of the *ton*. There is not a word
you could utter that they would not claim to be exceptionable,
and you know it." She rose to walk to the high-back chair still
facing the window. Turning to confront him, she trailed her
fingers along the back of the chair while studying his
expression.

"Why did you do it?" She leaned against the chair while she
waited for his answer. He had never looked more appealing
than now in the flickering light of the fire.

He studied the tip of one polished evening shoe before
meeting her eyes. "To tell the truth, I was piqued that you, of
all people, should consider me a bore. You see, I was quite
attracted to you last Christmas. It wounded my vanity to think
*that* was the impression I had made on you. I decided to get
even. Childish, isn't it?"

She slowly walked back to where he stood. " 'Tis no worse
than what I did in retaliation, I suppose. I was so angry, you
see. We . . . I felt you ought to be punished. Though I never
thought it would be so horrid. I expected you to be stung,
perhaps. I assuredly didn't anticipate your strong reaction. Was
it so very bad?" She peeped up at him through a fringe of
ebony lashes, her violet eyes beseeching him in a beguiling
way. His heart gave an odd lurch as he succumbed to the
appeal in those eyes. Then he recalled what had shocked him.

"But my mistress? You aren't even supposed to *know* of such things." Memories of the distasteful exhibition at the opera returned. He had to admit he was beginning to see a humorous side to it, though he wouldn't dream of confessing such to Sara.

"You forget my aunts. How could I not, living with those dear ladies?" Sara gave a gusty sigh. "I believe we are even now." She took a deep breath, then continued, "At any rate, you probably did me a favor by disposing of the three suitors."

"Not one of them was right for you." A gleam of amusement and something else quite indefinable lit his eyes while he watched her lovely figure parade back and forth in front of the fireplace.

She stopped, frowning up at him. "Should I submit my candidates to you for approval?" she sputtered. She glared at him, hating him for telling her the truth. Catching sight of the laughter in his eyes, she halted. "Now what?"

"There is an alternative, you know." He had discovered what that growing feeling was inside him. Now he watched her with eyes intent, as a fox might its prey.

"Alternative to what, pray tell?" She mistrusted the gleam she saw before those ridiculously long lashes concealed it.

"I doubt your uncle would deny the offer I made for your hand." He sounded most coaxing to her hopeful ears.

"You were not serious in that offer." She struggled valiantly with the desire to draw closer to him.

"But if I were serious? What would your answer be?" At her suspicious look, he added, "I believe Olivia is content with her new protector. She of a certainty is out of my life."

Sara clasped her hands before her lest she reach out to him. The love that had never really died flowed back through her with full force. Yet she was cautious. "Well," she said thoughtfully, "Aunt Milly says violets mean faithfulness."

His thumb traced a line along his jaw while he thought. "We could combine our print collections to have the finest in the land."

Sara had to chuckle at this novel manner of persuasion. "And violets. We could grow masses of them. My mystery is solved, and I am rather sorry to see it gone. Boredom faces me, alas." She feigned alarm as he stepped closer to her.

In a moment she discovered his arms about her in a very tight embrace. Bewildered, she met his gaze.

"I believe she discovered his arms about her in a very tight embrace. Bewildered, she met his gaze.

"I believe I have found a way to prevent my ever becoming a dead bore." His rough whisper thrilled her to her heart.

Warily she queried, "And what is that?"

"Marry me. I haven't been able to get you out of my mind since Christmas. Marry me, Sara, my little love."

A warm glow began to spread through Sara as he again claimed her lips in a kiss that set her tingling. It made the previous efforts pale into nothing. When at last she was able to speak, she looked up at him and said, "When?"

He threw back his head in a roar of laughter. "Oh, my dear, how precious you are. You know," he confided, "we must marry, if only to save both our faces. I am certain James is the soul of discretion, but one never knows who else might be listening." At her threat to do violence, he added, "Besides, I *do* love you quite to distraction, dear girl." He dropped another kiss on her tempting mouth, then continued, "Let me see . . . If I had my way, we would be wed this very hour, but there is the problem of a license. Can you manage to wait one week? Your aunts can arrange for a quiet wedding. I'll see to my Uncle George, the family bishop, as well as your uncle. Two such schemers as we ought to manage this with no trouble at all."

Sara's murmur was lost as she invited another of those wonderful kisses. Her scheme had won her the first—and best—on her list.